An Unex
for his Scarred Heart

—— ♘ ——

STAND-ALONE NOVEL

A Western Historical Romance Novel

by

Ava Winters

Copyright© 2021 by Ava Winters

All Rights Reserved.

This book may not be reproduced or transmitted in any form without the written permission of the publisher.

In no way is it legal to reproduce, duplicate, or transmit any part of this document in either electronic means or in printed format. Recording of this publication is strictly prohibited and any storage of this document is not allowed unless with written permission from the publisher

Table of Contents

An Unexpected Bride for his Scarred Heart 1
   Table of Contents 3
   Let's connect! 5
   Letter from Ava Winters 6
Prologue 7
Chapter One 10
Chapter Two 18
Chapter Three 26
Chapter Four 35
Chapter Five 44
Chapter Six 50
Chapter Seven 57
Chapter Eight 66
Chapter Nine 75
Chapter Ten 83
Chapter Eleven 92
Chapter Twelve 100
Chapter Thirteen 110
Chapter Fourteen 118
Chapter Fifteen 128
Chapter Sixteen 136
Chapter Seventeen 146
Chapter Eighteen 154
Chapter Nineteen 163

Chapter Twenty 170

Chapter Twenty-One 179

Chapter Twenty-Two 188

Chapter Twenty-Three... 197

Chapter Twenty-Four 206

Chapter Twenty-Five 213

Chapter Twenty-Six 220

Chapter Twenty-Six 229

Chapter Twenty-Seven 237

Chapter Twenty-Eight 246

Chapter Twenty-Nine 254

Chapter Thirty 262

Chapter Thirty-One.. 268

Chapter Thirty-Two 277

Chapter Thirty-Three 283

Epilogue 291

Extended Epilogue 299

   Also by Ava Winters 317

Let's connect!

Impact my upcoming stories!

My passionate readers influenced the core soul of the book you are holding in your hands! The title, the cover, the essence of the book as a whole was affected by them!

Their support on my publishing journey is paramount! I devote this book to them!

If you are not a member yet, join now! As an added BONUS, you will receive my Novella **"The Cowboys' Wounded Lady"**:

**FREE EXCLUSIVE GIFT
(available only to my subscribers)**

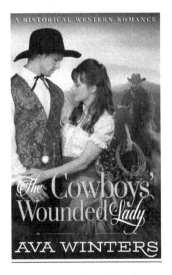

Go to the link:
https://avawinters.com/novella-amazon

Letter from Ava Winters

"Here is a lifelong bookworm, a devoted teacher and a mother of two boys. I also make mean sandwiches."

If someone wanted to describe me in one sentence, that would be it. There has never been a greater joy in my life than spending time with children and seeing them grow up - all my children, including the 23 little 9-year-olds that I currently teach. And I have not known such bliss than that of reading a good book.

As a Western Historical Romance writer, my passion has always been reading and writing romance novels. The historical part came after my studies as a teacher - I was mesmerized by the stories I heard, so much that I wanted to visit every place I learned about. And so, I did, finding the love of my life along the way as I walked the paths of my characters.

Now, I'm a full-time elementary school teacher, a full-time mother of two wonderful boys and a full-time writer. Wondering how I manage all of them? I did too, at first, but then I realized it's because everything I do I love, and I have the chance to share it with all of you.

And I would love to see you again in this small adventure of mine!

Until next time,

Ava Winters

Prologue

Summer 1880

The bitter taste in the wind caught her attention.

Nora jerked her head up to look toward the open window. The sun was beginning to set in the distance, creating for long shadows and vibrant colors in the sky. But, as she sniffed the air, she knew something was wrong.

It seemed as though the fear in her heart would never truly fade.

She scrambled over to the door, yanking it open to see where the scent could be coming from. Her eyes widened— she could see it, as well. There was smoke pluming high in the air, ash-gray clouds that were too thick and heavy to be safe.

A gasp escaped her lips as she looked below the smoke.

There was no way to deny the red haze of flames far off in the distance. Nora scrambled out onto the back porch, her mouth gaping as her heart sunk. There was a fire. And it had to be large for her to see so much.

It wasn't on her ranch. But any comfort she might have felt from that discovery was immediately weakened when she realized it was coming from next door. Their neighbors.

"No," Nora breathed in horror.

She could taste the bitter ashes once more. They were stronger now, and she had an inkling that it would only grow worse.

There was no time to hide nor hesitate. Nora's heart hammered as she ran back into the house. She breathed deeply as she hurried about to grab the one thing that mattered: Mattie. Little Mattie was still at the table.

"Nora?"

"We have to go at once," Nora said. It took all of her strength not to collapse in a state of panic. But there was no time. They had to move quickly. She scooped the child out of her seat and put her on her feet. Grabbing the girl's hand firmly, she started moving them back toward the door. "Now. Run, Mattie!"

The little girl grunted but obeyed. Her grip tightened on Nora's hand as they ran out the door. She didn't even turn around to lock it, let alone close it behind them.

Every minute mattered.

"Up you go," she said breathily as she heaved Mattie onto the buckboard seat. "Stay there!" Then she ran to the nearest stall, quickly readying a horse that could guide them. Even though it took a minute to prepare the animal, this would still be faster than if she ran. Nora prepared the horse, wiped her brow, and hurriedly joined the girl.

Then, they were off.

She gasped for breath as they went. Her chest heaved from moving around so quickly, as well as from the horror they were riding into. Nora prayed as they went, asking the Lord to help them and protect their neighbors.

"Don't be dead," she whispered under her breath. "Don't be dead, please, don't be dead."

She had lost too many people.

Just the thought of losing her neighbors made her eyes sting. But Nora didn't have time to brush away any tears at the moment. She had to keep her eyes open to be prepared. There was no time to dawdle.

A small ounce of relief filled her heart when the house came into view. It was not on fire. The house was safe, at least for the time being.

It was a different story for the barn, covered pen, and shed. All three were blazing. They were close to one another, within a couple dozen yards. Nora stopped for a minute to watch everything. Hundreds of thoughts ran through her mind.

Three buildings on fire was not an accident. It couldn't be.

But the idea that these were intentional fires sent a rippling fear throughout her body. Nora felt her stomach roll uneasily. She forced herself to climb down. Helping Mattie onto the ground, as well, she held the child close for safety.

Mattie clung to her tightly. "What's happening?" she asked tearfully.

Nora's heart pounded as she shook her head. "I don't know," she murmured.

She tried to comprehend the view before her, but she knew they didn't have time. Her eyes looked over the buildings with horror. The roof of the shed had caved in already, and the others were on their way.

Were there animals inside any of those buildings? People?

They had to find out. They had to stop this monstrous fire before it grew and swallowed everything. Nora coughed as she tasted the smoke on her lips. Something was terribly wrong, and she wasn't sure how they could fix it.

Chapter One

Spring 1880

A bead of sweat slowly slipped from her forehead down to the tip of her nose.

Nora did her best to ignore the itch, trying not to go cross-eyed as she attempted to stay focused on the fabric she was currently working on with her machine. The loud hum of the sewing factory echoed all around her; it was steady and terribly annoying. Like clockwork, a headache began to set in with the heat.

She had talked with her boss about opening a few of the windows, but he told her they were sealed shut. There was nothing they could do. She would have to work in the heat as long as she had a job.

So, she scrunched up her nose to take care of the itch, then concentrated on the task at hand. There was no time to dawdle or make mistakes.

Working at the factory was long, tedious work. The chairs were uncomfortable, the room was hot, and the loud noise of the other sewing machines always made her head hurt. Two years had passed since she had begged for the job there, and it had been this miserable ever since.

"Three o'clock!" the floor manager cried out as he rang a bell. "Three o'clock!"

Immediately, half the workers stood up and began to stretch their legs and arms. Then, they filed out for their late lunch break, leaving the rest behind.

Nora kept her head down, listening to their murmuring as they went. Nobody liked their job there. But they all stayed because they could earn more money the faster and harder they worked, something most of the other factories in Wilmington, Delaware didn't provide. In the beginning, Nora had practically only earned pennies. But, with time and effort, she had improved greatly.

"See you in a minute, Nora," a familiar voice sang to her as she passed by. It was only for Lauren that she looked up, nodding to her close friend.

Lauren was the only one there who was permitted to move about during the noon break as well as the three o'clock break. This agreement had taken a good bit of wrestling to achieve, but her husband was on the city council and had some sway. Enough time had passed that the young wife was beginning to show her swollen belly now, which also helped in the matter. Nora gave her friend a smile before Lauren left the room.

Then, she turned back to the drapes she was stitching. This bundle would be sent straight to New York City for the elite. It was soft in her hands, which meant it was expensive and she had to be careful with every stitch.

She dreamed of a beautiful life like that, where she could have similar maroon satin drapes. There would be people who helped her dress in the latest fashions, with all types of food for her to enjoy. None of this was possible, of course, but she liked to dream. And dreaming helped the time pass her by.

Only another five hours to go.

Ten hours of work every day wore her out. Especially if she found a side job to do afterward. Though she always asked about working more, the factory had set hours and refused to pay her anything extra. Nora began to calculate how far along she was to see if she might be able to complete another two or three on top of her current set of drapes. They paid more than clothing items, but also took longer to sew.

If she could somehow get another five sets of drapes done, then she would have enough for a hearty meal that evening. Her mouth watered at the thought of fresh meat from the market.

After all, this money she earned would finally be completely going into her own pockets. The debts of her father were paid at last. She could rest a little easier knowing that she didn't owe anyone any money.

But the fates seemed to have another idea in mind.

Nora was just about to finish up on her current running stitch when movement from the doors caught her eye. She didn't usually pay any mind to people that came and went. It was important to her to focus on her work. Except the person who entered the doors didn't belong in the factory, and that was why she immediately stopped.

Her blood chilled.

The man looked out of place. It was a rather drab building with gray walls and no decorations. Even the sunlight hardly cheered the place up.

Victor Rawls wore a fine dark blue suit, cut to fit him perfectly. His hair was combed back and oiled, and light glanced off the numerous rings he wore. The man looked wealthy in a way she had never seen anyone else do before; it was as if the world couldn't touch him.

And he was headed her way.

Feeling the blood drain from her face, Nora wondered how this was possible. She glanced around in the hopes that he was there for something else. But when she looked back, Mr.

Rawls was looking right at her. He was coming right over to her, for some reason.

It didn't make sense. This was the man that she had just paid off. She wondered why he was there, at her work. They shouldn't have to see each other ever again.

He was an older man who could make her squirm with just one glance, and she hated it. But last week, she had submitted her final payment.

And they should have never seen one another afterward. That's what Nora had supposed.

Except he was there, at her workplace, headed right in her direction. She felt her mouth turn dry. The relief she had felt all week in finally being free of his control began to fade away. Why was he there?

She looked around the room to find that no one else was paying much attention. They didn't know who he was, and they didn't care. Stopping her work, she stood up and went over to him so they wouldn't disturb the others on the sewing floor. Nora rubbed her hands together anxiously as she reached him.

"Mr. Rawls, it's a... You're not here for me, are you? We should have no more business together. I paid you everything my father owed you."

"Life is a struggle, is it not? I've been looking all over for you, Miss Nora." He fixed his jacket with an unconcerned air. "Unfortunately, you are wrong in that respect. While you may have paid off the original amount that your father requested in his loan, you've forgotten about the interest that was accrued over the years it took to pay off the original amount."

Her mouth dropped open in dismay.

Interest? She hadn't heard anything about that before in her few conversations with him or in the documentation. Nora ransacked her mind as she struggled to keep her composure.

This had to be a joke, after all. If it wasn't, then she still owed him money, and she still wasn't free. A lump formed in her throat, making it hard to swallow. The panic began to rise within her.

Shaking her head, Nora told him, "You never said anything about the interest. I don't have any record. I thought I paid you off, I thought—"

Mr. Rawls tutted.

"Years. It's been years," he repeated. "I'm expecting another payment tomorrow, seeing as you didn't bring one by yesterday. Business between the two of us shall resume. I expect in-person payments due every Tuesday at 8 o'clock in the evening."

Her eyes widened. He wanted her to keep paying him exactly as she had before? Nora could feel something heavy begin to weigh her down as she tried to imagine starting the cycle all over again.

Making those payments had nearly killed her. Two years of scrimping and saving just to stay alive had been terrible. She had hardly slept, never had enough to eat, and had prayed night and day for it all to come to an end soon. The idea of having to live like this all over again did not sound possible. She had been waiting so long to be free.

"I don't... but how much?" Nora stammered.

It couldn't be very much if it was just interest. She didn't know much about what that implied, but it couldn't be nearly what she had owed in the first place.

Thinking quickly, she wondered if she could convince Mr. Rawls to cut the payments into smaller increments for a little longer. The interest that he mentioned could only take a few more weeks. Then, in smaller payments, she could manage not to live such a horrible and lonely life.

"One thousand dollars."

She nearly burst into tears. Her mouth hung open as she stared at him. That was half of what she had already paid back. This meant that it would take her another year, if not a little longer, to pay it all back. She tried to imagine living another year like she had done for the last two, but couldn't. Her eyes stung at the very idea.

Nora tried to find her voice. "But... that's..."

He nodded. "A lot. Shame, isn't it?"

Raising her gaze to meet his, she felt the panic rise a little higher. "Please. How can this be the case? There was no mention of the interest. I thought what I paid was already everything. Are you sure that I owe you more? That much? I mean, I... Surely, we can work something out. I only have so much. It took me years to pay off what my father owed already."

Mr. Rawls took a small step back. With one eyebrow raised, he gave her one good look. It was a long one as he eyed her from toe to head.

Never before had she been looked at with such a lecherous leer.

Nora squirmed. Turning away, she ended up glancing at a few of the other women in the room. Several of them were looking her way. Most of them wore smirks, with a few skeptical glances. None of them made her feel comfortable or secure as they judged her for the man who stood before her.

"My offer of marriage still stands," he said, and he didn't seem to notice the other women in the room. His smirk grew. "You'd make a fine wife, sweetheart. And if you wanted to make that deal instead, I think I would be willing to consider your father's debt repaid in full. No more debt or interest to worry about. What do you think of that?"

The hum of sewing machines softened against the hiss of others in the room beginning to whisper. Someone must have heard what Mr. Rawls said, Nora supposed. That would not have been hard because he had a rather loud voice.

Ducking her head, she wished she could have forgotten about that.

It had been around the first anniversary of her father's death. She had gone to Mr. Rawls' office to beg for more time, since she had lost one of her jobs. The hotel had shut down, leaving her both without that extra income and without a home, since she had rented a bed alongside several other maids. When he'd told her that it wasn't his problem, he had offered to take her into his home.

But she couldn't do it, not with him. Marriage was far from her mind, and he was the last option she would ever consider. Mr. Rawls preyed on everyone and had a reputation around town for his ruthlessness.

A hot flush rushed up her neck at his offer. It felt like she was being mocked and belittled all at once. Nora wished for nothing more than to disappear in that moment.

"I..."

Before she could say anything, a familiar hand pressed against her back. Nora swallowed hard as she turned to find Lauren right there.

Her friend had returned. She hardly had time to realize that she wasn't alone any longer in this situation as Lauren spoke up to Mr. Rawls.

"I think Nora here has heard enough, sir," she said in a firm manner. "You've said your piece, and now I think it's time you left. If you're not employed in the factory, then you're not supposed to be here. Leave immediately, or I'll call Mr. Peterson, who owns this place. He won't take kindly to this and we don't, either."

That gave Nora hope. She looked at her friend gratefully, never having thought of that.

Of course, he wasn't allowed. It was one of the reasons she had been so jarred by his presence there. Those were the rules of the factory, though she wasn't sure she would have been brave enough to tell him on her own.

As for Mr. Rawls, he raised his hands in mock surrender. But it was the grin that left her on edge.

"Don't you worry, missus," he replied. "I was just getting ready to leave. As for you, Nora, I'll be seeing you again soon."

It wasn't until he disappeared from the room that Nora's tense shoulders relaxed. She wrapped an arm around Lauren for strength as she murmured a word of gratitude. Yet, even as the two of them returned to their sewing machines, Nora knew this trouble was far from over.

Chapter Two

He hadn't planned on this.

Granted, there was a lot that Joseph Bowman had not planned on. He'd tried hard to be prepared and to learn to expect the unexpected. Life was filled with enough trials and tribulations that he wanted to do what he could to manage such variables.

Except life kept finding a way to throw him off-guard.

Especially now, as he stood under the willow tree, looking at the small crosses placed before him. There would be headstones, eventually. That was the plan. But that was the only plan he knew of at the moment.

A shaky breath escaped his lips and he wished this was all some dreadful dream.

Unfortunately, he had pinched himself enough times to know that he wasn't asleep, and he wasn't going to escape this situation. He was trapped here in this strange world with so little. Less now, he supposed.

The wind whistled through the trees, ruffling the long branches. He tore his eyes away from the crosses to watch. It was a reminder of where he was and what would happen now. Though he hardly had an idea, he supposed he had best start working it out.

"A new plan." He forced the words out, though his tongue felt thick.

Joe, as he'd always gone by, didn't like it. He didn't want this. This was not supposed to have happened. He had worked so hard all of his life to avoid something like this. No matter how hard he tried, no matter how much he prepared himself, it didn't seem to change. There was still sorrow and pain to be found.

He felt something break within him.

Crumbling at the base of the tree's roots, Joe fell to his knees. He buried his face in his hands and tried to withhold the tears from falling. The loss he felt was overwhelming. Never before had he felt so alone in his life.

Though he had not lived in Nebraska, close to the rest of his family, for several years, he had always thought that he would have more time with his brother.

But now, Billy was gone.

He couldn't remember their final conversation. They would have shared parting words before he'd left to return to New York City, where he lived and worked. Perhaps there had been a joke and then a solemn moment where they knew it would be some time before they saw one another again. It's what he would have expected. But there was no way Joe could have known it would be their last talk together, the last time he saw his brother.

They should have talked a little longer, said a little more.

As he tried to recall all his past conversations with Billy, Joe continued to struggle with accepting this harsh loss. Their parents had passed away years ago, back in Pennsylvania, where they had grown up as a happy little family. But then they had gone their own ways. Billy had moved west to Nebraska to build a life with his own family. And Joe had gone east for his career.

It had been the right thing to do, he had told himself when he'd first made his way to New York.

But now, he began to second-guess his decisions. Being so far away meant rarely seeing what was left of his family. Part of him had done that on purpose, because of Billy's wife Sophia. It had been easier for him to stay away. He hadn't wanted to be any more lonely or heartbroken then, so he'd only visited once.

That first visit out to Nebraska had been for a funeral, as well.

"You should stay," Billy had told him one morning during his last visit. "You could help me run this ranch. Someday, it's going to be big and successful. I can feel it, Joe. And you have the brains here, don't you? Stay with us."

He hadn't taken the invitation seriously. Chuckling, Joe had merely shaken his head at the idea. "Me? Living out West? That's preposterous. I don't belong out here, Billy. I wouldn't have any idea what to do."

"That's a terrible excuse," his brother had been quick to point out. "You'll figure it out. You always have. I bet, with you here, we could finally turn over a proper profit and double in size within the year. Think about it. Family should stay together, shouldn't they? And what do you have in the city that you can't have here?"

It had been a question that Joe hadn't been able to answer then. He had thought of many attributes and businesses and experiences in New York City that would never be found in Nebraska. Though he had tried to convince his brother to bring his family to visit several times, they had never been able to find the time. So, his brother had no idea what he was talking about when it came to the city lights and opportunities there.

And yet, perhaps Joe hadn't understood Billy, in return.

Because he didn't have family in the city like he did in Nebraska. All he had was the busy job and the busy life filled with parties and events. Yet, he didn't always enjoy either of them. Taking that trip out West, away from his business, had been a breath of fresh air that he hadn't known he'd needed at the time. Even now, Joe knew he would have enjoyed the chance to come back out to visit under different circumstances.

Happier circumstances.

The job was a good one, but a career was nothing when it meant he was always alone. Joe pondered how different his life might have turned out to be in the last four years since Billy had made that offer.

"Maybe," he had responded instead. "I'll have to return to the city one way or another. If I find myself craving the wide-open world, however, then I'll let you know. Deal?"

"Deal."

It might have been fun. He would ride a horse through fields unbothered by other humans. He would learn to be a cowboy and explore what it was like to manage a ranch. It could have been an adventure that he explored with his family.

But now it was too late.

Sophia had died four years ago. And now, Billy was gone. Joe felt more alone than he ever had in all his life. Through the past heartache and grief, this was a new pain that he dearly wished to be free from.

"Uncle Joey?"

He took a staggering breath. Hurriedly, he climbed to his feet. Brushing the dirt off his clothes and drying his face, Joe turned around to see little Mattie looking up at him with her big brown eyes.

Only seven years old and now an orphan.

She would need him. He had only arrived the afternoon before. They had met up for a few minutes, but they were both suffering on their own. Joe had no idea how to talk to the child through his grief.

She had the soft blonde hair of her mother, pinned back due to help from the Camerons. Audrey and Dan Cameron lived on the ranch just west of them and had been minding Mattie since Billy died. They were the ones who had sent the telegram to Joe. He had arrived and found the growing girl so much bigger than the three-year-old he had seen before. Children were hard to talk to, and he hadn't been able to find any words to say to her then.

Nor in this moment, either.

"Mattie." His voice sounded rough as he struggled with his words. "What are you doing here?"

Her eyes dropped down to look away and she fiddled with her dress. It was a dark blue one. There hadn't been time to put her in anything for mourning. But Joe supposed folks didn't have time for that out West. Only the pastor had worn black for the funeral they'd had just a few hours ago.

"Audrey said to come get you," the girl mumbled, just loud enough to be heard. "She said it's time to eat."

"I'm not hungry." He said the words before he caught himself. Joe winced and shook his head. "I mean, I'll just... All right. I'll come in a moment. You can go back now," he added when she didn't budge.

Too late, he noticed that she was hesitantly eyeing the fresh pile of dirt before the crosses. Joe's heart sunk right into his stomach. He hadn't meant to sound rude. But, as he opened his mouth to apologize to his niece, Mattie took off running back to the house without a word.

His shoulders slumped.

Now it was just the two of them. Him and Mattie. Except they were strangers to one another and clearly didn't know what to say. He was her guardian now, but he hadn't had much time to think about what this would mean for the two of them.

When he'd heard the news, he had booked the next train out to get to the ranch. Fairwell, Nebraska was not his home. He would be there for the funeral, clear out the ranch, and then take his niece back to New York City with him. She was young and energetic and so she would adapt even more quickly than he had when he first arrived. It seemed like a good idea, and reasonable for the two of them. Surely, she would want to be far away from a place filled with the haunting memories of her parents.

But as Joe reluctantly stepped out from the shaded tree into the glaring sunlight, he saw the world around him.

It was a different world compared to the one he had seen four years ago upon his prior visit. His brother had done a great job in that time, building up the ranch into something impressive. Billy was a smart, hard-working man no matter what he said about himself. Joe had been surprised to see how pleasant the cattle operation had grown during those years. Arriving to see his brother's ranch should have been a thrilling moment where he could see all the progress that Billy had made.

Instead, it was painful. He kept expecting to find his brother coming around the corner or talking in the next room. But Billy wouldn't be doing any of that anymore.

Joe tried to swallow his grief as he headed toward the house. He rubbed his hands together anxiously, trying to mentally prepare himself for company.

The Camerons were helping out and he couldn't be more grateful. They had done so much already and continued to make sure that both he and Mattie were eating and sleeping. He couldn't rely on them much longer, Joe knew, and he appreciated their kindness.

On the way to the house, he glanced up to see movement over by the bunkhouse for the ranch hands. There were a couple of them around the building just a hundred yards away. Joe squinted, recognizing the foreman, Ezra Moody. But he couldn't recall if he had met anyone else. They were taking good care of the ranch, in the meantime.

It was a good thing, he thought to himself, for he didn't know what he would say if they needed anything from him.

That was when it dawned on him that they would, eventually, ask. The ranch hands would need him. He owned the house and the ranch now, and he was Mattie's caretaker. Joe slowed down as he looked around him. A new weight began to descend on his shoulders.

The ranch hands lived here. This was their home more than it was his.

There were grasslands out where the cattle lived. He knew there was a river around there, as well, one that flowed especially well during the spring, though he couldn't recall where it was. He hadn't planned on needing to explore the ranch, but he had seen enough to see its growth.

A well had been put in over by the stables, plus a water pump up by the house. His brother loved modern conveniences and had written him three letters that year explaining his water pump, even though Joe had them in the city.

Just over one hundred and fifty acres for a sprawling, booming ranch. He wondered how many cattle were there. They enjoyed the flat valley, but Joe recalled his brother saying once that there was a grove of trees not too far from the house that several cows enjoyed wandering into.

There was so much out here that Joe didn't know what to do with. The ranch could stay put if he left. Surely, someone else would buy it. They would take care of the animals. But what about the ranch hands? He hadn't considered this.

What was he to do with them if he took Mattie up to New York?

His mouth dried at the prospect of putting all these men out of work. He doubted any of them would be able to purchase the ranch if he put it up for sale. Except he hadn't considered any other ideas. He made it to the wide porch around the house as he struggled to accept that there was even more pressure on him now.

He had just lost his brother, but he had gained a lot in return.

Joe would give it all back to Billy in a heartbeat. He didn't know what he would do now, with so many folks depending on him. Weighing the options, he made his way into the house to try and eat something. Perhaps, with a little food in his belly, he could begin to think more clearly.

Chapter Three

Nora stared at the train that had just pulled into the station.

She clutched her two bags that now carried everything that she still owned. Her heart thudded against her ribs. Was she really doing this? Leaving Delaware forever? This was the only place she had ever known, and now she would never return.

Closing her eyes, she thought back to when the decision had been made.

It had only been three months ago when Victor Rawls had crept his way back into her life. He had showed up at the factory with those dark eyes, hanging around like a vulture waiting for her to finally give up the ghost. She was left with no choice but to start making payments to him again or marry him. If she tried to fight it, Nora had no doubt that she would be tossed into a jail cell for the rest of her days.

She had still been shaking when she'd made it back to her small apartment. It was on the outskirts of town, surrounded by others struggling to make it day by day. Everything was dirty and it smelled like death. Though she tried to clean up her tiny home as best as she could, there was only so much she could do. So, Nora had gone into her home with Lauren following behind her.

The apartment had a table and two chairs on one side. The other side included her cot, which was tucked away behind a curtain she had hung up to hide her bed from guests. Or rather, from Lauren, because no one else ever came to visit her.

She had a window seat that she loved, but it was the only thing Nora liked about her little apartment. It was small, with hardly any amenities—which only worked once in a while.

"I'm making us tea," Lauren had proclaimed after locking the door behind her. "Take a seat."

Nora hadn't needed to be told twice. She'd collapsed at her table before dropping her head into her arms. A small groan escaped her lips when she closed her eyes.

His face came into her mind, haunting her. A nauseating feeling washed over her, making her wish that she had eaten recently enough to throw it back up. But she hadn't had anything since her morning break at the factory, hours ago. Her stomach rumbled, but the idea of food left a bitter taste on her tongue.

The shock was finally wearing off. She had hardly finished the project that she had begun before Rawls' arrival by the end of the day, unable to do anything more. It meant she had earned close to nothing for the day.

But she didn't have time to think about that yet. She couldn't get that man's face off her mind. She shuddered and shook her head.

"Another year," she had whispered before looking up to her friend that evening. Nora felt cold all over as she tried to imagine living like this for any longer, with the weariness and exhaustion. "Twelve more months. I don't know if I can do that, Lauren. It's nearly killed me already. All those extra jobs. The long nights, the days without food, I... What am I supposed to do?"

Her dearest friend looked over to her with a sincere expression. Lauren sighed and shook her head. "I'm sorry, Nora. I don't know. I've been thinking all day. Do you think you could take him before a judge about this?"

"How would I afford a lawyer?" Nora pointed out. "Most likely he would win, anyways. And then I would have more debt on my shoulders. From the lawyer and from not paying him all the while."

Lauren groaned. "I just don't believe that's possible. I don't know much about banking or interest, but that's too much. Too much, Nora. How can it be so much? After all you've done?"

Burying her head back into her arms, Nora felt the same way. They had talked about this during their long walk to her home. Neither of them could seem to understand that this was happening to her again—another debt she had to pay off in order to be free.

What if Victor Rawls never let her be free?

She jerked up as a horrible thought came to mind. He could tack interest on top of the interest, couldn't he? She could pay him off over the year only for more interest to accrue. It would become a never-ending cycle of her constantly having to pay Mr. Rawls all that she earned. This would leave her destitute, struggling to survive for the rest of her days.

Perhaps she would never be free.

"It can't be true," Nora murmured as a cold inkling of fear began to drip down her spine. Her hands balled into fists, her fingernails leaving crescent shapes dug into her palm. "He would practically own me."

Lauren whipped around. "No. Don't you say that, Nora. We'll figure something out. I know it. You won't marry him, promise me that. Promise me you won't marry him."

A lump formed in Nora's throat as she tried to imagine accepting the man's proposal so that she would no longer have any debt owed to him. He had teasingly mentioned in the beginning that she was a beauty and would look like a fine lady on his arm. If the debt was washed out, there was a fair chance she would never have to work another day in her life with him as her husband.

But then another shudder rippled through her.

Even if her financial debt was removed, there would always be something else. He would hang threats over her head and would never make her feel safe or happy. She couldn't marry him, no matter what.

"I won't," Nora assured her friend. "I couldn't. I would rather die." Her eyes closed. "Which is what I'm worried will happen. This debt will never be over, Lauren. What am I supposed to do?"

"Leave."

She opened her eyes as Lauren joined her at the table with two cups of tea. Her friend was beautiful in her own right, with dark hair and dark eyes. There was a warmth to her cheeks as her belly swelled, and she always had at least half a smile on her face.

But now, she appeared serious. "Run away," Lauren added before nudging the teacup over to her.

To where? Nora stared as tears began to well up in her eyes. She couldn't leave. Her parents were buried here. This was the only home she had ever had, and she couldn't just walk away because she was scared. Could she?

And then, there was the thought of leaving Lauren. Sweet Lauren, who had always been her friend and her support. She couldn't imagine never seeing her again.

"That's crazy," she stammered. She shook her head, drumming her fingers on the table. "I can't just leave you. You're my only friend in the world, Lauren. I need you. And I want to be here for you, as well. Your family is growing, and I—"

The teacups were set to the side as her friend took her hands. "I know. I've been lucky, Nora. Feel this?" Lauren set Nora's hands on her large, curved stomach, where it only took a second before they could feel the movement of the babe within.

Nora inhaled sharply in amazement. "Oh."

"That's life right there," her friend pointed out to her. "I have a child that I will bring into the world soon. Only four months to go. This baby will have a happy mother and a wonderful father. Daniel and I are going to work hard to be good parents. This is the life we want. But look at the life that you have now. That can't be the life that you want, can it?"

She had made a point that Nora grudgingly recognized. "I know, but…"

It was clear that her friend was pointing out to her what she might miss if she continued to work, day and night, to pay off the debt without doing anything else. It shut her off from making more friends, enjoying activities out in the city, let alone meeting anyone.

Of course, she wanted a family like Lauren had.

This was all Nora had ever wanted. Her mother had died from pneumonia when she was young, and her father had died in a factory incident just over two years ago. Most of her life had been lonely. Nora would give anything to have a chance at what Lauren had. She and Daniel were happy two years after their marriage and now they were going to be welcoming a child into their lives.

"You deserve a chance at this, too," Lauren told her. "I'm happy, Nora. I want you to experience the same joy I have felt. But I'm afraid you won't ever have that if you stay here."

Though Nora opened her mouth to argue that there was always a chance, she didn't have any words to refute Lauren's point. She hesitated as she felt the baby move again. It was an incredible sensation. There was life in her friend's stomach.

She thought of her own life and couldn't help but admit that Lauren was right. There was no chance at a life for her there in Delaware. She would always have Mr. Rawls hovering over her shoulder, just waiting to pounce. If she didn't pay off this debt immediately, then she would never be free. She would never be free of debt or free of Mr. Rawls. That would control her life until the day she died.

"But I don't even know what I would do," Nora stammered as she tried to imagine leaving.

"You need to think about yourself." Letting go of her to take a sip of tea, Lauren offered a raised eyebrow. "Don't worry about me, just remember that. Focus on going far from here. You could go West, Nora. Can you even imagine? There's a whole world out there, ripe for the picking. Travel into unknown lands. Or even board a boat for England. You could do anything, if you really wanted to."

That had never occurred to her before.

She thought back to the days when she'd had time to daydream. Nora would come up with thrilling adventures that would send her off to find hidden treasure, to save others around her, or to meet exciting people. She had always wanted more than what she had in that moment.

Looking around, it was clear that she now had close to nothing. Her tiny home had very little furniture. Much of it had been found in the trash so she wouldn't have to pay for anything. There were rats in the walls, and she hadn't slept well in years.

She didn't have much and it wouldn't get better unless she did something about it.

Nora took a deep breath. "You're right. I will. I'll get out of here, one way or another."

It took them three days to make a plan. Nora was walking Lauren home after work when they stopped at the market to purchase a few baby bottles. They had paused by the books and magazines as the idea of becoming a mail-order bride was born.

"This makes sense," Lauren had told Nora when they brought the magazine back to her little apartment. "Think about it. You'll get far away from here. This could give you a home, security, and a roof over your head. Surely, there's a decent man out there looking for a young, pretty bride like yourself."

So, Nora put out her information and found someone to correspond with.

William, or Billy, Bowman was a rancher in Fairwell, Nebraska. He wrote her an introductory letter saying that he was a hard worker and wanted to find someone to spend the rest of his life with. The man had been married before, he explained, and had a young daughter who deserved a mother.

Nora was circumspect about this idea, and she had spoken more about her desire for honesty and absolute confidence about this decision than about her looks and her history. But Billy didn't seem to mind. She could see right from the start that he was a kind and light-hearted gentleman.

It took only three letters from the man for Nora to know what she wanted to do.

He had been through such pain in losing his parents and then his beloved wife, Sophia. The man made it clear in his letters. But he also spoke of his adoration for his daughter, the love he had for his ranch, and the hope he had for the future. He wrote clearly and simply in a way that drew her heart out West. The thought of moving for a man like Billy Bowman brought her comfort rather than fear. He was a good man who needed a wife for himself and a mother for his daughter, Mattie.

So, she'd responded that she would be coming out West to him. She wanted to be that wife and mother. Her heart was full at the prospect as she packed her bags to leave.

Nora quit her jobs one by one, praying she would never have to slave away like that again. She sold the few items she didn't need before cleaning out her home for someone else to claim.

As regards Mr. Rawls, Nora had debated a long time about what to do.

She made a few more of the payments that he had requested. But she'd said nothing about her intention to move, or that she would no longer be paying him anything. When she'd delivered her payments, she had brought Lauren in the hopes of the man not asking her about marriage again. He'd teased at the subject, but nothing more. And neither of them had said a word about Nora leaving town soon, to never return.

And now, she was leaving Delaware.

There was a tearful goodbye with her dearest friend in the station before Nora boarded the train. She looked out her window and waved to Lauren.

Her friend quickly wiped away her tears before waving back.

They would write to each other, Nora knew. And she hoped that someday they would see one another again, but something told her that might not happen. The train finally began to move, and Lauren disappeared.

Nora took a deep breath. She leaned back on her bench and prayed to the Lord that she really was headed for a better place, where she could have a family at last.

Chapter Four

Joe found the photo first.

The letters were right beneath it in a thick envelope that sat in his brother's chest at the food of the bed. It was a photo of a woman that was not Billy's wife.

Joe studied the picture. Whoever she was, she was young, with light curly hair down to her shoulders. She looked back at him with parted lips and arched eyebrows, making him feel like she was trying to figure him out.

He turned the photo around to see a name scribbled on the back.

"Nora Gilmore." Joe said the name out loud. No one had mentioned her to him before, including Billy. So, he had opened the envelope and sorted through the few letters. Nothing could have prepared him for this.

A mail-order bride?

Billy had never mentioned that he was looking to marry someone else. The man had always talked about being focused on his ranch and his daughter. Joe couldn't imagine his brother marrying anyone after Sophia.

As he read her letters, however, he began to get an inkling of what more had been going on in his brother's heart before his untimely passing. Miss Gilmore thanked him for his kindness and honesty, especially about how he had painted his home and his family. She mentioned Sophia by name and how much she hoped that they could find some form of happiness together when she arrived.

Joe inhaled sharply as he realized that her arrival was expected the day after tomorrow.

It had only been two days since Billy's funeral and three days since Billy's death. No one had known to reach out to her before she began her travels.

How could he tell this hopeful young lady that Billy had passed? She would arrive thinking she was meant to be a bride, only to find out she hadn't even had proper time to marry him and become his widow.

Joe picked the photo back up to study it. She was rather beautiful. He liked her round little nose and the curve of her lips. Just as he began to wonder if Billy had a complete photograph besides this one that only showed her neck and head, he caught himself shamefully admiring an attractive young woman who was about to discover all her hopes were dashed.

This was no time to think of a pretty woman when he had to make plans to go to town for her and tell her the news.

He stuffed the letters in his vest pocket and left.

The day was growing late, and he knew he should go pick up his niece from the Camerons' home. He made his way over on a spare horse and dismounted in the Camerons' yard.

There was Audrey, in the kitchen window.

She waved to catch his attention. "There you are," she called. "Come inside, Joe. Welcome."

Giving her a nod, he fixed his vest and started up the steps.

He didn't like letting himself into others' homes, though it seemed normal for those out in the West. Joe grudgingly stepped through the door and walked over to the kitchen. It was a large space that looked very much like the one at his brother's house.

The Camerons had settled down ten years ago. The couple had built this home when they were hardly in their twenties. "Excited newlyweds" was the term that Audrey liked to use. They had made a lovely home that eventually included a loft and a cellar.

Billy had soon purchased the land right next to them once he'd married Sophia. The four of them had become quick friends. Sophia had admired the Camerons' home so much that Billy had based much of their home off of it.

As he walked into the kitchen, he was reminded of this all over again.

The window let in natural light that glanced off the pots and pans that hung on the far wall. They were set up over a small cabinet that held the dishware. In the next corner was a cast iron cook stove, which was currently being used. He could smell lemon and a hint of something else, though he couldn't quite place it.

Against the other wall below the window sat larger equipment like the coffee grinder, a butter churn, and a basin set up for a sink.

"Come in, come in," Audrey said. "My lemon pie should be ready soon. I hope you're hungry. And Mattie is here, of course. She's right… Mattie? Mattie, did you find the towel?"

Mattie came running into the kitchen clutching a white towel in both hands. She smiled hopefully at Audrey before noticing her uncle there. To his embarrassment, her smile faded and she dropped her arms.

"Hello, Mattie," Joe offered hopefully. He tried to smile but he wasn't sure it was helping.

"Hello, Uncle Joe." She shifted her weight anxiously from foot to foot. "Do I have to leave now?"

His stomach churned, wondering if he was such a sorry figure to be around on his own. But then he glanced at Audrey and knew that it had to mean a lot for Mattie to spend time with her neighbor. After all, the two girls knew each other well. They hardly knew him. And he was most assuredly not at his best at the moment.

"No." Joe swallowed when the woman glanced over at him. "No, we don't. We can stay for a while. Did you, er, help Audrey with her lemon pie?"

"She sure did," Audrey chucked as she took the towel from the young girl. "Tell your uncle what you did, Mattie."

The child hesitated. She took a small step closer to Audrey, who began to use the towel to clean up. When Mattie found that her friend wasn't going to do the rest of the talking for her, she slowly found the courage to speak up.

"I made the mengue," Mattie mumbled. Her golden hair fell in her face as she looked down.

Joe hesitated before he realized what she was saying. "Do you mean the meringue?"

His niece nodded furiously. "With the egg whites and everything. I messed up first, but then Audrey helped me. She even let me help with the crust."

"That's wonderful," Joe said as he worked hard to keep a smile on his face for her. "I bet it's going to be a delicious pie. It sounds like you had a good day, is that right?"

She nodded before turning away to watch Audrey clean. Joe tried to find something else to say, but he didn't get much more from her. The two of them struggled to talk until Audrey's husband, Dan, returned from his day of work.

Joe didn't want to take up any more of the couple's time, but they insisted on hosting supper. It was a quiet and delicious meal. Joe asked Dan about his ranch and they talked business for the evening, even until Mattie dozed off in the nearby rocking chair.

She held her toy doll in her arms and slept. But even from there, Joe could see the circles under her eyes.

"Well?" Dan asked him after a moment of silence. "Have you made up your mind?"

Joe swallowed as he glanced over at his niece. He knew nothing of children. That much had been made blatantly obvious over the last couple of days. In the letters he used to exchange with his brother, Billy had talked often about how much he wanted to give Mattie every chance in the world. Joe wanted to do the same, for his brother and for his niece.

"I think I'm going to stay." He cleared his throat noisily as he gave Dan a weak smile. "I know nothing about running a sprawling ranch. Yet I think that's what's best for Mattie. I wanted to sell the ranch and take her back to New York City, but I think I owe it to her and to myself to try and continue my brother's legacy."

A weight settled on his shoulders as he thought back to Billy's offer for him to stay four years ago. He couldn't go back in time to change his mind no matter how much he wished he could.

"That's wonderful," Audrey volunteered. "I think your brother would have greatly appreciated that."

Joe scoffed before he could help it. Shaking his head, he shrugged and put his hands on the table. "I don't know about that. He said I should stay the last time I came here. Back when Sophia died. For years, I thought about changing my mind. But I didn't, and now he's gone."

"Billy wasn't mad at you," Dan said slowly. "You know that, don't you?"

"Your brother wasn't like that," his wife added confidently. "The whole town knew and loved Billy. He was a good, selfless man, who will be greatly missed. He wasn't the type to hold grudges."

The words were kind, but Joe wasn't sure he believed them. He hadn't explained, but they didn't know what it was like four years ago. Joe had left after telling Billy that he would never live out west. He said he had a good life and a better career in the city compared to minding a small ranch. It had grown tense between them, though they never talked about it. So, he had left Nebraska and remained in the city, wallowing in his loneliness for letting his pride get the better of him.

And, because of his stubbornness, there could be no reconciliation.

Billy had surpassed him in every way and now he was gone, leaving everything behind for Joe. He didn't deserve any of it, and he wondered if he would ever be the type of man that his brother had been.

"I'm not my brother," Joe mumbled. "But I should do what I can to keep him alive."

Would he have still been alive if I had accepted his offer to stay here? All accidents are preventable in one form or another. It could have been me instead, at the very least. Then, Mattie wouldn't have lost both of her parents.

"Like the ranch." Joe cleared his throat before cheating a glance over at his sleeping niece. "For Mattie's sake, I'm going to stay here. *We* are going to stay here. I didn't need to stay in the city, anyway, and I could use a change. How hard can it be?"

Audrey clapped twice at the news. "Good! We're happy for you. And we'll be here to help along the way. Won't we, Dan? Mattie will be happy here, she always has been. Besides, this home is her remaining connection to her parents. Oh, you'll be happy here, Joe, I'm sure of it."

From the corner of his eye, he saw Mattie stir. The sun was setting and it was growing late. He realized they had best head out for the night. He ran a hand over his shirt before standing, only to hear a crinkle in his vest.

It was the letters.

"Right. Nora Gilmore," he breathed softly. Then, he looked up at the confused couple. "Billy was going to remarry. Did he tell you this?"

Though Dan hesitated, Audrey clasped a hand over her mouth. She looked over to Mattie before turning back to Joe. When she did, she had tears in her eyes. "Oh, I cannot believe I forgot. Dan, how could we? Billy told us he had found someone to accept his proposal. A sweet young lady. Was that her name?"

"He was thrilled," Dan said hoarsely. "Even Mattie was."

His wife nodded as she sniffled. "She was. She wanted a new mother. Mattie had begun to draw a card for her, I remember. It's around here somewhere. I... oh, goodness. Yes, she's been so withdrawn. A week ago, she was dancing everywhere. But now..."

The three of them looked back to study the small child who had suffered through so much in her few years.

"She's on her way," Joe confessed in a low tone. Pulling out the papers, he showed them her picture. "It was too late to reach out. She'll be here soon, and I can't imagine sending her back, but I don't know what to do. Billy won't be here for her."

Dan shook his head. "I still can't believe he's gone. He's done so much. Losing Sophia was hard, but he put his energy into building a great ranch. And raising sweet Mattie over there. Billy always said that the ranch was for Sophia, even after she was gone. I think you're doing the right thing. Your brother would want you here."

It was a kind gesture, even if Joe didn't completely believe that at the moment. He nodded his thanks before glancing at the picture. "Maybe. He wanted her here, too. But I'm not looking forward to giving her the news. It's going to be a horrible shock. What am I supposed to do, marry her?"

There was silence for a moment before Audrey cleared her throat.

"You could," she offered. "Of course, there's no need to pressure her. But, if she's looking for a new family, then perhaps you should seriously consider that."

His eyes widened as she gave him a small shrug. She looked completely serious, even though he hadn't been serious about the idea. While he wasn't married, Joe hadn't expected to take over every aspect of his late brother's life. Besides, that wasn't what Miss Gilmore had agreed to. Nor had he.

Though he opened his mouth to protest, Joe stopped. It was a possibility, he supposed. At least something to be considered. He swallowed hard. At twenty-six years of age, a lot of men his age were married. As were all the women. Though he'd had options in the city, he had never thought much about courting. There wasn't anyone that he had loved, after all.

But they could have a marriage of convenience.

This would give the woman a home, a husband, and a child.

Joe glanced between Audrey and Dan as he thought about what could be done if they decided to take this route. It seemed incredulous. But stranger things had happened.

"I could ask her," he said finally. "At least give her some time to decide. But she was planning to come straight to the ranch, I'm sure. Is there any chance she could stay here upon her arrival?"

Dan nodded to his wife, who looked at him hopefully. "Yes. We're your friends and we'll do what we can to help; however we can support you, Joe. You and Mattie."

Everything in his life was changing so drastically and so quickly. He could hardly believe this. Joe eventually scooped his sleepy niece in his arms and took her home after thanking the Camerons profusely for their hospitality.

He laid awake for most of the night, wondering what might happen next.

Chapter Five

The world swept by her in a blur.

Nora could hardly believe she was doing this. There wasn't a single part of her that could have predicted her leaving Delaware for the Wild West.

Folks talked about the wilderness that was beyond the cities and towns. There were stories of natives who didn't live in houses, cowboys who traveled for miles every day, and huge buffalo that could feed a family for weeks on end. She had heard so many stories that she didn't know what was true and what was not.

All she knew was that she was about to find out.

The train ride had been more pleasant than she had anticipated. Though she grew weary of sitting in her spot for days on end, Nora couldn't deny that it was nice to have time to herself and there was nowhere for her to rush off to. She slept when she was tired, ate the food Lauren had prepared for her when she was hungry, and watched the world pass her by.

It hadn't taken long for civilization to pass her by. They had traveled through several cities filled with large buildings and smoking factories only to eventually leave it all behind for mountains and prairies.

While Nora accepted that the world was big, she couldn't have imagined she would get to see so much. There were moments when she stared out her window in amazement, wondering if she was still asleep. Mountains disappeared into the clouds and there were lakes that disappeared beyond the horizon.

There was no one to bother her. Though people walked about and talked with their traveling groups, no one really ever talked to her. Nora liked it that way. She was busy with her thoughts.

Her heart pounded in her chest as the train conductor called out the next stop. It was Nebraska.

My stop. We're there already?

Nora looked up as the folks in her compartment began to stand and stretch. Everyone was talking. Most of them didn't appear to be getting off at this stop, but they wanted to take a quick look around while they had the time. They talked loudly and excitedly about their various destinations, reminding others of all that they would experience.

She sat there for a minute before realizing that she had to get up.

It was her stop. If she didn't get off now, she would end up somewhere else and more alone than before. Her legs felt weak as she grabbed her two bags from the overhead shelf.

Stepping out into the aisle, Nora took a deep breath. So much could happen once she climbed off the train. There was a world out there waiting for her, and a brand-new family. It all seemed like a dream. She could hardly believe she was doing this. Never before had she considered what it meant to be a mail-order bride.

Now, she would find out.

Making her way to the exit, Nora descended the steps before making it onto solid ground. She could hardly believe it. After letting out a deep breath, she raised her head to look around.

There was a little town just ahead of her.

It was smaller than Wilmington, but still bigger than a few other stops they had made along the way. Many of them only had one row of buildings that were surrounded by dusty hills. She had no idea how they managed to survive.

As for Fairwell, there were at least two streets before her. Plus one at the other end, she believed, so perhaps it was actually a minimum of three.

A little town with sturdy buildings on either side, all of them with at least one window and a triangular roof. She could see a few signs set up ahead. They were too far away to read, but she liked the idea that they were big enough to need an occasional sign.

This would be her new home.

Nora could hardly believe what she was getting herself into. She looked around the layout as she contemplated the logical consequences she would face by living out in the west. There would be fewer people, fewer shops, and so much that she didn't understand.

"You can do this," Lauren had told her confidently before they'd parted. "I promise you, Nora, you are more capable than you could possibly dream of being."

She was grateful to have such a supportive friend. But she wasn't sure she felt the same way. It had taken all of Nora's strength to board the train. During her ride, her thoughts had strayed often enough that she didn't worry. But now that she was here, in this strange and unfamiliar place, she found herself questioning what might happen next.

A family. She could still hardly believe it. After seeing Lauren's relationship with Daniel grow over the last couple of years, Nora had prayed that someday there might be someone out in the world for her so she could have a similar relationship. Though she still hardly knew Billy, she found herself feeling hopeful for their future together.

Nora gasped as she remembered.

He had sent her a photograph with his first letter.

She put down her heavier bag to look for the photograph, knowing she had put it somewhere that would be easy for her to pull it out. Her eyes glanced quickly around the train station to see if anyone was watching her. But no one stood out to her as she located the photo on top of her letters.

There he was. William Bowman made for a friendly face. His large nose didn't make him quite as handsome as society might look for, but Nora thought it was endearing. He had made jokes about it, as well, so he knew it was big and accepted it. For that, she had found his humor and tenderness more attractive than any photograph. Above the nose were dark, hooded eyes that Billy had explained were usually gray with a hint of blue. It was a full portrait of him seated in a chair wearing his Sunday suit. The shirt was wrinkled, she supposed, but she didn't mind.

None of it bothered her, for she had read his letters and corresponded with him. That was what mattered to Nora. Anyone could look however they desired, but it was their heart that was most important to her.

And she could tell that Billy had a good heart.

Nora looked the picture over for another moment before she lifted her head to look around. There were still a few people at the station. It had no roof, so the sun was warm on her back as she wondered if Billy was nearby.

He had promised to meet her at the station, after all.

But no one had that nose. Nora's brow furrowed and she felt a twinge of concern. He was nowhere to be found. Perhaps he was late? She picked up her bags to move a few feet forward.

It was then that she noticed a man walking directly toward her.

Nora blinked and looked around, wondering if she was imagining the man looking at her. He was a fairly young and handsome man. Tall with muscular shoulders, he wore a trimmed beard with tapered sides to emphasize his strong jawline and sharp cheekbones. He had dark blond hair that fell across his brow. His dark, hooded gaze was so striking that her heart skipped a beat.

There was something familiar about him, but Nora couldn't think of where she might have met him before.

In either case, she knew she should turn away. She was about to marry a fine and decent man, and there was no reason for her to be thinking about other men. Even if he did dress well in a finely cut dark suit and polished shoes.

"Miss Nora Gilmore?"

She jerked to attention as he said her name. This man knew who she was. Nora felt her brow crease in confusion. "Hello. Yes, that's me. I'm sorry, do I know you?"

The man stopped before her. Tugging nervously on his jacket, the man hesitated before shaking his head. "No, you don't. You see, I'm Joseph Bowman. Billy's younger brother. I wish it hadn't come to this, but I'm afraid I have some very grave news."

Her heart turned cold. Nora opened her mouth as she tried to find something to say but couldn't. Something told her she didn't want to hear what he was going to tell her.

"My brother died a week ago." He cleared his throat. "A stampede on his ranch."

Nora stared at him.

This can't be possible. It can't happen. How could it? I ran away from everything in Delaware for this life. And it's just gone?

She struggled to process what he was telling her. The man she was supposed to marry was gone before they'd even had a chance to meet. All her hopes of having a happy and safe life here were dashed to pieces. She had hoped for love, if not at least friendship. There would have been a safe and happy home for her. They were supposed to be a family.

"I see," Nora started to say, but her voice broke.

Suddenly, she inhaled, thinking of little Mattie, the daughter she supposed she would never have. Billy had spoken lovingly of his girl who clearly needed him. Now, the girl had lost both of her parents. Nora was an orphan as well, but at least she'd had more years with her father.

That poor child. Heavy emotions washed over her for the girl who had to be suffering. Mattie had been through so much. She had to feel so lonely and lost. Nora could hardly fathom her pain, and she wished dearly for something better for the girl. She didn't deserve that sorrow. *If only I could have been here for her earlier.*

Nora felt drawn to the young girl, even though they had never met. And now, she supposed, they might never meet. Her throat grew tight as she looked back to the man before her. He, too, had to be suffering.

She studied the circles under his eyes and wondered what might happen next.

Chapter Six

He didn't know what to say to her or what to do.

Joe shifted uncomfortably, wondering what had happened to him. Back in the city, he was confident, always ready to talk to people whether he knew them or not. He was regularly invited into social circles because of his quick wit and storytelling.

But now, his tongue was tied. And he was tired.

Terribly tired from tossing and turning at night over what might have been. He dreamed of his brother, of Sophia, and his parents. Every night, there was someone telling him what he should have done better, and he woke up every morning feeling like a failure. *It's the icing on the cake, telling this poor woman about my brother. She doesn't deserve this.*

"I only came out here myself recently," Joe blurted when the silence between them grew too awkward. He winced before explaining himself. "That is, I came when I heard. The neighbors sent me a telegram and I left immediately. I'm from the East, you see. New York City. I live there for work. I'm a businessman. I helped companies with their financials and taxes to... well, never mind that. I'm not a rancher. But I'm going to be. I decided to stay."

The young lady furrowed her brow as she attempted to follow his story. "Stay?"

He had woken that morning feeling that it might not be too warm, with the clouds in the sky. But now it felt like the hottest day of summer as he stood before her. "Right. On the ranch, you see. I'm staying for the ranch. I'm going to run it. My brother's ranch. I never lived here, before, so I didn't know about you beforehand. Billy never told me. We didn't talk too much, you see, since I was so far away."

"Oh."

Scratching his chin, Joe tried to remember what he was trying to tell her.

It had been a stressful morning.

He had started it off begging Mattie to eat. But they reached a stalemate and had gone over to the Cameron house because he didn't know what else to do.

That was the only place she wanted to be, and she would only speak to him if she was in the mood. Dan had been out with his cowboys already, but Audrey was there at the door before they climbed the steps.

Mattie ran off to feed the chickens and so he had stood on the porch talking with Audrey for a short while before they'd decided that perhaps Mattie needed time to grieve without him in the way. With Dan's support, Audrey would come to stay at the Bowman ranch house to watch over Mattie. That way, the young girl could be at home with a friend. In the meantime, he would stay in the cabin just behind the main house. It had been used for storage, so he just needed to clean out a few items and then he could put a cot in the corner.

The entire time, he had felt like he'd been punched in the gut.

Billy would not have been happy to know that he had agreed to finally run the ranch only to have his daughter wanting to be somewhere else to avoid him. Though Audrey assured him that the girl was simply shy, Joe wasn't so sure.

What if he could never make her happy? He could have taken her to the city where she would have been miserably stuck with him in a strange place. Even now, they were stuck together and both unhappy.

"She's grieving," Audrey had reminded him. "And so are you. The two of you just need time, that's all."

Of course, they were grieving. He felt the stab in his chest every day. But he had thought that the two of them would come together during this hard time.

Instead, he worried that Mattie was more alone than ever. Joe had spent much of his adulthood alone and was used to it. But she was only seven years old and going through so much. He wanted to be there to help her. Except he couldn't if she didn't want him.

"What if she never warms up to me?" he had asked Audrey. "What are we supposed to do? I can't ask you to take care of her forever."

The woman had kindly shaken her head and patted his shoulder before standing up to face the day. "Don't worry. We love Mattie, but she's yours now. It will take time, I think, but give it a chance. People are complex, and children are even more so. Now, don't you have someplace to be?"

Joe had glanced up at the sun as it rose in the sky before them. He squinted and frowned before realizing it was time to head into town.

So, he had hitched the horse up to a cart and made his way along the two miles into town to meet Miss Gilmore at the train station. He had rehearsed his words over and over in the hopes of being prepared for her.

Yet it hadn't worked out at all.

There he was, struggling to tell the young lady what she needed to hear. One minute, he couldn't say anything, and the next he couldn't stop talking. Joe swallowed hard before wiping the sweat from his brow.

"I read your letters," Joe blurted suddenly when silence fell again. He saw Miss Gilmore's eyes widen. Immediately, he realized his mistake. Taking a small step back, he tried to explain himself. "I didn't mean to. I didn't know what they were. That is, I... I was going through my brother's things, you see. I shouldn't have read something so private, but... well, that's why I didn't have time to send you a letter, you see. There wasn't a chance for me to reach out to you."

Miss Gilmore nodded slowly. "I understand. I suppose I should thank you. Coming out here to tell me what happened. And I'm sorry for your loss," she managed after a moment.

He saw her shoulders slump. There was worry and sorrow in her eyes. He could see it as plainly as his hands before him. Joe's gut tightened.

Poor woman.

She was prettier than her picture, he noted. Taller than he had expected, though still several inches shorter than himself. But most folks were, since he was over six feet. Even though he was the younger brother, Joe had been taller than Billy for more than ten years.

Her sloped shoulders were downcast, but it didn't stop their emphasis of her small waist. She had a graceful hourglass figure that was apparent even through her simple dress. Her hair was a light blonde, more flattering than he had imagined.

As for her eyes, they were deep-set and hazel, with large flecks of green. They sat right below expressive eyebrows that furrowed as she tried to understand what Billy's death meant for her.

That was when Joe remembered his offer.

He grimaced, hating how forgetful he felt in this moment with this lovely young woman. "Billy was excited to marry you, from what I understand. The neighbors knew and told me that he was... well, he would have been thrilled to have you here. I just wish he was the one meeting you. From your letters, I know you've been through some pain yourself."

She glanced up at him before nodding. "I have. But I don't want to add to yours. I suppose I should..."

When she took a step back, he took a step forward. "Stay. You can stay with me."

"Stay?" Miss Gilmore repeated.

A hot flush crept up his cheeks as he nodded. He fidgeted with his jacket once more. "Yes. It's only right, I think. The two of you had a partnership, a deal. He was looking forward to this, and I can't imagine you would want to turn around now. If you're really interested in staying here, in having a life, I... I think it's only right that I offer my hand in turn." Her eyes widened, but he forced himself to continue. "I'm trying to honor my brother's promise. I'm not married and I'm not Billy. It might be a different type of life, but I thought I could at least try to do right by you. And him. Both of you."

She blinked slowly. "So, you're..."

But she left the question hanging between them as the tension grew.

"I don't need a wife. I mean, I wasn't looking for one," he hurriedly amended. "I'm not looking to build my own family or anything. You could have your own place in the house, a room to yourself. I'm learning to run the ranch and, of course, there's Mattie. She could really use a mother. I need help running the household, you see. And I don't know anything about children. I could use some help and thought you might... want to... help."

Though he had brokered deals that carried the weight of professional relationships and thousands of dollars, nothing could have prepared him for this moment.

It had to be the most pathetic marriage proposal in all of history, Joe supposed. He cleared his throat and cheated a glance up at Miss Gilmore when he paused to take a breath. Wondering what she thought of his offer, he simply hoped she wouldn't laugh at him.

"I see," the young lady said at last.

She still sounded dazed, as if she wasn't quite listening.

Joe nodded slowly, for he had felt the same since that fateful telegram. He studied her as she lowered her gaze. Her nose twitched and he saw the slightest clench of her jaw.

When she said nothing more, Joe wondered if he had pushed her too far. He thought about all that he had said. It had been a lot, more than any person should have to deal with in such a short amount of time. This had to be quite a punch in the stomach for her as it had been for him. Expecting her to make a decision about her future like this was unreasonable. After all, they didn't even know each other.

He took a step back to give her some space.

Then, Joe took a deep breath and tried to smile when her eyes flickered up to his face. "This is a lot. You must be exhausted, Miss Gilmore. This is obviously all very overwhelming. After having traveled for so long, I'm sure you could use a chance to rest. There's no need for you to answer me immediately about this, I think. Please, take your time. You don't need to rush; you can stay here for as long as you like. I've made arrangements for your stay already. The neighbors have agreed to let you stay at the main house on the ranch. Audrey will be staying there, as well. I won't. I'll be in a cabin. That way, I won't intrude, and... Is that all right?"

She took a minute to consider the offer. Lifting her gaze to study him again, Miss Gilmore inhaled deeply before she offered a tentative nod. Joe hardly dared to breathe when she spoke again.

"I think that's agreeable. Thank you, Mr. Bowman."

The knot in his stomach loosened just a little bit, giving him hope that perhaps this meant things might grow easier for all of them. He could only pray.

Chapter Seven

Nora followed Joseph Bowman over to his horse and cart.

She allowed him to help her onto the headboard, where she sat next to him for the bumpy ride through town and down the lane.

They passed through more greenery than she had ever seen in all her life. It surpassed everything on her journey over. There were farms with tall fields and prairies that went on as far as she could see. In the distance were dark mountains that appeared so small to her. This was a brand-new world that she had entered, but she could hardly acknowledge any of it.

Mr. Bowman glanced at her every now and again.

She could feel his gaze, curious and tentative, before he looked back to his horse. He seemed to be as uncomfortable as she felt. The man was dressed like the businessman he claimed to be. When they were leaving the streets of town, she saw that no one else wore a suit. Only Mr. Bowman did.

He cuts a fine figure, even through his discomfort.

But she tried to brush the thought away. He was handsome and young. She could see the stiffness in his shoulders and wondered what was going on in his mind.

He had offered to marry her.

Nora could hardly believe it. Accepting anything that had just taken place at the train station was a struggle. Every time she looked up, everything felt like a strange dream. She could see that the world continued to move on all around her. Except she couldn't do anything about it. She couldn't say anything; she could hardly move.

AN UNEXPECTED BRIDE FOR HIS SCARRED HEART

What was she supposed to do?

All she knew was that she couldn't turn around and return to Delaware. That was the only thought on her mind.

In the meantime, she tried to grasp that the man she had come to marry would no longer be there to greet her. He wasn't at the train station and he wasn't waiting for her at his house. She thought of his photograph, expecting to see Billy appear and tell her none of this was really happening.

Mr. Bowman at last pulled off from the main road.

She looked up to find a wooden fence before them with a sign hanging overhead for the Green Valley Ranch.

That was the place that Billy had told her about. He had written an entire page about all the hard work he had put into building it up. There were times when he'd worked all through the night. He had jammed two nails into his hands, but he had merely washed them and wrapped them before returning to his work.

Billy had been proud of the home he had built. In his last letter, when he'd asked her to come out there to join his family, he had promised her that she would come to love the ranch as much as he did.

They followed the trail over to a large house. It had a wrap-around porch with curtains fluttering in the open windows. There was a second floor with even more windows. It appeared to only be an extra room or two, surrounded by red brick chimneys. This had to be the size of the entire boarding house where she had moved when her father had first died. Her room had been very cramped and had not included any windows.

But she didn't feel the thrill that she had hoped to feel upon seeing something so beautiful. Instead, Nora felt numb inside. She hardly bothered to look around when Mr. Bowman stopped the horse and came around to help her down.

"Here we are," he said after clearing his throat. The man was nervous, it was plain to see. She wanted to tell him not to be, but she wasn't sure how.

Nora had no idea what to do with herself in the presence of a man she had never met. Though she had recalled Billy mentioning that he had a brother, at the moment she couldn't remember anything else about him. It was as though her brain had simply given up working.

The man tied the horse to a post by the barn where they'd stopped. He gestured loosely toward the house and took a step forward, then wavered a moment, eyeing her arm as though about to escort her up.

At the last minute, he remembered her bags and turned back to the cart for them. He hefted them up easily before heading toward the house.

She followed behind, slowly and surely. The path was uphill, allowing her the chance to stretch her legs after her long journey seated on the train. Nora found that she could breathe more deeply, and the air tasted different. She stared down at her feet as they kicked up dirt on the path until she heard the sound of a swinging door.

Looking up, Nora found two girls stepping out of the house.

The taller was an older woman, perhaps in her early thirties, with a tall, thin build. She had wispy hair falling over her shoulders and a wide smile that she directed toward Nora. They had never met, but the other woman seemed happy to see her.

Beside her was the small figure of a child. It had to be Mattie. She wore a soft blue dress and clutched something in both of her arms. Though she stood back in the shadows, Nora could make out the little girl's thick strawberry-blonde hair and round cheeks set in a delicate frown. Her eyes were glued to the ground as though she was trying to ignore the world around her.

Nora didn't blame her.

"Ah." Mr. Bowman stopped at the steps. He set one of her bags down to give a short wave to the girl. When she didn't reciprocate, he hesitated before rubbing his neck. Looking back at Nora, he managed a tight smile. "Nora, this is Mattie. Mattie, this is Miss Nora Gilmore. Do you remember? Your father told you about her. And Nora, this is Audrey Cameron."

She didn't have a chance to respond before the other woman hastened down the steps with her arms outstretched. Nora was wrapped in a hug before she knew what was happening.

"I can't imagine what you're going through right now," Audrey said. "It's been a horrible week for all of us. I wish we could have met on happier terms. Billy was thrilled to have you coming out here. Know that, won't you? He was just so happy. Oh, you would have loved him. Very cheerful man. He's done a wonderful job of raising his daughter, you know. Well, he did." Audrey finally stepped back. She offered a smile before taking Nora's hand in hers to lead her up the steps. "Mattie? Do you want to say hello to Miss Nora?"

Her heart thudded loudly in her chest.

This was not supposed to be happening was the only thought she could comprehend. Though she appreciated the kindness she was receiving, everything felt wrong. Nora could feel the pattering of her heartbeat against her ribcage. It didn't feel good.

She felt out of place. This family was supposed to grieve in peace. But here was the neighbor, trying to make everything better.

And now, she was there, interrupting everything. Nora struggled to recover from her initial shock.

Especially with little Mattie before her.

Nora turned to the child to find that she had her father's strong brow. Then, there were her eyes. They were a sweet blue, but clouded with so much pain. The corners of the girl's eyes crinkled as Mattie lifted one hand to offer a short wave before wrapping her arms around herself once more.

Swallowing hard, Nora wanted to wrap the child close to her chest so all her sadness would fly away. She was such a little girl. It broke Nora's heart to know how miserable she must be. Losing her mother had been difficult when Nora was young. But at least she'd had her father for a few more years.

"Hello, Mattie," Nora managed thickly. "It's a..." *This cannot possibly be a pleasure after all that has happened.* "I'm glad to finally meet you. I'm so sorry for your loss."

The child only shrugged before turning to Audrey.

"Why don't we go inside?" The woman looked around at everyone as she patted Mattie's shoulder. "I have a lemon pie just waiting to be eaten. You must be hungry, Nora, so I've prepared a lovely supper. Joe, why don't you take her bags to her room while I lead these ladies into the kitchen?"

"Of course," he said from behind Nora. "I'll join you all shortly."

Everyone gathered inside. While Mr. Bowman wandered down the next hall, Nora allowed herself to be whisked into a grand kitchen. It was large and filled with all sorts of decent cookware. Lauren would always take her window shopping, where they would dream of the lovely things they might own one day. And now, those things were all right there.

Nora sat down at the table with Audrey and Mattie. Mattie stared at the table as she clutched what appeared to be a shirt, at a closer look. She didn't have to guess to know this had to be one of Billy's shirts, meant to bring the little girl some comfort.

"Delaware, right?" Audrey spoke up in the silence as she brought the pie to the table and began to dish out slices. "I've never been so far East, you know. I grew up in Tennessee with my husband, and we moved out here with the plan to make it to California. But, somehow, we just never left. Not that we mind. We live just west of here, you see, and love it. We fell in love with the land and we've had a good little ranch going for us ever since. I feel that we've been very fortunate. Especially so to know the Bowmans. Billy made for a great neighbor, as did his wife. And Mattie is a dear, as well."

The other woman kept the conversation going for most of the afternoon. She asked a few questions to Nora and Mattie, all of them simple to answer. Nora wanted to be of more help, but nothing came to mind.

Eventually, Mr. Bowman returned, and they ate their supper. Nora offered to help clean up, but Audrey told her not to worry about it. Instead, she was directed to her bedroom and sent to bed early.

She didn't expect to fall asleep. But her eyes closed once she landed on the comfortable pillow.

The night passed her by and when she woke up, the sun was shining all over again. There was a warmth to the day that told her she must have slept for a long time.

Nora changed and made her way out of the room. Though a guest in the house, she didn't want to take this time at an advantage. She made her way into the kitchen to find Audrey and Mattie already there cooking and cleaning. There was food set out of her. She ate and then began to help tidy up.

If I can keep myself busy, she reasoned, *then maybe everything will begin to make a little more sense.*

She wasn't sure if this would work, but Nora deemed it worth a try. She spent the next couple of days hovering nearby Audrey and Mattie.

It was Audrey who did most of the talking, which Nora was grateful for. She needed time for reality to sink in. Over the next couple of days, she began to slowly accept her situation. Audrey's friendly chatter became comfortable as Nora discovered that she talked to set everyone at ease.

"In the silence," Audrey had explained, while they watched Mattie collect eggs as they stood by the kitchen window, "we feel the pain more closely, I think. At least, that's how it is for me. Mattie's a sensitive child. She needs to know that life continues through these hardships. When she talks, I listen. She can talk about her father or the animals or anything else. But, in the meantime, I talk in the hopes of bringing her back to the moment. I don't want her getting lost in her head. Or do you think I'm being silly?"

Nora hurriedly shook her head. "You're not. I think I understand. And that would have been nice for me." She offered a pained smile when the woman turned to her. "My mother died when I was Mattie's age. Then, my father passed away two years ago. Being orphaned is confusing and terrifying. But Mattie has her uncle, and she has you. I wish I'd had that."

Though she had Lauren, her friend still had a life of her own and had not always been able to be there when Nora wanted someone. She had accepted this as a part of life and didn't like to ask for help like that, anyway.

But Mattie needed this. She needed people like Audrey in her life to give her hope. At first, Nora had thought perhaps the woman was insincere or anxious about the silence. But Audrey proved to be a wise woman and Nora found herself grateful to have someone like her there on the ranch.

And, of course, there was Joe.

That's what he preferred to be called. She'd made the mistake of calling him "Mr. Bowman," and he had quickly shaken his head. That was what he was called back in the city, Joe told her. But not on the ranch. He was just Joe now.

He seemed to be a decent man. Quiet and hardworking, he was hardly around as he was trying to learn his way around running a ranch. The man came home caked in sweat and dirt most days before washing off by his little cabin that sat beside the barn. Then he'd come up to the house tentatively, not wanting to interfere, before disappearing for hours into the study.

Usually, she only saw him at meals.

Joe was extraordinarily polite, almost more than necessary. He was always offering to help with the smallest tasks when he had a moment. Then, at supper, he would try to lure Mattie out of her quiet and withdrawn attitude.

He tried so hard. Nora felt her heart breaking for both of them over the horrible loss they had experienced. Though her heart hurt, she knew it was nothing compared to the misery that Joe and Mattie had to be experiencing. Joe was clearly struggling, though he did his best to hide it. And little Mattie was scared. She would jerk her head up every time someone started to move away, as though worried they would leave her forever.

Nora could hardly believe the situation she was in. She felt for all of them but didn't know what she could do to help. They hardly knew each other.

As the shock finally began to wear off, Nora began to look for ways to be of help to everyone. There had to be something she could do to be useful.

Chapter Eight

Joe had done a lot of dumb things in his life. But now, he worried this might have been the worst.

He wanted so hard to be able to do everything that Billy had hoped for him. Joe hardly slept as he struggled to learn his way around the ranch. He had started to read all of Billy's notes to have a grasp on everything that had to be done at one point or another. A hefty notebook had been purchased and his hand ached from writing so often.

But that was only in accordance with the work he did in the study.

The majority of his time was spent outside under the warm sun with the cattle and horses. There was always work to be done, whether something broken needed mending or the cattle needed to be moved to another range.

Fortunately, there was a foreman who knew how to keep everything running in the meantime.

"It's a lot of work." Ezra Moody had peered at him when Joe had announced that he was going to stay and run the ranch. "And I do mean a lot of work. It's a job. Do you understand that? How much time have you spent on a ranch?"

"A few days," Joe had grudgingly admitted. "And I'm aware of that. Billy always said it was the hardest thing he had ever done. I accept that I have a long road ahead of me, Ezra. This might even take me years. But I'm ready and willing to learn. I want to do right by my brother. The question I have for you is if you can do that, as well?"

Business was the one thing that he felt he could talk well about. Making this statement made the foreman raise his eyebrow, clearly intrigued.

Ezra Moody was nearly sixty years old, though he could probably pass for forty. Barrel-chested with bowed legs and the thickest mustache Joe had ever seen on a man, Ezra always had something in his mouth. Joe knew he didn't stay in the nearby bunkhouse with the other ranch hands—he had a sneaking suspicion that the foreman just slept on top of his horse. The man was tough, honest, and a hard worker. Billy had hired him for those reasons, and Joe could see the truth in the man's face.

"I can," Ezra had agreed. "I was hired to do a job, wasn't I? It's a right handy job and I'll keep it so long as it's here. The boys will stay, too, so long as the terms of the job don't change," he added pointedly. "Same pay. Same responsibilities."

Joe had no qualms with this. In his brother's letters, he had read how Billy offered a slightly higher wage than most ranches around the area. He did this with the expectation of getting more work out of the men, and he had been able to build his profits. It had been hard in the earlier years, when everyone was still newly hired, but the ranch hands tended to stay once he gave them a good wage, and that kept them loyal to the ranch. That wasn't something Joe wanted to change. He knew the benefits of keeping employees happy, and he would accept those terms.

"They will," he assured Ezra. "Once the final paperwork has come through, I'm going to set up updated records for everyone here. Nothing will change at the moment besides the fact that I'm taking over Billy's place. I don't intend to alter any of his plans at this point, because he had a smooth plan working out. And he had you on his side, which I know was a great benefit."

That made the man grin. "Sure did. I think this can work just fine, then."

Joe had felt confident about everything until later that afternoon, when his foreman had pointed out that he should probably start meeting all the ranch hands. He only knew a few of their faces and even fewer names.

It was a fair point. He couldn't be a good boss that the men trusted if they didn't know who he was. Climbing into the saddle, he had made his way out into the valley as the men came together for their noon meal.

Ezra had given a short whistle to get everyone crowded around.

"The ranch is here to stay," he announced. The uncertainty in everyone's faces had immediately dissipated. Some of them cheered and clapped, talking to each other in relief. Joe saw their grins grow and then fade as Ezra continued. "This here is your new boss. Joe will be taking after Billy, after all. Joe, here are the boys. We've got Chuck as the cook, right over here with the apron on. Then there's Ryan, Pete, Taggert…"

The introductions went on. It was a sprawling ranch and Billy had around twenty men working for him at all times.

Joe tried to smile as he nodded to each man while trying to memorize their faces and names. He fidgeted absently with his vest and caught a few glances directed his way. Most of them were curious, but a few just frowned and turned to look at one another.

Any confidence he had begun to feel about his decision was quick to dissipate. Never in his life had he felt so insecure.

Swallowing hard, he wondered how Billy used to do it. But, then again, Billy was the charismatic one between them. Joe had always worked hard at every little thing he said and did to make sure that he presented his best self. He had worked tirelessly to achieve success back East, garnering quite some attention. He was even friends with the mayor. He'd left behind a large group of friends and partnerships for this ranch.

And the men there were clearly questioning if he was up for the challenge.

Joe couldn't blame them, because he didn't know, either. He had no idea what would happen next for any of them.

But he couldn't just stand there and do nothing. Ezra was his employee, just like the rest of them. They would all have to get used to working with him there now. Joe steeled himself for what might come next.

"Thank you, Ezra." He gave the foreman a nod before turning back to the men. "Thank you for your hard work and service during this time. It has not gone unnoticed. I'm sure you're all well aware of my inexperience here." Someone snorted, but he couldn't find the owner of the sound.

Joe paused before he continued talking. "Please don't take that for stupidity. I will be fixing that by working with each and every one of you one on one over the next couple of weeks so that I can learn from everyone. I don't intend to tell anyone how to do their jobs, since you were hired knowing how to do it. I will uphold the same standards that Billy maintained. So long as there is honesty, hard work, and good will, then we won't have any problems. I won't stand for anything less. I expect your full cooperation as I take up ownership, and I expect loyalty to your job and this ranch."

Silence settled among them. Joe looked around to see quite a few men were looking back at him. But they weren't mocking stares—rather, they seemed to be listening to him.

He cleared his throat and gave them a nod. "Good. If any of you have any problems, please come straight to me. I'm not interested in learning anything second-hand, at this point. That's all I have to say on the matter for now. In the meantime, Chuck, what are you serving us?"

The men had turned to the cook with their full attention as the topic changed.

Once everyone had eaten together, they headed back out to the cattle. Joe spent the day shadowing Ezra while he worked and made plans to spend the next day with Ryan to take care of the calves.

If he wasn't out in the fields with the ranch hands, Joe was usually in the study reviewing past notes. He was glad that he'd reminded Billy over and over again to keep track of everything. It gave him an idea of important purchases that had to be made, connections for beef and farmers, and instructions on how certain things were done around the ranch.

Usually, it was Audrey who came knocking on his door to remind him that he needed to eat something. But, once Nora arrived, she took over that role. It was a pleasant change, even if neither of them knew much of what to say to one another.

"I'm going into town tomorrow," Joe told them at supper. "Does anyone want to join me? Or need any supplies?"

Audrey nodded. "You need more salt. And if you could fetch some new needles, that would be perfect. Mattie needs some new dresses, and I don't have enough to share with Nora. Besides, she should have her own sewing supplies here."

He nodded before looking over to Nora. "What type of needles?"

"I..." She trailed off, glancing at Audrey and then back to him. "I can make any needle work. Whatever they have here I should be fine with. Being a seamstress taught me a few tricks," she volunteered.

Of course. He wondered how he could have forgotten. "Right. Well. Why don't you come to town with me? You can see for yourself. And see if you need anything else."

"That's a great idea," Audrey proclaimed.

"Oh, I don't know," Nora said hesitantly. "I don't want to waste your time. And if Audrey and Mattie need me, then I..."

Joe glanced at Mattie, who was playing with her food. She had spoken up just a few minutes ago to recite the names of all their chickens. Then, she had even answered him about what she had done for the day without prompting from Audrey. He liked to think that was a sign of improvement. But she still looked downcast, with her lower lip sticking out.

"We'll all go." He turned to Audrey, who gave them a smile. "It'll be nice to go around town, I'm sure. A nice change of scenery."

So, the following morning, he brought out the wagon and saddled up two horses for it. The ladies came out of the house with their bonnets and baskets. Joe first hoped for some company, but all three girls ended up taking seats in the wagon together.

He shrugged it off and nudged the horses forward. It was a pleasantly quiet ride. Though he could hear the murmur of them talking behind him, Joe couldn't make out most of the words. Still, he enjoyed hearing the occasional sound from his niece, relieved to know that she at least felt safe somewhere.

They soon arrived in town, and he waved the ladies off as they headed to the haberdashery. Joe turned the other way to get some equipment fixed at the blacksmith's shop. The man explained it would take him an hour or so, giving Joe time to do something else.

There wasn't much more for him to do. He went to the general store to pick up salt and flour. Once those were loaded into his wagon, he decided to stop over at the saloon for a drink. Though he wasn't much of a drinker and preferred it only in social settings, the world was weighing him down and he could use something to relax the tension in his shoulders.

"Whiskey," he answered when the bartender asked him what he wanted. "Neat."

Soon, there was a chilled glass in his hands. Joe stared at the amber liquid thoughtfully before taking a sip. The taste was bitter and sweet all at once.

"Looks like you've had a rough day. Or year, maybe." A voice came out of nowhere, talking to him. Joe looked around to find a man settling into the seat on his left. He had black hair and scruffy beard with a crooked hat that he tipped toward Joe. "Hey, there."

He nodded warily. "Hey."

"I don't mean nothing by it," the man added after a moment. Then, his lips curved into a smile. "Life is tough here. You look like you're new in town. Visiting?"

Joe sighed as he took a small sip of his drink. "No. I've actually just settled down here. The Green Valley Ranch, if you've heard of it."

The man's eyes widened before he leaned back. "Well, well, well. I was wondering who might take over since that Billy boy died. Huh. Hard work, hm? The name is Harlan, by the way. Harlan Kane. Welcome to Fairwell, stranger."

Joe shook hands with the man, noticing the unnecessarily tight grip. "Thanks," he mumbled before staring back at the counter. He had enough going on that he didn't feel the need to catch up with every stranger he met. "Joe Bowman."

"Ever run a ranch before?" Harlan asked him while he flagged down the bartender. "I'll take two bottles of beer. One for me and one for the gentleman here."

Joe glanced down at his clothes. He was wearing his suit jacket. It was weird going without one in public, even if no one else wore them about. For so long, the professional garb was his way of life. Changing it now felt uncomfortable. Perhaps he was overdressed, all the same, for a place like Nebraska.

Then he looked up as the bartender returned.

Quickly, Joe waved a hand out. "Thank you, but no. I appreciate the gesture," he added to the man beside him. "But I'll just be having a glass of water after this. I don't drink often."

The bartender turned away to fix the offering. As for Harlan, he took the beer left on the counter and quickly opened it to take a long swallow. He breathed out deeply before speaking up again.

"Are you sure? You might change your mind. You've never run a ranch before, have you?"

Heat crept up his face. He hadn't thought it would be so obvious. "Well, I... I'm learning. But I suppose, yes, it's my first time. I spent the last couple of years back East."

"Ah, the cities." Harlan gave him a knowing look. "Where there are lights, women, and money for the taking. I should have guessed. But I'm thinking you should also guess by now that a ranching operation is different than any type of business back east. Are you sure you're wanting to take a ranch when you know nothing? You might scuff those shoes."

A flash of annoyance washed over Joe before he glanced down. Harlan was wearing worn-out leather boots that climbed up his calves. As for Joe, he wore his nicest shoes, which were already covered in dust.

"I don't know," Joe said slowly in response to the man's question. "I don't really know."

Harlan stayed around for another minute before he left, taking his drink with him. Joe remained at the counter, alone with his thoughts. He didn't like that. Joe stared at the rest of his drink with frustration. After all, Harlan Kane was right. The two men didn't know each other, but only one of them seemed prepared. And it wasn't him.

As Joe headed back to see the blacksmith, he felt the unease building inside him.

No one was ready to take him seriously about the ranch. They didn't believe he could do it because he knew nothing about the work out there in the west. Even though he had made the decision to stay, he wondered if it was wrong.

What if I'm not cut out for this life?

Nebraska was not New York. They were completely different worlds, and Joe struggled to make sense of his choices. New York City had treated him well for the last couple of years. He had a good job, social influence, and respect from folks in the upper social circles, who valued him for the skills he already had.

He would be lying to say he didn't miss being back East.

But as Joe turned down the road to see little Mattie walking around with her head up for the first time in days, he found himself unable to turn away just yet. Behind her trailed Audrey and Nora, chatting. Joe watched them thoughtfully.

He had to try this out, for everyone's sake. He promised to give things a better chance. Yet, in the back of his mind, he couldn't help but wonder what kind of fool he really was.

Chapter Nine

"What do you think of him?"

Nora looked up at Audrey after hearing the door close to the study down the hall. Joe had come in the house, his face dripping wet after he'd rinsed it in the rain barrel right outside, and he had headed off to get more work done.

Joe hadn't been wearing a jacket, so his shirt clung to his skin and emphasized the thick muscles in his shoulders and arms.

He never seemed to stop, making her wonder how he did it. She was fairly certain that the man rose before her. He probably stayed up in his cabin, as well, since he was always taking a book back and forth between the two buildings.

Her life of working several jobs at a time in Delaware had been thoroughly exhausting. She was so relieved to find herself at the ranch, where the work was hard but much more enjoyable. There were no angry bosses, no crude men hovering around her, and no deadlines meant to make her panic. It was a satisfying change—so satisfying that much of the labor she put in lately didn't even feel like work. Especially with Mattie and Audrey beside her.

Yet Joe pushed on without a break. He never complained. Or, rather, he seemed to say very little.

She didn't know what to make of the man. They only saw one another at meals. He stumbled over his words if he spoke too much to her, but otherwise seemed quiet and even aloof. It was as if he wanted to give her as much space as possible while focusing on something more important.

A week had passed since her arrival in Nebraska.

Studying the hall where she had last seen Joe, Nora shrugged and wondered if he ever gave her a thought. She wondered what he thought of her, or if he cared anything about her. He was a busy man who was diving into his work, possibly because he was struggling to accept his loss. She hoped that wasn't the case. He seemed to be dealing with the pain all right, though Nora knew she didn't know him well enough to make a definitive decision on that.

He was just a mystery to her.

"I don't know," Nora admitted finally when she couldn't find anything more to say. "He's kind, I suppose."

Audrey nudged her as they kneaded their separate balls of dough. "Surely there's more than that. I know he's not Billy," she added, "but his brother spoke kindly of him. Billy thought highly of Joe and always had something good to say about him. The man works hard and cares for his family, don't you think?"

"Of course," Nora agreed before biting her lip. "He does seem kind. But I feel as though we've hardly talked. I don't know where I would begin…" Trailing off, she shrugged. "I'm sorry. I don't know, Audrey."

The other woman offered a sympathetic look. "I understand. Please don't think me cold, Nora. I'm simply trying to look out for you. And for Joe and Mattie. Time for grieving is important. But it's also important that we don't forget to live."

Nora looked at her friend for a minute, wondering about Audrey. The woman was thoughtful and gracious at all times. Nora didn't know how she did it. All she knew was that she was grateful to have a friend out there. They had spent so much time together, drawing close in their budding relationship. It helped her to feel less alone.

"You take care of everyone," Nora murmured. "How do you do it?"

Shrugging, Audrey pressed her knuckles into the bread dough. "I always have. My parents worked tirelessly and, as the eldest, it was my job to take care of my siblings. All ten of them, mind you. It's second nature to me. Tears have their place, anger has its place, and so does happiness. Dan says I can be too calm sometimes, but I would like to think I've just learned to be prepared for both miracles and disasters," she added with a lighthearted wink.

That earned a chuckle from Nora. "It's very clear you have. I wish I could be more like you."

The two of them talked as they made bread for that evening's meal. It reminded Nora of all her time with Lauren back home, where they were always talking about their hopes and dreams. Nora thought the two women would become fast friends and found herself wishing that they could meet someday.

She wasn't particularly certain how that would happen, but maybe, someday, it could.

"I'll set the table if you let Joe know supper is nearly ready," Audrey offered. "And I'll find Mattie, I think she's curled up in the hallway with a book."

Nora exchanged a bittersweet smile with the woman before nodding and heading down the hall. She looked over her shoulder to see the little girl curled up in the far corner. Mattie was fiddling with her father's old shoes and putting them on her own feet. It was a tender and heartbreaking scene.

Her eyes began to mist up. She wanted to scoop Mattie up in her arms, but she knew she couldn't go scaring the child. Mattie was finally beginning to talk to her. Yesterday, she had gone out to pick some vegetables and the little girl had agreed to join her when Nora had invited her. After Mattie had gone to bed that night, Nora had talked for a good hour to Audrey about how hopeful that made her feel for the child.

But there would still be hard days.

When Mattie looked up, Nora waved to her and forced herself to keep walking away. She passed two doors to find the study.

It was quiet. She closed her eyes, pressing her ear to the door. Sometimes, she wondered if Joe was still there, because she could hardly tell. After a moment of hearing nothing, Nora hesitantly stepped back and rapped her knuckles three times on the door.

"What is it?"

"Supper time," Nora offered loudly. She rocked on her heels. "It's nearly ready, if you would like to join us."

There was the sound of footsteps before the door flung open. Joe looked at her for a moment. She couldn't tell what was on his mind, with his impassive expression. The man stared at her for a minute before finally blinking.

"Right," he said at last. "Supper. I'll be ready. I just need a few more minutes."

Nora nodded. "Of course, yes." She watched a strand of hair fall across his forehead. It caught her attention and for a moment, she could think of nothing else. Her fingers itched to brush it away. Then she blinked and thought of something. "Do you have paper?"

Opening the door wider, Joe glanced behind him at a wall covered with books on bookshelves that climbed all the way to the ceiling. Nora could hardly believe how many books there were. It was unlike anything she had seen before, and it intrigued her.

"I have a lot of paper. What type were you considering?" Joe asked her.

Her gaze flickered back to him. "Right. Paper to write on, Joe. Do you have any to spare? A pen, as well, if that's all right?"

The door opened completely as he took a step back. "Of course. Feel free to look around, if you'd like," he added. Joe always said that.

She took a small step inside, but ventured no further. There was a calmness to the room that left her curious. But she was still hesitant to enter, not certain of how to act around Joe. He made his way over to his desk, which was large and wide. But she wasn't sure that any surface was left uncovered with all the books and papers he had piled there.

There was the sound of paper being moved about before he finally straightened up and brought her several sheets of paper with a pen and an inkwell.

"Thank you," she told him politely as she caught him looking at her with curiosity. "It's for a letter. I want to write to a friend of mine back home," Nora explained. "She'll be wondering how I am."

Joe gave her a small smile. "Then she'll be glad to hear from you. I can take the letter to town tomorrow. There are a few drifters around looking for extra work and I thought I would take a few of them on for a while."

"Oh?" Nora hadn't known about that. "Is there a lot of work to do? I'm sure I could help out if you need something; I'm stronger than I look."

He just shook his head before telling her, "That's all right. You have more than enough to do here. But thank you, Nora. That's very generous of you. I know being here can't be easy," he added after a moment.

Not knowing what to say, she shrugged. Nora fiddled with the items in her hands before finally telling him, "I would rather be here than anywhere else right now."

She caught him looking at her again. But that was because she hadn't moved and he still had work to do in the study, she realized. Flushing, Nora hurriedly stepped back. She ducked her head low before thanking him and rushing off. She put the items that he had loaned her in her room and then returned to the kitchen, where Audrey was trying to encourage Mattie to practice reading a recipe out loud.

This was a lovely home, she thought to herself, if still unfamiliar. But, with time, she knew she could get used to it.

It was during supper that night, as Nora looked around at everyone, that she knew she had to make up her mind about whether or not she would stay. These folks were going through enough, and she couldn't keep accepting their hospitality in such a manner. Even though she was helping around the house, Audrey couldn't stay there forever. Joe and Mattie deserved to know whether or not she would stay. Otherwise, if she grew close to them and then left, she worried she might cause more pain than they were already in.

Nora cleaned the kitchen after supper and hurried to her room to work on her letter to Lauren. Her good friend would be wondering if she had arrived and what was going on. There was so much to tell her. Nora had been too busy with adjusting to the life there to write, but she had to make a few minutes to assure her dearest friend of her safety.

It was a relief to put her thoughts and feelings to paper. She hadn't been able to talk to anyone about what she was feeling. The shock of the loss had already been experienced by everyone there and Nora hadn't wanted to cause anyone more grief.

And she wrote about Joe's offer. This would be a marriage of convenience, he'd told her. Not the marriage that she had planned for with Billy, she knew, but at least it would be a marriage.

Was that enough?

Even if there wasn't love, Nora supposed, there might be other positive things to a marriage with Joe. She could stay with Mattie. The poor child needed hope and gentleness. Audrey had done so much for the family, but she had a life to get back to with her husband. That meant Mattie would be alone often if Nora left.

And Joe would be alone, as well as herself.

Where else would I go? I couldn't return to Wilmington.

Victor Rawls and his leering grin suddenly came to mind, causing Nora to shudder. If she returned, then he would certainly find her. Then she would most likely end up in more trouble with him than she had been in before.

At least here in Fairwell, she was free of him. Perhaps that had to be enough.

Though she might not have love, she had her freedom. Nora contemplated her options as she wrote down her thoughts and ideas. There had to be an answer in there somewhere. She could feel her chest constricting as she found her thoughts turning back to Mattie more than anything. All she wanted to do was ease the young girl's pain and sorrow. Every time Nora looked at her, she saw a young version of herself. She had endured so much and wished something could be done for Mattie now.

By the end of the letter, Nora realized she had made her decision.

She was going to stay.

Taking a deep breath, she stared at the letter as the pieces fell together into place. It made sense and was her best option. Joe was an honest and decent man. Even if they never loved one another, she knew she would have a decent home. Perhaps she didn't need children of her own, for she would have Mattie to care for.

Nora found herself adding one more paragraph to the letter for Lauren.

She shared about the beauty she was beginning to discover in the land around her, as well as her hopes for her future with her family. Joe would make a fine husband and Mattie would have adults who loved her and watched over her.

It was a long journey ahead of them. But Nora was hopeful. She folded her letter carefully as she thought about what it might be like to have a family again.

Her heart grew full, telling her that there was hope ahead of them.

Chapter Ten

"Here is the letter," Nora told him that evening after he had given her the paper.

Joe stood in the hall, having been called back by her just before he could make his way into the study. There was some more work that he wanted to get sorted through before the night was over. His stomach was full from a delicious supper and he wanted to work while his mind was still alert.

Now, he accepted the folded note from the young woman. He saw it was indeed meant for another woman in New York City. For a moment, he wondered what was said on those pages. Was he mentioned?

Then, he told himself he was being silly.

"Right, your letter," Joe said as he forced himself to pay attention. He managed to put on a smile for Nora. "Of course. I can take it to town first thing in the morning."

He started to turn, but he stopped when she opened her mouth. Then, she closed it. He waited, wondering.

"Yes?" he asked when she didn't say anything.

Inhaling deeply, Nora worked hard to bring a smile onto her face. Her eyes searched his face as though she were looking for something. Joe couldn't help but wonder if she found it. "I... May I come with you?"

His eyebrows lifted in surprise.

"Of course," he offered. Joe cocked his head, wondering why she'd asked. She was welcome to come and go as she pleased. There was no need for her to be shy. Even if they weren't particularly friendly with one another, he would not refuse her a request like this. "We'll leave first thing in the morning. Is there anything you need? Something I can help you with?"

A tight smile graced Nora's lips. There was a pink tinge to her cheeks as she said, "Well, yes. I thought perhaps we could go to church. If your offer is still open, I would like to accept."

For a moment, he didn't know what she was talking about.

And then it dawned on him.

"My proposal," he said out loud. "You would want to... That is, we will be married?" He realized what a fool he sounded like once the words were said. Heat climbed up his neck. Tugging at his collar, Joe nodded. "Right. Yes, we can do that tomorrow."

Nora looked at him for a moment before she offered him a tentative smile. "All right, then. Well, good night."

"Good night."

He watched her walk back down the hall and turn away. The young woman was gone, leaving him all alone. Joe held the papers absentmindedly as he thought about what had just happened. It was slow to sink in.

The offer of marriage had been a polite gesture. He had meant it from the beginning, but he wasn't sure that he had understood what it meant. After all, he had never been married. And the offer was not because he loved Nora. It was because, like everything else, she was meant for his brother.

Sighing, Joe walked into his office and took a seat. There was a lot to think about.

He was still thinking about it the following morning as he put on one of his nicer suits, combed his hair, and made his way out to the Cameron property. It would be best to have some proper witnesses to the occasion. He couldn't think of anyone better than Audrey and Dan.

The two of them were more than happy to help out. They brought their horses around to the house, where Nora was helping Mattie.

"Good morning," Nora said when she met them on the porch steps.

She had brushed her hair back into a thick braid around her head. It showed off her hazel eyes and hopeful smile. She wore the same dress that she had worn on the day of her arrival, but it had been cleaned up and starched, with a ribbon added around her waist to emphasize her fine frame.

Perhaps they did not have love. But she would make for a beautiful wife. One who had also proven to be kind, helpful, and generous through her deeds.

"Good morning, Nora," he responded. Forcing himself to look away, he glanced down at Mattie, who was wearing her nicest Sunday dress. "And good morning, Mattie. Both of you ladies look wonderful."

"Thank you," Nora offered as she put a hand on Mattie's shoulder. "Isn't that nice of him to say?" The young girl nodded shyly before ducking her head down. Licking her lips, Nora met Joe's gaze again after taking a deep breath. Her smile looked hesitant, but it was still lovely. "Well, I'm ready."

She didn't need to specify what she was ready for.

Joe nodded before moving down the steps to make way for them. He had the wagon and the horses prepared for their journey into town. There was his list of supplies, his boxes, and the little family he had somehow inherited.

Everything had changed so drastically in his life in such a short time. Joe mused over this new life as he listened to Nora talk to Mattie on their drive.

She spoke about the small things, trying to draw the young girl out of her shell. Nora discussed the weather and the landscape and how different everything was compared to the life she had lived before coming there. Though the words were meant for Mattie, Joe found himself paying close attention. He was curious about the young woman. While he felt he knew something about her from her letters that he had read, it was different to have her there beside him.

The journey into town ended sooner than expected.

With the Camerons joining them, Joe supposed that they should be married first and then they would finish with their errands. So, he guided them to the church, where their party knocked on the doors.

Soon, the pastor arrived. He looked around at the party curiously. The man would definitely recognize the Camerons, as well as Mattie, but he hesitated when he looked at Joe and Nora.

"Good morning," the pastor said. "Audrey, Dan, it's good to see you. And little Mattie, you're always welcome. You must be her uncle. I'm Pastor Simmons. How can I be of service today?" he asked when he turned to Joe.

"I'm Joe Bowman," he answered. "Billy was my brother. This is Nora Gilmore, whom I have come here to marry. We apologize for the lack of notice, but we were hoping you might have a few minutes for us?"

Pastor Simmons stared for a moment in surprise. "Oh. Ah. Of course! Well, certainly. Come in, my children."

The man was covered in wrinkles and thin gray hair that didn't look like it had been combed in a few days. But he had a cheerful demeanor as he ushered them inside. He gave Mattie a wink and shook hands with everyone as they stepped through. The six of them made their way down the aisle, where he stopped and looked around at them.

"Well, it's always a lovely day for a wedding, is it not?" Pastor Simmons asked. Beaming, he picked up his book. "I'll have my couple up here, and the rest of you can take your seats. Unless you would like to stand?"

Dan shrugged and took a seat. His wife followed, and she beckoned to Mattie, who joined them.

It left Joe and Nora together. He faced her and felt his heartbeat begin to speed up.

The pastor began to talk about the importance of the various virtues of marriage, though Joe's thoughts began to wander once again. He thought back to his years in the city. There had been plenty of women and several opportunities for him to marry someone. But he had never cared to grow serious with any of the women he'd met.

I could never have the woman I truly wanted. So why would I settle for anything less?

Now, he tried to tell himself that he wasn't settling. This was not why he had offered his hand in marriage to the young woman. He was doing it out of principle.

And perhaps it was time that he married. Marriage didn't have to be solely for love, after all.

"Welcome, Joe Bowman and Nora Gilmore," the pastor said after clearing his throat. "Today, we seal you two into a union before God and before these witnesses. This is an important step in following God's plan for each of you that will affect the rest of your lives. It is an opportunity for love, service, and growth. Will you take each other's hands?"

Joe couldn't remember if this was necessary. But he nodded and obeyed, putting out his hands for Nora.

She accepted. Her hands were slightly rougher than he had expected. They were also small and held tenderly to him as she offered a tentative smile.

Pastor Simmons continued to talk, putting them through the rites of marriage. As he proceeded, Joe felt the numbness beginning to fade away. He found his heartbeat hammering in his chest as a small shiver of delight ran up his spine.

He was not returning to the city. New York was in the past. Though he'd thought he would be bothered by this, Joe held little concern. He had written a few letters to be sent today, alerting all the pertinent parties that he would not be returning. His job was over, his friends were left behind, and his apartment would be bought by someone else.

Was this the life that Billy had wanted for him?

It seemed so hard to believe that after all these years of avoiding his brother, he was now taking over much of Billy's life. The sensation was strange. Joe had tossed and turned in worry that he was only taking what his brother had left behind. He was there to pick up the pieces of what had fallen apart.

But now, it felt different. Now Joe felt as though this was what Billy had wanted all along.

The anxiety he had felt earlier was gone. The beating of his heart began to calm as the pastor asked him if he accepted Nora Gilmore as his wife.

"I do," Joe said.

Then, the pastor asked Nora the same question about Joe. Her eyes crinkled up at him. And, as she cocked her head, Joe could see the gold flecks in her gaze. "I do," she answered.

Just because they didn't love each other at the moment didn't mean they couldn't find some form of happiness, Joe supposed. Peace entered his soul as the pastor marked the wedding ceremony complete.

"You may kiss your bride, Mr. Bowman," the pastor added.

The peace immediately dissipated. Nora offered him a shy smile, but Joe wasn't sure what to do about that. So, he leaned forward and gave her a kiss on the cheek. That was polite enough, wasn't it?

"Congratulations!" Audrey cried out. Clapping quickly followed.

The noise distracted both Joe and Nora as they turned to their guests. Nora pulled her hands from Joe's and went over to the others.

Now, he felt dazed all over again. Shaking his head, Joe turned to the pastor and put out a hand.

"Thank you," he said. "I know we didn't provide you any time to prepare, but I appreciate your help."

Chuckling, Simmons shook his hand. "The Lord works in mysterious ways and I won't stop His work. I'm simply glad to be of service. She seems like a fine woman. And I'm glad that Mattie has a family here," he added with a serious expression. "She needs people who love her. It will be good for her, I think. Shall we see you and your family on Sunday?"

Joe hesitated. He had never been good at attending on a regular basis. But, glancing over his shoulder at Mattie, who now held Nora's hand, he wondered if he might have to change everything in his life.

"I believe so," he answered. "Thank you again for your time."

The marriage certificate was signed and then pocketed away so Joe could put it with his records. Everyone said farewell to the pastor before heading out.

"I'm so glad we could be here for this," Audrey told him as they crossed the street. "Thank you for letting us join you. I think the two of you make a very fine couple. There are a lot of struggles ahead as you adjust to this new life here, but I believe you both will be content."

"Thank you," Joe said as he considered her words. "I think."

Dan chuckled, clapping a hand on Joe's shoulder. "Don't forget, we're here for all of you. Come by anytime. We have a sick calf to get back to now. But, like she said, thanks for the invitation. We'll be seeing you."

They waved before making their way to their horses. Dan and Audrey sat tall and proud on their horses, showing what an exemplary couple they made. Soon, they were gone, headed back for home.

This left Joe with his new wife and his niece.

Although they had spoken earlier and he knew they weren't strangers, suddenly, he wasn't sure what to say. It felt as though all this pressure was beginning to weigh on him. He had a lot to keep up, now, as a guardian, husband, and rancher. As the two young ladies looked at him, he found himself praying that he would once again find that peace again he had begun to feel just a short while ago.

In the meantime, there were errands to run.

He rubbed his hands together. "Well, I suppose we had best make our way to the general store."

"Of course." Nora nodded. She glanced down at Mattie and then back at him. "Where might that be?"

The three of them started down the street. He put his hands in his pockets, not sure what else to do with them. Every now and again, Joe would glance over at the two girls, as if to make sure they were still there and still real.

Part of him wondered if his life could change in any more ways. He hardly recognized his life now and could hardly comprehend the thought of anything more happening.

Chapter Eleven

He paced about his office.

She was late. It wasn't like her to be late. If anything, Nora Gilmore usually stopped by his office early.

Running through potential excuses that might explain why she wasn't there to pay her debt, Victor Rawls clasped his hands behind his back and paced around the room. From one corner to the next, he tried to imagine what prevented her from coming to him.

"She'll be here," he told himself. "She has to be."

Where else would she be?

Nora Gilmore was a beautiful young woman who had no one to depend on. She was perfect—stunning, gullible, and naive. Her lips were plump and the way her eyes widened in fear around him made her irresistible. It was impossible for him to forget her.

The name had been mentioned by her father before the man's passing. He'd said he had a daughter who was helping him pay off the debt that he had owed over the last couple of years. The man had said it was just the two of them, and he didn't know what he would do without her. He had relied on her greatly and had mentioned often in their few meetings that he was hopeful for her bright future.

And then, he'd died.

What was left of the debt was not much. But the interest had added up over time, and it had been high. Victor had generously warned the man, who had paid little attention. He needed money and needed it fast. No one else had been willing to give the man anything, so Victor had offered him a fair loan with high interest, which he hadn't even balked at.

There was a grace period of three days after the funeral.

And then, he'd sent a letter to the same address, to a name he hadn't yet put a face to. Not until she showed up at his office the first time with the letter in hand and her first payment.

Victor remembered that sunny morning perfectly. Her eyes had been watery and red, but that did nothing to disguise her beauty. She had been hesitant and soft-spoken when she'd offered him some of the payment.

It had been a pittance.

"That's all?" he had asked her.

"I'm sorry," Miss Nora had said in reply. "It's all I can manage for now."

He had tutted, taking a seat at his desk. "Well, if this is how your payments will play out, then I'm afraid you'll be paying off this debt for the next twenty years."

Those pretty red lips of hers had opened in surprise. He'd almost leapt across the table to kiss her right then. Then, a little crystal tear had slipped down her cheek. "Twenty years? But I can't... I couldn't manage that."

"Then you'll need to pay more."

It was as simple as that. There was something elegant about numbers that Victor Rawls had discovered when he was a young boy. They were clever and simple all at once. And, if he worked hard enough, he could make them work in his favor. Even as he stood before the young Miss Nora, he was analyzing his options to see how he could get the most out of this situation.

"I..." Nora had managed as her bottom lip trembled.

She'd been close to tears. Such a vulnerable young woman. Victor had trailed his gaze over her before making his way around the desk. He'd sat on the edge of it, close enough to breathe in her flowery scent.

"It's hard," he had said sympathetically. "To lose family like this, to owe this much, it's very hard. But there's no reason this should send you to the poorhouse. Wouldn't you agree? If you can make payments on a regular schedule, then I suppose I can be rather flexible with the paperwork."

Her eyes had widened with hope. "Really? I can keep paying. I'll take another job. I'll take two. I'll do whatever it takes, I promise."

Memorizing every part of her with his eyes, he'd nodded absently. It would be rather appetizing to keep seeing her. But what if he could have more? Victor believed in opportunity. As in, there was always opportunity so long as he tried for it. He could have anything he wanted.

Like Miss Nora Gilmore.

"Of course," he'd agreed with a smile. As he spoke, he was thinking fast. "Anything to make it easier for you. Though, from what I understand, it's a difficult market we have out there. It's hard to find a job. After all, this will take years to pay off either way. It was a good-sized loan. Why, it'll take the best years of your life," he had added softly. He'd sighed out loud before leaning forward. "You know, I would hate for that to happen to you. Now, I'm an understanding sort of man. I can make some allowances. What do you think about a different form of payment, hm, Miss Nora?"

His eyes had trailed down her body, liking the way it moved. Eventually, he'd looked back up to her face as her eyes widened. Victor didn't have to be any clearer for her to understand what he was thinking.

She'd stood up, shaking her head. "Excuse me? I am not... No. You misunderstand my concern."

Then he had put out a hand, his heart skipping a beat. Though disappointed, he'd been quick to move past it. A man like him couldn't dwell on refusals. She may not agree to everything, but surely there was something she might.

"I meant marriage," he'd said with a forced chuckle. "A young lady like yourself is vulnerable right now. You've been through a lot. You need help in the world. So, I could be there for you. Don't you need protection? And I'd clear away your loan. Every last penny, so you would never have another thing to worry about."

Hearing his calming voice had made the young lady pause. She'd been comforted for a moment. But only for a moment.

"Marriage?" Nora had repeated in shock. Then, she shook her head while she began to back up. "No. No, I don't think so. Thank you for the offer. That's kind. Very kind of you. But I couldn't possibly... no... I'm sorry, I should go."

To his great misfortune, she'd left before he could say anything more. She'd had her head ducked low and clutched her bag as though he might attack her.

That was a preposterous idea. He would never do such a thing. Victor huffed and sat back down at his desk. Though he had plenty more responsibilities to worry about, he couldn't stop thinking about the pretty young woman.

He would have her, one way or another, someday.

That was their first meeting, but not the last by any means. She owed him a lot of money and though she clearly began to bring in more income to provide heftier payments, it was not enough to clear her out of the debt.

Until, two years later, she'd managed it.

Victor thought long and hard about what could be done about this. He wasn't ready to let her go. He hadn't had her yet; it was beginning to drive him crazy. Nora thought she was better than him as she paid off her debt. It was obvious in the way she'd rushed to have the debt paid once and for all.

But he wouldn't have it.

There had to be something he could do. Victor went over his papers, he went through his plans, and had finally came to an idea. He'd erased the documentation of what Nora Gilmore owed. The young lady still had to give him the interest from the loan, after all. She had years left to pay the money back; in fact, she might never be done. So, it would be in her best interest to give up the fight. By this point, he was fairly convinced they were meant to be together.

She was meant to be his.

And yet this was the first time she had ever missed a day in his office to submit a payment. Victor Rawls paced back and forth as he wondered if she was late or not planning to show up.

That was impossible. Of course, she would show up.

But why had she not yet arrived? She was never ill, so that couldn't be it. Perhaps she was bringing him a gift. That would be nice. It could be that she had finally seen the error of her ways and knew it was time for them to wed.

Or could it be that friend of hers who had convinced her otherwise?

Victor stopped with a snarl. That other woman, clearly with child, was getting into business that was not hers. He remembered how she had looked at him as if he were a cockroach she wanted to stomp on.

He paced for the next hour, waiting and wondering.

It eventually became clear that Nora Gilmore was not going to be coming by his office. Victor kept everyone away as he stewed over what could have happened. As the day progressed, he only grew more frustrated. It didn't make any sense that she hadn't shown up. She hadn't said anything about being gone. No matter what he tried to come up with in his mind, nothing made sense.

He couldn't let her go.

She owed him. Victor couldn't sleep through the night, knowing she might have slipped through his fingers. He tossed and turned, only growing more aggravated as time went on. By morning, he felt as though he were going mad. He dressed and shaved and headed straight for the factory.

Nora hadn't mentioned her other jobs. Though he knew vaguely of her other work, he had no details to go on. But the factory kept records, and he had followed her once to see where she went after she left his office. Victor had wanted to make sure she wasn't about to meet with anyone else.

He waited by the doors. Women trickled in with a few men, bustling about with their heads down and tongues waggling. They disappeared inside without coming out. And yet none of them was Nora Gilmore.

This could not be.

Victor tugged on his coat jacket and went right in. He held his head high. Because of his fine clothes and good stature, no one would think to stop him. This was a skill he had learned many years ago and had since put to good use.

It was a large textile factory of five stories. The first floor, taking up two levels, held eight large spindles that were controlled by several men. This was an open layout with a door at the next end leading up the stairs. The next floor held offices for those who managed the factory. He knew the type, for it was all desks and papers. These were his type of men, if they made something more than pennies compared to his own earnings. So, he moved on to the next floor: to the sewing portion of the factory.

Where there had been constant shouting on the ground floor and disgruntled discussions on the next, this floor offered a tense silence of women with their heads low as they concentrated on their work.

Frowning, he looked around for that familiar face.

She had to be there somewhere. His body buzzed with energy as he grew more and more impatient. He had been waiting much too long for her. No woman had a right to demand more of him. Nora had better be grateful for all that he was doing. They would have that life together, just like he had told her. He had been patient long enough. It would happen, one way or another. He would have her and the money.

If only he could find her.

Though she wasn't to be found, Victor did see that other woman. The one with child. She was one of the few smiling in the room, making chatter as the worst of women did.

His eyes narrowed in distaste.

There was something about her that he didn't trust. Recalling the way she had talked down at him before, he knew she was trouble.

Yet she had to know something. He could see it in her eyes. And one way or another, she was going to tell him everything she knew.

Chapter Twelve

A week passed.

The days were long, but every moment was short. Nora hardly knew how she was doing it. How any one of them was doing it.

Every morning, she woke up beside Joe with the vague memory of choosing to marry the gentleman. He would jerk up, as well, often looking around in confusion before hurrying up and out of the room. There was so much work to be done on the ranch, and he was struggling to keep up with it all.

She couldn't blame him.

Nora was busy, too, with the cooking, the gardening, and more. There was always something to be working on. Though Nora expected herself to grow weary of the work and annoyed with all she had to do, that never came. She liked this work. It was more fulfilling than anything she had done in a long while.

Growing her own vegetables to put into her cooking was exciting. Audrey had brought over a book of recipes for her to use and Nora liked trying them out, for it felt like a game to her.

The house was a big place for just the three of them. Though simple, there were corners that had not been cleaned in a long time. So Nora tried to find time to sweep the corners, dust the ceiling, and polish everything so it shined.

And then there were the animals.

While Joe tended to the horses and the cattle, the smaller ones were left to Nora, who learned quickly to care for the eight pigs, twelve chickens, thirteen sheep, and two goats.

Each animal was particular in the way they ate, moved, and behaved. She was beginning to pay close attention so she would know their ways.

"That's Petunia."

Nora looked up from where she was feeding the pigs. "Petunia?"

With a nod, Mattie gestured to the largest one. "Next to Flora."

The young girl still lived very much in her shell. Only once in a while, with Audrey, did she run around and talk loudly like other kids her age. When Nora first arrived, Mattie wouldn't say anything. But she was beginning to speak up a little more each day.

And now, Nora had learned that every animal there had a name.

Mattie was a sweet child. If permitted, she would spend all day out with the chickens so that she could pet them. All she wanted to do was find a quiet corner with an animal and not be bothered. Nora understood this desire and often let the girl alone. But she still tried to be inclusive and supportive.

The poor child needed people to trust. After losing both of her parents, she needed patience and love and so much more. Nora was constantly thinking about what she could do for the girl. Joe didn't seem to know much, but he tried. The only problem was that he treated Mattie like an adult instead of the terrified child she was.

So, Nora tried.

She nodded and smiled, trying to remember what it was like to be a child. She invited Mattie to do everything with her, and she didn't fight when Mattie shook her head. Having lost both of her parents as well, Nora had a good idea about the pain that the girl was in.

It was hard. Sometimes, she still wasn't sure how to move on with her own grief. There were nights where she laid awake, staring at the ceiling as she questioned the world around her. Little made sense. The last two years had been so jarring and strange. And there she was, out in the Wild West, with a husband to support and a child to take care of.

She was just glad to be free again.

Anything was better than being weighed down with Victor Rawls creeping over her shoulder. That was the last thing she wanted.

Yet in the moments when Nora was alone, she couldn't help but worry about him.

Was he angry? Furious for her disappearing? Certainly, he couldn't do anything now that she was out of town. She was out of the state. There was no way for him to find her. Though she knew she was safe now, part of her couldn't keep from looking over her shoulder.

"Nora? Can I…"

She blinked, looking down at Mattie, who fumbled with a wash rag that was being used to rinse off the potatoes. "Yes?" Nora asked her softly.

"Since you married Uncle Joe, does that mean… you're staying here forever?"

Putting the bowl down on the table, Nora looked at her. Worried filled her soul as she looked at the troubled young child. "Why, Mattie, of course. I'm sorry that wasn't clear before. Yes, I am staying. So is your Uncle Joe."

Joe Bowman was a good man, no matter how little she really knew him. He had made it clear through his actions in his drive to learn how to manage the ranch, along with taking care of Mattie. The man was always polite and courteous. The two of them had few opportunities to speak with one another, but even in their small talk, she could tell he was someone good. He tried hard and did all he could to help those around him.

He was almost too good.

There wasn't enough time for her to find any of his flaws. She told herself it wasn't a problem. It was only that she felt weighed down with her own mistakes and failings, and she didn't feel she could share them with him.

She hadn't told him about Victor Rawls. Part of Nora didn't ever want to say anything. But there was another part of her that made her wonder if that was wrong.

They knew so little of one another, she reminded herself. She could tell him in time. Perhaps by then, her worry would have faded away. And then it would be just a bad dream that she had survived.

Nora told herself this over and over most mornings. As she cooked alongside Mattie, she tried to turn her attention more toward the young girl who needed someone there with her. Mattie needed love and patience and kindness. She needed to know someone was listening. The two of them worked together to prepare that evening's supper and then began to clean up.

Nora was showing Mattie how to sweep when Joe stopped by.

"Good afternoon, ladies," he said with a smile. Then, he held up a few papers in hand. "I just came back from town with the mail. There is a fence that needs mending, but I should make it in time for supper tonight. And, Nora, there was something for you. Here."

Jerking her head up, she felt her heart quicken at the sight of a small square envelope that he set down on the table. Nora clutched the broom tightly with one hand as she picked up the paper with the other.

It was from Lauren.

Her eyes widened with hope. She was finally hearing back from Lauren. A picture of the young woman came to Nora's mind and she smiled. She missed Lauren dearly. Life had been so busy lately that she hadn't had a lot of time to dwell on her past life. But Lauren would always be in her heart. The two of them had been friends for too long to go quiet.

And after all, it was because of Lauren that Nora was out here in Nebraska.

She wanted to read the letter right then.

But, feeling Mattie's gaze on her, Nora looked up and offered the girl a smile. She nodded and turned to Joe to tell him, "Thank you for bringing it to me. And that sounds perfect. Supper should be ready soon."

"Great," he ventured, his eyes cautiously searching hers. "It smells delicious."

Nora offered him a hopeful smile. But since she didn't know what else to say, she pulled the letter close and kept her lips pressed tightly together. He was just standing on the other side of the table, close enough for her to see the bold coloring in his eyes and the slight dimple in his right cheek. She hadn't seen that before. Her heart skipped a beat before she noticed the unease growing in her stomach.

"Well," Joe said after clearing his throat, "I suppose I should go. I'll be back soon."

She nodded and watched him leave. The man fixed his hat on his head as he headed out the back door, disappearing into the sunlight. She watched him for a minute before turning her attention back to the kitchen.

Mattie was looking at her with a cocked head. Her eyes were narrowed at Nora as if she could see something that Nora could not.

"What?" Nora asked. "Do I have something on my face?"

The young girl hesitated before shaking her head. "No. I don't think so."

She felt her face just in case. There were all of her features, still in their respective places, and just a small dab of oil on her cheek. Nora rubbed it off, wondering if that was what Mattie had been looking at. And if she had seen it, Nora noticed, surely Joe would have. She wasn't sure how she felt about that.

"Well," Nora announced as she tried to pull her thoughts together, "I think we should finish cleaning the kitchen. How about that? Here, let's have you finish sweeping. There you go, dear."

The two of them tended to the kitchen, tidying up the mess they had made while cooking. She tried not to think about the letter in her pocket, telling herself that she could save it to read later that evening while alone. Nora directed them to cleaning the dishes afterward, all the while keeping an eye on the food set over the fire.

Once she had Mattie busy, however, Nora couldn't take the anticipation any longer. She excused herself into the hall to read the letter from Lauren.

My dearest Nora,

I hope this letter comes to you at a cheery time. Your last letter was rather concerning, due to everything that has happened in such a short amount of time.

But I am hopeful. I want you to have the life that you deserve, even if it is far from me. Nebraska sounds like it is a beautiful place. I shall look for paintings of the landscape, though I fear they will not do your words justice.

Joe sounds like he is handsome, and Mattie sounds like she is darling. The two of them have been through so much pain that my heart hurts for them as well as you. But I find some comfort in knowing the three of you can create a new family that is happy and hopeful. You deserve it, Nora, don't forget it.

Please enjoy yourself and do be safe.

I write this with a word of warning. I didn't want to tell you, but Daniel says it is best that you are made aware of something that occurred the other day. It was just after I received your letter.

Don't alarm yourself, but Victor Rawls made an appearance at the factory.

That nasty man was looking for you, it seems. I wanted to slap him as hard as I could when I saw him enter the room, but, of course, there was little I could do. As I said, don't fear. No harm came to me or anyone else. I tell you this with the hope that you are kept in the loop of his dastardly deeds.

Rawls searched for you but could not find you. When he couldn't, he came up to me. I was hard at work and had no time for the likes of him. But thinking of the way he treated you brought a fresh fury into my soul.

'Where is she?' he asked me. Or, rather, demanded. I don't believe Rawls has a nice bone in his body. 'She owes me money.'

After that, it quickly became a mess. I'm still not quite certain of all that I said. I believe I called him a fool and a snipe, but that might be all. Rawls will never reach you, and I wanted to make certain of that.

I suppose I should tell you that he did threaten me. He thought he could take my job from me.

But he cannot. The only reason I would leave this job is if I wanted to. I am a good worker, and those are often invaluable, I like to think. Thankfully, our boss, Mr. Peterson, agreed. Though Rawls spewed insults and his own claims, all of which were very false, Peterson practically kicked him out of the building.

'Get out of here,' he said at one point that I can recall. His face was so red, I thought he might burst! 'Never show your face here again!' It was very kind of Mr. Peterson to be so supportive about everything.

Rawls disappeared after that. I didn't see him on my walk home, thank goodness. When Daniel returned, I told him everything. You know how I hold no secrets from him. We talked all night and agreed never to tell Rawls. His intimidation tactics are futile.

I won't tell him, Nora.

This is your new life and I want you to enjoy every moment. You deserve it. I only wish I were there to see you smiling. Focus on your happiness and what you have. It's time that you enjoyed your life.

Be happy, Nora.

Your dearest friend, Lauren.

Nora read it over once more, wondering how this could have happened. She hadn't expected to hear about Victor Rawls again. But the man was persistently still in her life, one way or another. Though she wanted to listen to what Lauren was telling her to do, all Nora could see was that terrible man's face in her mind.

Would Victor Rawls never let her be free?

She returned to the kitchen to help Mattie polish the silver. But even as she tried to engage the young girl in conversation and focus on finishing supper, Nora's thoughts kept turning back to the letter.

What if Rawls never left her alone? What if he came for her? What would she do with the debt she still owed? There was nothing that could be done then. She didn't make any money, as she managed the house on the ranch. She wouldn't have anything to give him if he chased her all the way west.

Feeling the panic rise, Nora forced herself to swallow it down.

Of course, Rawls wouldn't come out there for her. She was being ridiculous. Just because he had haunted her for so long didn't mean she needed to let it continue. This would consume her if she wasn't careful.

And the only way to rest easy about this was to tell her husband.

Just the thought of having it out in the open brought her some peace of mind. Nora couldn't let this hang over her forever. She would feel him hovering like a dark cloud over her, as well as Joe. That couldn't happen.

Still, it took her a while to come to terms with the idea of telling Joe.

She fought her feelings for the next couple of hours, thinking about all that might happen once she confessed her past. They hardly knew one another. What would he say? What would he think? Perhaps it wasn't the best idea. Maybe she should wait. Nora debated this even as she set the table and heard Joe enter through the back door. She would recognize his footsteps anywhere now.

"Welcome back," she offered to him with a cautious smile. "I hope you're hungry."

Joe nodded. "Starving."

The three of them ate quietly. Joe tried to start some light conversation, but Mattie was quiet again and Nora couldn't stop thinking about how she needed to talk to him. She just didn't know where to start.

But as evening set in and they left Mattie in the sitting room, Nora glanced over at him as the two of them dried the dishes. She had to start somewhere.

What if he was furious with her? There were so many doubts in her heart that worried her.

"Joe?"

He looked up from where he was drying the large pot that now sat on the table. Nora inhaled deeply as she mustered up her strength. He had to know. One way or another, she had to tell him. Her husband deserved the truth.

Chapter Thirteen

Every day was a strange experience for Joe.

He felt as though he was constantly falling behind as he tried to grasp an idea of how to live this new life. He wondered how his brother had done it. Though they had talked about the ranch work in their letters, nothing could have prepared Joe for the constant labor.

It was refreshing to spend every day outside; he liked that more than he had anticipated. But every day brought him new challenges. There were skills to master, basic lessons that he needed to learn in order to run the ranch properly. It was a race that had started without him and he was trying to catch up.

But at least it was enjoyable.

The ranch hands were tough but honest. Mattie was quiet and hopefully growing more comfortable. And Nora was sweet and caring. She clearly worked hard, as well. The evidence of her work was obvious. Their house was always clean, with the sweet scent of freshly baked bread constantly hanging in the air.

He didn't know how she did all this, but she was doing a wonderful job.

She said his name and he drew himself out of his thoughts. Joe looked at her now as she stood by the sink, a large bucket filled with water and suds. Her hands were covered in soap, with her elbows dripping water onto her apron. But she didn't seem to notice or care.

Rather, she had a troubled expression on her face. Her brow was furrowed, and she bit her lips. Joe cocked his head, wondering if something was wrong.

"Yes, Nora?" he asked when she didn't say anything more. "Is everything all right?"

"Yes. Or no. That is... I mean, I think so," she mumbled.

He turned away from the large pot and dried his hands. With his brow drawn, Joe looked at her worriedly. He had no idea what could be bothering her. His eyes drifted down to the sink beside her and then he glanced out to the sitting room.

Perhaps it was Mattie. Was something wrong with his niece? He thought back to supper and ran their time together over in his mind. There had been little conversation. And none of the food was ruined or wasted. What could it be? Then, Joe wondered if he had messed something up.

Just as he was growing carried away with his thoughts, Nora gave a loud and heavy sigh. She flicked one hand to get rid of most of the water before reaching into her apron and bringing out a letter.

It was the one he had given to her earlier.

A small rectangle that had traveled west from somewhere else. He hadn't paid much mind to it, not wanting to invade Nora's privacy. He hadn't seen who it might be from, for there was no name at the top except for Nora's. But now he wondered if he should have. Joe hesitated while he pondered whether something bad had happened.

"Are you sure?" Joe took a step forward to get a better look at Nora, who was now staring at the ground. "What is it, Nora? You can tell me."

At least, he wanted her to feel that she could talk to him. Wasn't that important in a marriage? They hadn't had a lot of time together to talk about such matters. But they had been brought together in a union that they had both agreed to enter. It made sense to him that they should be honest and true to one another as they moved forward.

"Well, I..." Nora started, then stopped.

He could see the hesitance in her eyes. She was conflicted over something, perhaps that had to do with that letter in her hands. He cocked his head while he considered his options. He could demand she talk, which offered no guarantees. Or he could wait until she was ready to say something.

"I'm listening," Joe assured her. "You can tell me whatever you want."

There was a spark of light in her eyes when she looked up at him. Nora glanced down at the letter and then returned her gaze to him. Something dark in those eyes was holding her back. But he had no idea what it could be.

After all, they hardly knew one another.

This was something he thought about most nights as he climbed into bed beside her. It was only proper for a married couple to be together, after all. The bed was big enough and there was a large wardrobe that fit all of their belongings quite well. Even though they did this, however, it felt like something was missing.

He wanted to talk to her. Most nights, he would lie awake trying to summon up the courage to say something to his wife. There was so much he wanted to know about her. He had so many questions. All he knew about her was from her letters to his brother. They were kind and friendly and thoughtful. Still, there was so much to her that he wanted to discover.

Yet, night after night, he couldn't seem to open his mouth to her.

But now she did.

"There's something I need to tell you," she mumbled, repeating her earlier statement.

Joe waited patiently.

Nora struggled with her words as she opened and closed her mouth several times. Her gaze flickered up to meet his before quickly turning away. She swallowed loudly and then let out a sigh before finally talking.

"I came here for a reason. Besides being married. I came to get away from someone."

He fumbled with the towel as he tried to think about what she meant by that. His chest tightened with unease. Joe searched her face for clues and waited for her to continue.

"There was... My father... For the last two years, I've been paying someone back for my father's debt. It took every penny I had. I worked three jobs to survive," she went on after a long pause. "And just when I thought I was finally free, he said there was more that I owed him."

"I see." But he wasn't sure that he did. Joe studied Nora carefully as he considered what she was telling him. There was debt in the family for some reason. But surely that couldn't be a terrible thing that troubled her so?

She inhaled sharply. "I couldn't keep paying, Joe." Nora grimaced and looked away. "It would have taken two more years. It was killing me, and I... I couldn't. I'm sorry. I should have told you sooner. This should be all in the past. But my friend, she wrote this letter, you see. She said that he was looking for me."

"Well, debts are supposed to be paid," Joe offered awkwardly. He knew the business well, having moved money around often himself while in the city. But immediately he realized his mistake as Nora's shoulders dropped. He took a step toward her, wishing he could take it back. "I didn't mean…"

Sniffling, Nora managed a jerky nod. "I know. I know. I never would have done such a thing. But… but he's a dangerous man and I didn't know what else to do. He threatened my friend, and I can't stop thinking about him. Please. This was the only way for me to get away from him. He's controlled my life ever since my father passed and I knew even if I paid off the last debt, it would never be enough. He would never stop. I had to get away and becoming a bride was the only way."

Her hands were clasped together as she took a tentative step toward him.

Joe wavered, not sure of what to think.

He was so taken aback that he struggled to accept what she was saying. There was a debt laying on her shoulders that she had skipped out on? It hardly seemed like an honorable thing to do. Especially if it was something that could affect their marriage in any way.

This was something that she should have mentioned. Billy would have probably still married her either way, but it was the principle of the matter.

And if Joe had known? He didn't know what to think.

He fought with his emotions as he tried to come to grips with what had just been shared. Though he wanted to be upset with her for hiding this from him, Joe couldn't be mad. When he looked up at Nora, he could see her eyes brimming with tears. This deeply affected her in a way that he clearly didn't understand.

So, he thought more about what she had said. Caring less about the debt, he considered how her voice had nearly broken as she had confessed the truth. The letter in her hands was damp and crumpled now with stress. She watched him, anxious and afraid.

"You couldn't pay him back?" Thoughtfully, Joe repeated her words out loud.

She shook her head. "He said it was the interest of the loan. I thought I had already paid that, but he told me I wasn't done. A thousand dollars in interest, he said. Almost the same amount of the original loan."

Joe started in surprise. That was a massive sum. He thought quickly as he calculated the numbers. What sort of loan had been provided that would require such high interest? No one he knew, whether in a proper office or not, would request that in a loan. That was madness and he doubted that anyone would ever be so desperate as to accept such an offer.

There was an itch in the back of his mind that told him something wrong had happened. Only he knew nothing of the matter but what Nora had said.

He looked at Nora thoughtfully. Any irritation he had felt a moment ago was gone. In its place was a low-burning anger in his chest at the thought of someone taking advantage of her. She didn't deserve that. The fear in her eyes was obvious. Joe felt his hands tighten into fists, wondering how anyone allowed that lender to be permitted on the streets.

"Who is this man?"

Her brow drew close together in confusion. "Him? Victor Rawls. He lived in my town."

Joe gave a short nod. "Well, he's not here, is he? And he never will be. This is our home, and I understand you did what you thought you had to do."

The young woman before him gave a small sigh of relief. She kept the letter close to her bosom as she held it with both hands. The fear was beginning to fade from her eyes.

Joe glanced down at the towel he still held. The pot beside him was dry and it was time to move on to another one. But before he did so, one other thought came to mind. He didn't like this surprise and he didn't want any others like it. This could cause trouble. They didn't have the time for such matters.

"Are there any more secrets I should know?" he asked her.

Nora gave him a slight frown. "What do you mean?"

Rubbing the back of his neck, Joe sighed. "I mean that I accept what you did, and I don't want it to be a problem. That was in your past and I understand your desire for freedom. But we're married now, aren't we?"

"Yes," she answered with a note of hesitation.

He nodded. "Right. So, if we want this marriage to work, then I want us to be honest with one another. It's the least we can do." Then Joe cleared his throat just as he realized he was speaking as if he were in a business meeting. This was nothing like his work in New York City, however. Taking a small step toward Nora, he softened his tone. "Especially for Mattie's sake. I want us to be honest and open. We need that here, especially after all we've been through. Hiding won't help anyone."

"Of course," Nora replied hurriedly. She put her letter away and moved forward as well. Her eyes searched his face hopefully as she bit her lip. "I don't have any more secrets. I don't think so, at least. And I do want this to work."

His heart skipped a beat. Joe nodded to her. She was nearly within arm's reach and he had the sudden urge to sweep her off her feet. But instead, he clenched the towel tightly. "Good. As do I." He offered her a smile that she eagerly returned.

Nora's eyes were bright and hopeful. She looked more beautiful than ever. He wondered if he could stay right there for an eternity. The two of them looked at one another before he realized that he had nothing else to say. Clearing his throat, he turned back to the table to put the pot back in its place until the next time it was used.

The two of them soon finished up the dishes, with her washing and him drying. Joe joined them in the sitting room for the first time in a while. He sat by the window with his book to read quietly.

Nora and Mattie sat on the sofa together working with needles and yarn. They were making new rugs for the house, it seemed, and neither of them knew much of what they were doing. But he listened to the two of them talk quietly, whispering to one another. Joe caught a few words and glanced over at them frequently.

He liked seeing how happy they appeared. The two of them were clearly beginning to bond. This gave Joe hope for the future. Especially for Mattie.

Chapter Fourteen

"Do you have any plans for today?"

Nora looked up from where she was putting on her boots at the edge of the bed. There was Joe, standing at their mirror, fixing the buttons on his shirt.

As usual, he was rushing to get ready for the day and most likely a few minutes behind the rest of the ranch hands. There was so much to do and yet she knew how hard it could be to find the desire to get out of bed. She wanted nothing more than to flop back down and drag the blankets over her head.

They didn't usually say much in the mornings. There was always something else on their minds, she supposed. Nora wondered if he was trying to get her to say or do something in particular. She wavered for a moment before deciding to answer.

"We'll be preparing some preserves," she volunteered. "The blackberries bloomed early, and I want to can as many as possible."

He glanced over at her and then nodded. "That sounds tasty. Will you leave a few fresh ones out?"

A smile crept up her lips. "Of course. And perhaps a pie for after supper?"

"You're reading my mind," Joe told her. Their gazes met, and she was able to see that dimple of his once again when he smiled her way. Nora's heart fluttered and she forgot about the boot she was attempting to lace up.

"Perfect," she managed to say at last.

Joe gave her a nod as he straightened his sleeves and opened the door. "Well, I had best be off. We're tending to the dam in the river today and I have a lot to learn." He offered a sheepish smile, then looked at her thoughtfully. "Perhaps I'll be back to join you and Mattie for the noonday meal."

Inhaling deeply, she nodded. "That would be lovely. We'll set a place for you, just in case."

He flashed her one more smile before heading out. She heard his footsteps move down the hall toward the back door, which creaked as it opened and shut. It had just been a short conversation. This meant nothing, Nora told herself. But the fluttering in her stomach didn't go away as she returned to lacing her boot. Her mind spun as she thought about the night before, when she had confessed the truth about her past.

Joe had taken it better than she'd anticipated. There had been a flash of anger in his gaze that had quickly subsided into something else. Nora hadn't known what to expect, but she wasn't sure it could have gone any better than it had. He had believed her and was now putting his trust in her. No more secrets, he'd said. And that's what she intended.

They hadn't talked much after that.

But it had meant something to her, and she had the feeling the same went for Joe. He was a good man and was doing his best. Together, they could make a good life out there. Though they both had a lot to learn, she knew they were ready for whatever came their way.

Once she was finished putting on her shoes for the day, Nora woke Mattie and the two of them walked outside. It was a bright, sunny morning that seemed to carry a lot of promise. She milked the cows while the child collected eggs from the chickens. More and more, Nora was enjoying the smell of fresh hay and, she found, and the bright mornings.

They tended to the animals before washing up and returning inside.

Nora knew that Mattie still wasn't up for talking much, but she knew that with time, the young girl would grow more comfortable around her new family and move forward.

"What shall we eat for breakfast today?" she asked out loud. "Eggs and sausage? How about some beans, as well? I think that should be good. We need to make more biscuits, I'm afraid. Do you remember the recipe we used last week?"

The young girl thought for a moment before slowly nodding. "Extra milk, right?"

Nora gave her a wink. "You know it. How would you like to whip those up while I start on everything else?"

Mattie's eyes widened. "Me? On my own?"

"Of course," Nora told her as she handed over the nearest pail of milk. "If you have any questions, I'm here for you."

They shared a smile before returning to their respective responsibilities. Nora focused on getting the sausage and eggs ready. She pulled the meat out from their small icebox, a luxury she'd never had growing up, and stoked the fire. Once she had that settled, she moved over to their stove to prepare that, as well.

It had taken her a few days, with Audrey's assistance, to figure out how to use it. But even now, Nora was hesitant. She and her father had never had much. The meals they ate were simple and never seasoned. Only on holidays was there enough money for a treat.

And now, it felt like she lived in a new world of possibility.

There was a full-sized kitchen just waiting to be used. She could wash dishes inside, cook a few items at the same time, and do so much more. It had been overwhelming upon her arrival. But now, Nora loved it. There was something freeing about being in the kitchen and taking charge over what might happen next.

A few minutes later, as the heat grew, the savory scent of sausage along with the musical sound of sizzling began to emanate from the pan. Nora switched from the stove to the fireplace to keep an eye on the food.

Mattie was right there beside her as she prepared the biscuits and set them to bake. There was a proud smile on her face at having prepared the dough all by herself. Nora had kept an eye on it over her shoulder and just out of the way. But she hadn't needed to say a word, for the young girl knew what she was doing. They worked alongside one another very well, Nora thought, and hoped dearly that Mattie might come to agree someday.

"Are you hungry?" Nora grinned at her as she brought the skillet over to the table. "Mm, I could eat right out of this pan."

That garnered a small giggle. "You can't do that."

"No?" Nora chuckled. "Perhaps not. Bring me that fork, won't you, please? The sooner we get this food on our plates, the sooner we can eat!"

Mattie had nodded to that statement. "Good," she proclaimed decidedly. "I'm starving!"

Both of them brought all the food over so that they had everything ready for them to eat. A few of the biscuits looked a little darker than necessary, but Nora assured Mattie that they would still be tasty. She had done a wonderful job, and Nora didn't want that smile to come off the girl's face.

They were starving. Nora and Mattie dug in eagerly after saying grace.

Though she meant to try and engage the young girl in conversation, Nora's stomach was growling too loud for her to do anything else. And Mattie didn't seem interested in talking as she piled a few biscuits onto her plate.

Afterward, the two of them cleaned up and wrapped the remaining biscuits for later. As Mattie did that, Nora washed her hands while glancing out the nearby window.

"It's a warm day," she said out loud. "We shall need our hats. Wide-brimmed ones, for our bonnets will not protect our necks. Are you ready to go berry picking, Mattie?"

"Yes," the girl said as she agreed eagerly. But then she stopped to think. "Can we eat the berries as we pick them?"

That garnered a chuckle. "Of course," Nora assured her as she reached out for a towel to dry her hands. "We have to make sure they taste delicious, after all. But we can't eat too many, for we'll need most of them for later."

"Later?" Mattie cocked her head in curiosity. "What for?"

The two of them headed out of the kitchen and into the hall to retrieve their hats and baskets that were waiting for them.

"Oh, for many things," Nora assured her. Audrey had found the recipe book belonging to the former woman of the house and had shared it with Nora. Mrs. Bowman, Billy's late wife, had written out very clear instructions describing how she took care of all the fruit and vegetables on the farm. Altogether, it made for very intimidating projects. But today, it would just be blackberries. Nora felt certain they could do this.

Mattie accepted her hat. She studied it with a slight frown before saying, "I think my mother used to take me out to do this. And she did something with cans?"

Pausing, Nora looked over at the child, who looked more confused than sad. She wondered if that was a good thing. Her heart ached for Mattie, who had lost both of her parents much too young. She wanted to wrap the girl up in her arms for safety and warmth. If only Nora could take away all the pain.

"Yes," she said finally. She didn't know what else to say. As she tried to think about what she wished had been said to her when her mother passed, Nora offered the girl a gentle smile. "Yes, she did. And today, we're going to collect berries and use them like your mother used to. We will preserve them and make jam so they will last for a long time. Not all the blackberries will be picked today, but there are several bushes that are calling our names. The bushes will need some help; they haven't had a lot of care over the last couple of years. So, we'll pick the berries and come back out tomorrow to trim them."

Mattie nodded along as she listened carefully. She cocked her head and squinted up at Nora.

"I think my mother would have liked that," she said after a moment.

Nora felt her heart softening. "Yes?"

The girl smiled. "Yes. I remember she liked berries very much." But then her smile faded as a troubled expression crossed her face. "I shouldn't talk about her, should I?"

The question caught Nora off-guard. Picking up the baskets, she wondered what the girl was so worried about. Her heart ached as she saw the pain in Mattie's eyes. "Why wouldn't you? Mattie, no one will stop you from talking about your parents. Either of them. They were very important people, especially to you. When you talk about them, you're keeping them alive in your heart. No one will force you to talk about them or to be quiet about your parents. We all want you to be happy. And if talking about them makes you happy, then it makes me happy, too. I, for one, would love to hear more about this lovely mother of yours."

It was the last statement that seemed to seal the deal for Mattie. Her eyes widened brightly as she offered Nora a broad smile. "Okay."

"Wonderful. Now, let's go pick some blackberries," Nora said. "We can talk more outside."

They made their way outside beyond the garden toward the nearby hill. The blackberry bushes were just out of the way and off the path. Nora had been very curious about them when she had arrived and had stopped by them several times in the hopes that they were ripe for the picking. A few of them had been sour, but just the other day she had tasted a sweet, juicy berry that told her all she needed to know.

"Four. No, these five," Nora said as decided she inspected the berries. She pointed them out to Mattie, who nodded and set her pail down by her feet.

It was only a couple of bushes, but the bushes were as tall as Mattie and twice as wide. They were weighed down heavily with blackberries that were just waiting to be plucked. A few of them had already fallen to the ground without being put to good use.

Nora remembered going to the gardens as a child with her father. He had liked to point out the trees as they passed by, having learned their Latin names some time ago. The man had taught her all about trees and bushes. So, while she knew little about berries or flowers, Nora knew that these bushes were growing wild. They would need to be trimmed soon to be properly cared for. Picking them clean of berries was the first step to doing that, and the most delicious step by far.

"Mm," Mattie hummed as she worked. "I forgot how good blackberries are."

Chuckling, Nora peeked around from the bushes. "Well, hopefully you will never have to forget again. If we do this right, Mattie, then we shall have enough blackberries to last us until we have more born on these stems."

"Really?"

"Really," she assured the child with a wink.

Mattie beamed as she got back to work. It was simple enough work, though they both wound up with a few scratches on their arms and some color on their lips. Nora teased the child lightly as they started back to the house, thrilled to hear her giggling. It brought joy into her heart to hear that sound.

Once they had four pails of berries, the two of them set everything in the kitchen and washed up. From the root cellar, Nora brought up the cans and jars that she had been carefully sorting through. She had done some light reorganizing, for it was a haphazard mess, and hopefully everything would be sorted, cleaned, and freshened up before winter.

"Here we are," Nora proclaimed. She set the bundle down carefully and then looked around. "All right. Let's work first on preserving them. We'll prepare, let's see, this many jars. Then we'll make our fruit vinegars. And finally, our preserves. How does that sound?"

The young girl glanced around the crowded table before offering a shrug. "How do we do that?"

"With your mother's help, remember?" Nora pulled out the recipe book and brought it over to her. "See? Her name is right there. She wrote everything down so she could keep track of her recipes. And I think she may have wanted this for you."

Mattie touched the pages softly. "There are so many recipes."

"Then we had best try some out."

They quickly got to work. The jars were cleaned, and while they were left out to dry, Nora and Mattie rinsed the berries. Then the blackberries were put into the jars along with a mix of syrup and water. A few notes were made on the recipe pages to include spices, but Nora wasn't sure about being too creative just yet. She was still hoping she could make this project work in her favor. Doing her best to stay enthusiastic, Nora worked fast and hard. Once the first group of jars were set up, they were boxed to go down to the root cellar.

"Now what?" Mattie asked as she bounced on the balls of her feet.

"What, aren't you tired of this?" Nora chuckled. She glanced down at her fingers to see them stained purple and blue from the berries.

The young girl shook her head. "No. I could do this forever!"

Grinning, Nora assured her, "Good, because we still have more to do. Can you please bring out the vinegar? I'll start the fire."

It was a good day for Mattie, for she was more talkative than usual. Nora still did most of the talking, but she was already ready and patiently waiting for Mattie to say something. She could sense that the girl was beginning to trust her more each day. It brought hope into her heart that perhaps she might be able to help Mattie heal from her sorrows.

She thought about this a lot as they worked. Steaming the blackberries, Nora poured in the vinegar and taught Mattie how to strain everything afterward. Then, they added the sugar and boiled everything until it turned into a syrup.

"Well?" Nora asked as the young girl tentatively tasted their concoction. She glanced down at the recipe. They had followed it perfectly, but she couldn't stop worrying something had still gone wrong. "How does it taste?"

"Very good," Mattie proclaimed. "It's tart and sweet."

Finally testing it herself, Nora found that Mattie was correct. This fruit vinegar was delightful. She looked at the syrup thoughtfully as she thought up all the recipes they could use this with. There were so many opportunities ahead of them.

Then, Nora looked at Mattie and grinned. The young girl had accidentally smeared blackberry juice across her cheeks.

Yes, Nora realized, they had a lot of opportunities—in preserving blackberries for the year as well as building a life together.

Chapter Fifteen

Harlan Kane was not happy.

Smoking his cigar, he eyed the doors impatiently as he waited for his men to arrive. They were late.

They claimed it was hard getting away from their jobs, but that was nonsense. Everyone knew that the Bowman ranch was easy work now, with the brother working the land. Joseph Bowman had no idea what to do; he wouldn't notice if two men were missing from their labor.

Of course, Ezra Moody would.

He gritted his teeth in a grimace as he thought about that man. Moody had worked for him, first, when he'd arrived in Fairwell. The man was a good foreman. He had a way of building solutions before problems were a problem. But the man wasn't perfect by any means. He had a mouth and was willing to fight for what he wanted.

"I quit!" Moody had spat at his feet that day with a burning in his eyes. "I won't work for a man like you, if you can even call yourself that."

"You can't talk to me like that," Harlan had retorted in return. "I'm your boss. And the mayor! I'm kicking you out of town. Right now, Moody. Get out and never come back. I'll have your hide if you dare."

That had garnered a scoff from Moody, who had shoved his hat on his head, mounted his horse, and left that very moment.

It was supposed to be over after that. Harlan remembered fuming for the weekend as he balanced his work in town with managing his ranch since the foreman had left him. He might have been the de facto mayor, but there was still work to be done.

They had rarely agreed on how the bigger problems were meant to be solved, since Moody could be slow. Then, when he had the time, he started telling folks in town what kind of fool and cheat Moody could be.

"Ezra Moody?" Chuck Barnsworth had overheard him talking to the blacksmith. "The foreman? Why, my boss just hired him on. You know Billy Bowman, don't you?"

The Bowman ranch was a problem.

It had been a problem as it started to grow. It had been a problem when Billy hired on Ezra Moody. Even now, it was a problem.

Not that it was supposed to be. Harlan couldn't believe how much he had to do in order to make this all stop. This was taking up too much of his time. Building his own ranch had not been this difficult, he swore. All he did now was play a game of cat and mouse. There were moments where he enjoyed it, certainly, but he didn't like how long this was taking him. And he especially didn't like that he had to wait on other folks.

As he took a puff, Harlan wondered about the next steps of his plan.

There were options.

If only he could get rid of Ezra Moody. That would do half of the job. Then, he could more easily get rid of Joe Bowman. The new boss of the ranch, and the one who clearly had no idea what he was doing. Harlan could still recall seeing the weariness on the man when they'd met at the bar just the other week. Joe was struggling. And if Moody was removed from the mix, then Joe would no longer have anyone to lean on.

He would sell in a heartbeat.

This was something that Harlan had put a lot of thought into. His first idea had been to cause a stampede. He had done it once before, and it hadn't been hard. Animals liked to stretch their legs and they were easily spooked. All it would take was a few minutes of secretive work and then, suddenly, it was nature taking charge. He could do this when Joe Bowman was in just the right spot, and all would be well for him.

But then he had decided against it. Two stampedes that killed the two Bowman brothers was rather risky.

Folks might ask questions. Stampedes happened, but to have it be what killed both ranch owners could appear a little suspicious. And he didn't need anyone asking questions like that.

That was how he had decided it would be best to convince Joe Bowman to sell the ranch, instead. Harlan had the money, even if he didn't want to part with it. He could do something on the right side of the law.

Once he had that ranch, he would own half of the town.

And he could really kick Ezra Moody out of Fairwell for good.

Moody had helped him grow his ranch, expanding the property and bringing on more cattle. But it was nothing compared to what the man had achieved on the Bowman ranch. Harlan was infuriated just thinking about it.

"You cheated me," he told Moody once, when the man had made a rare trip to town. "How is the Bowman ranch already the size of mine? You never did a day of honest work for me! My ranch should be twice its size. But it's nothing. Nothing compared to the Bowman ranch."

The foreman had merely shrugged as he hefted up a large bag of oats. "I did what I could. It's not my fault you're a blind old bat. I could have done the same, but you never gave me the rein I needed to make anything happen. Perhaps with your next foreman, you'll trust what he tells you."

"Trust?" Harlan had snarled. "What kind of trust is this? I kicked you out of town and you're still here!"

"Because you can't stop me," Ezra Moody had told him simply. Then, he'd tipped his hat and walked off.

Harlan recalled railing at the man until he'd disappeared down the street. But Moody had never looked back at him to respond to a single word. It still left a bad taste in Harlan's mouth just thinking about that day.

It wasn't right. It wasn't fair. He had been working on his ranch for twice as long as the Bowman ranch had been around. There had been some growth, but that had stopped in the last three years after Moody left. The Bowmans had the biggest ranch in town and it seemed ready to keep growing. This drove Harlan mad, knowing that the Bowmans couldn't have any idea what they were doing. It was pure luck.

Luck that they didn't deserve.

He wouldn't have it. The only dream he'd had all his life was to build a sprawling ranch empire in Nebraska. And it was going to happen one way or another. All he needed was the Bowman ranch. That was the key to making it all come to life.

And he had been close.

Joe Bowman had no idea how to run a ranch. The man dressed like he belonged in an office. He spoke like a fancy city man, and he was probably only surviving because of Ezra Moody. This man didn't deserve that ranch.

He had been close to selling. Harlan had his resources and knew this to be true. Joe didn't know anything about the West. He knew even less about ranching. Of course, it would make sense for him to scoop up his niece and flee east.

Then Harlan Kane would have been ready to buy from a desperate man.

But that hadn't happened. Someone had come to town. A mail-order bride, from what his men told him. It had surprised everyone, especially Harlan. How had Joe brought someone out West so quickly? Had they known each other previously? None of it made sense to him. Yet it didn't prevent Joe Bowman from marrying the girl.

And now, they had settled down on the ranch.

It made his blood boil. They were making a happy little family on the ranch that belonged to him. Joe Bowman had made it clear he was now running his dead brother's ranch. He had a wife now and a child to care for. Though he knew nothing of ranching, the man appeared determined to learn.

"He's green," Harlan had proclaimed when he'd realized what was happening. "He knows nothing! Being a cattle rancher takes hard work. It takes gumption. And that man has nothing!"

But no one had been around to hear him.

Perhaps because of that, Joe Bowman still continued to manage that ranch. Harlan didn't understand it. The man stayed. And the ranch was still thriving.

Moody probably had something to do with it.

"Boss?"

Harlan snapped his head up with a glare. Holding his cigar, he glanced around the room quickly and then gestured for the men to sit down beside him. "It's about time!" He scowled at them. "Where have you been?"

The two men glanced warily at each other before shrugging. Pete and Ryan were distant cousins who had come to work on his ranch ten years ago when they were just young boys. They had been desperate for a new life of freedom, which Harlan had given them. He'd taught them how to manage the cattle and how to live on a ranch. Now, they were in their mid-twenties, half his age, and loyal hands.

A man always needed an extra card up his sleeve.

And that was what Pete and Ryan were. Two years ago, they had followed after Ezra Moody, proclaiming that they simply couldn't work for Harlan Kane any longer. It had taken some convincing, but Moody had that kind of forgiving heart. So, he had taken them back with him onto the Bowman ranch.

It was just what Harlan had wanted. He had spies in enemy territory after that.

They had started with some light sabotage before Harlan had realized that Billy would never sell. That had been his only mistake in not trying to stop the man any earlier. Billy Bowman was a simple man who wanted nothing more than to work on his ranch with his family. And, since his wife had died there, he would never leave willingly.

So, the stampede had been necessary.

"We were working on a fence," Pete explained. "We couldn't get away with the boss there."

"The boss?" Harlan narrowed his eyes.

Ryan jumped to the rescue. "Bowman, he means. We mean Bowman, since you're our boss. You're our only boss. But he's right that we couldn't go. Bowman was there the whole time and we couldn't get away with him there."

That just made Harlan shake his head. "Why would he be there? It was just a broken fence."

"The one I tore down the other night," Pete assured him. Then he wrinkled his nose. "Bowman keeps wanting to learn everything. He has eyes everywhere, it seems. Like he knows when something is wrong or broken. Then he tells everyone that he has to be there when it's fixed. Says he needs to learn, or something like that."

Scoffing, Harlan slumped in his chair. "That's ridiculous. A rancher doesn't have to worry about that nonsense when he has his ranch hands."

Both Pete and Ryan glanced at each other and shrugged.

"That's what he said," Ryan mumbled in response. "But we're here now, aren't we?"

He narrowed his eyes at them carefully. The older these two grew, the more outspoken they seemed to become. And he didn't like it. But he shrugged it off, deciding there would be time enough for this later.

"Yes. So, tell me what you've accomplished," he ordered.

There were a few other folks around, so the three of them leaned in to talk quietly. No one else needed to hear about what was being done to sabotage the Bowman ranch.

It had to be small things that no one would guess was intentional harm. But it had to be enough that it caused trouble. There needed to be delays, accusations, and more to make it worthwhile. Pete and Ryan told Harlan what was happening and assured him that there was contention. The trouble was mostly contained, but they'd heard a few other men beginning to complain.

"What about Bowman?" Harlan asked impatiently. "He's the one who has to be convinced. He has to know that the ranch isn't worth his time."

The two young men rarely had any good ideas. They were too small, like breaking part of a fence. But Harlan was more creative. He suggested fraying ropes and leather. He thought up lies for miscommunication to seed doubt and trouble. The three of them talked for the next hour about everything that could be done.

So long as it frustrated Joe Bowman into agreeing to sell that ranch, Harlan didn't mind what happened.

They were getting close. He could feel it. Smoking his cigar, he told the two young men about a few more ideas for them to implement. This was going to work; he could feel it in his blood.

Joe Bowman would sell. He would realize he was a fool to stay out there, and he would take his new family back to the city.

And when he knew this to be true, Harlan was going to make him an offer that he wouldn't dream to refuse.

Chapter Sixteen

"Joe?"

He blinked, jerking to attention.

Uncertain whether he had been lost in thought or falling asleep, he lifted his head to look blankly at his wife.

She was standing at the table, alongside Mattie. Nora wore her blue dress, which was his favorite, and the yellow apron that was now stained from all the blackberries that they had picked for the day. She was drying her hands on a towel as she glanced from him over to the jars laid out on the countertop.

Nearly a hundred, he supposed, if not more.

"Hm?" he managed from his seat, where he had sat down a minute ago.

Mattie took a small step forward and pointed at the glass that had been set before him. Joe had already forgotten about it. They had prepared him a blackberry lemonade to drink while they waited for supper to finish cooking.

Two pies, Nora had said a moment ago. Or had it been longer? Joe wasn't sure. Every part of his body ached. All he wanted was to fall asleep wherever he could, even if it meant on the dirty floor. His brain felt foggy as he looked from both women and then to the glass.

"Ah," he managed. "Right. Thank you."

"Supper is nearly ready," Nora assured him after a moment of awkward silence. "Why don't you go lie down? It looks like you could use some rest."

A wave of irritation washed over him. Of course, he was tired, Joe thought. How could he not be? There was never enough time for sleep. And there was always more work on the ranch. If it wasn't a sick animal, then it was new branding or new horseshoes. Sometimes, it was mending the dam or a fence. The cattle had to be checked on frequently for illness or injury. The land had to be looked over for poisonous plants or other problems. There was always something to do or something to fix.

He supposed he could stop helping the ranch hands. But he had given his word and didn't like to go back on it. This meant something to him. He had told everyone he would stay, right? So, he had to. He must.

"Fine," Joe muttered before getting up. He left the lemonade behind as he went to his bedroom and collapsed.

When he had come and married Nora, he hadn't realized how crowded his life would feel. If he was outside, he was with the ranch hands. If he went inside, the women were there. It was a struggle to find peace and quiet after living so long by himself in the city. Granted, there was noise there, as well. But that was different.

Even though he had closed the door, he could hear the clatter of tin and glass in the kitchen. Joe sighed and put his pillow over his face.

Life was not bad. He knew this. But it was an adjustment he'd had no time to prepare for. The ranch life was busier and yet slower than his time in New York City. Every day, he saw the same faces over and over again. It hardly seemed reasonable.

All of this weighed on him, day after day. Though he could usually push it down, it sometimes grew too heavy to ignore.

There were moments where he considered picking up and leaving, like he had originally intended.

Yet every time he thought this, his brother's face came to his mind.

"You should stay," Billy had told him three years ago. "Build this ranch with me. I mean it. I want you here."

But Joe didn't want to be there. Not then, at least.

Sophia had just been buried and the pain was terribly fresh. He had avoided visiting after she had married his brother and broken his heart. It hurt him still. Sophia had been all he had ever wanted. But she had chosen Billy. So, it was Billy who had built a good life out West, a life that Joe had hardly understood.

That wasn't something he had ever talked to his brother about. And Billy hadn't tried to speak about it too much, either. Though he'd hinted at in a few of their letters, Joe had ignored it and his brother had eventually stopped.

Joe slumped in his bed. It was because of her that he hadn't been able to stay here. And it was because of her he had not been there to keep his brother from dying. Or rather, it was his selfishness. He was only using Sophia to avoid the truth and he knew it. Closing his eyes, Joe sighed as the regret washed over him.

New York City had provided him a good life. But it was nothing like this ranch. If he had chosen family over that busy life, what would have happened?

Though Billy had spoken often about the hard work he accomplished on the ranch, Joe didn't feel that his brother had ever mentioned how frustrating it could feel. In the city, he knew when he was succeeding. But a ranch required more time and more effort.

It felt as though he were failing every day. He knew nothing about the land and even less about animals.

And, if possible, less still about Mattie.

He had first stepped inside to find Mattie and Nora giggling about something. That had been a sweet moment to see, but he couldn't stop himself from feeling hurt. He was Mattie's uncle by blood. But she would hardly look at him or give him the time of day.

Along with a few of his ranch hands. They gave him strange looks at some of the questions he asked them. Joe could see them whispering, probably questioning if he should be their boss.

This had never been the case in New York City. There, he had been admired for his knowledge and capabilities. Joe was much more suited to the East than he realized. The upper social circles he enjoyed with their weighty conversations and delicious delicacies were something he was beginning to miss more every day. And at least there, he was seen as more than competent.

But Nebraska was making him question everything.

What if he wasn't cut out to be a rancher like Billy had hoped? Perhaps he was just fooling himself about all of this. Continuing his brother's legacy might not bring him the closure he had been looking for. Had Billy dealt with all these problems before?

"Our ropes are fraying," Pete had told him the other day. "What do you want us to do about that?"

He hadn't known what to say. "Mend them, I suppose?"

The young ranch hand had given him a look as though asking if he were crazy. "What? How?"

"How do you usually mend it?" Joe had asked uneasily.

His ranch hand had narrowed his eyes. "We fix the frayed edges. But it's not like we can just keep it as is. What do you expect us to do, put wires in the rope? It would ruin everything."

"That's right," Ryan had piped up. "It's damaged now, too damaged for repair. You'll need to turn it into a smaller rope, split that in two. And then get a whole new one. Unless you want to tear it apart a bit and then rebuild it with more string?"

Both of them had turned to stare at Joe, waiting expectantly for his answer. He hadn't known what to say. And he could have sworn the two young men knew this, too. It felt like a test.

A test he kept failing.

"Do that," he said with a nod. "Mend it that way. And if you can't get that to work, then split it in two and we'll try to find use for some short ropes. Don't forget to add it to the list for when I go into town next, gentlemen."

Pete and Ryan had tipped their hats to him as he walked away, feeling more flustered than he'd expected. It seemed like a simple type of problem with an easy solution. But he had no idea if that was right.

That wasn't the only problem. There was the dam that needed to be rebuilt. They had worked on that for most of the morning. But the stones were heavy, and he didn't understand the small levers that were being used. Joe had lost his footing a few times and ended up completely soaked to the bone. No one had said a word, but he could tell that some of his men had wanted to laugh.

It was a baptism by fire. That was what this was, he decided.

Every day brought new problems and lessons and trials. Joe had thought he was ready for it all, but he was beginning to doubt himself. He wasn't accustomed to the long, hard days spent under the hot sun.

"Another one?" Joe had asked that afternoon when Ryan and Taggert stopped by the men at the river to mention that one of the wire fences needed fixing. He had turned to Ezra, who frowned as well.

"We rebuilt those fences just last harvest," his foreman said. "What could have caused this problem?"

Taggert and Ryan had just shrugged as the latter said, "Looks like an animal ran into it."

Sighing, Ezra made his way out of the running water. "Fine. I'll see to this. Take my place, men."

"I'll come with you," Joe decided. He shook his dripping hands as he waded out of the thigh-high waters. "A breakage is unusual, you say?"

Nodding, his foreman clapped his hat on his head, and they started walking to where Ryan had pointed. "This early on, yes. My fences last at least three years—I build them strong in the beginning. But there's been a lot of problems lately that are unusual, I'd say. There aren't typically this many issues."

This was a surprise to Joe. "Really?"

"There are days where I could stay abed if I wanted," Ezra admitted. "As well as you or Billy. Right now, we rotate so three men are working at any given time. That used to be five or more. But there's a never-ending parade of issues that keep popping up. I don't like it. There's not time enough to do everything."

Though Joe thought that might bring him comfort that this wasn't usual, he couldn't help but wonder if part of this was his fault. He was far out of his depth here in Fairwell. Everything was strange and difficult.

This adjustment was much more than he had expected. Joe thought about this as he grabbed the wires, gloves, and tools to mend the fence with his foreman. They found the breaking point and trimmed the wire back a few posts. What was left was tied tightly around a nail.

Ezra brought out some new wiring and added another line of it just to be sure. They made their loops to connect the different wires alongside one another, making it stronger than before. They made another loop at the other end, then checked for any kinks in the wiring. When they didn't find any, Ezra decided it was good to go. The work seemed simple enough, but Joe was sweating by the time they finished. And with the sun beaming down on them, he was mostly dry from his last fall in the river.

Everything they did was hard work.

Joe liked to think he was tough, but all of this was so new to him that he felt like a fool every day. And he didn't like it.

He dozed for the next hour. Every part of his body ached. Though dry in his wrinkled clothes, Joe could feel the sweat clinging to his skin. When he woke up to a knock at the door, he was still feeling rather cranky.

"What is it?" Joe called.

"Supper is ready," Nora replied. She paused before adding, "Would you like to join us?"

Though he considered staying put, Joe knew he needed to eat. His stomach rumbled at the thought of a home-cooked meal. He sighed and climbed off the bed. Rolling up his sleeves, he opened the door. Nora looked at him hesitantly and he shrugged in response.

She led the way quietly back to the kitchen, where the three of them ate quietly. Nora offered grace, and that was it. Joe kept his head down low while he shoveled food in his mouth. Then, when he was done, he went to the front door to take off his boots.

The door was locked and he was about to make his way to the office when he heard a new sound coming from the kitchen. Joe paused and looked through the doorway.

It was Mattie. She was laughing as she shook her head. Water droplets fell everywhere.

Beside her, Nora giggled before flinching at the water. "Whoa, Mattie!"

"You started it," Mattie teased back.

They were both smiling. This struck Joe like he had just run into a wall. He stared as it suddenly hit him that he really wasn't alone. There was a family there for him. A family that was finding joy through the pain and troubles.

Nora and Mattie were bonding. This brought joy to his heart just as it brought pain. He wasn't there to bond with them. Instead, he was caught up in his thoughts, as usual.

Joe grabbed the wall for support as he realized that though he had allowed the family to be there with him, part of him had never really accepted the fact that they *were* there. He hardly talked to either of them, for he never knew what to say. But he hadn't made much effort, which was only making it worse.

Joe swallowed. He had to come to terms with this new mistake of his.

The ranch was a lot of work, and an easier task to focus on than building a relationship with his niece, who was practically his adopted daughter. Nor had he given much mind to Nora. They were much more complex than running a ranch.

But now, he saw the two girls laughing together, and he wished he was with them.

He was seeing them in a whole new light. They were more than just people in his house, more than folks he needed to be polite to so they would get along. They were his family, and they wanted to be happy. And they would do that whether he was with them or not.

A lump formed in his throat.

Not wanting to be left out like this again, Joe realized he had to do better. He wanted to be there for Mattie and Nora. They were his family. Though he had known this all along, perhaps he hadn't given it enough thought.

The ranch had a foreman and ranch hands. But his family was not a ranch. They would be around longer and they needed him there in more than just body. He needed to be there in mind and in heart.

Nora was a good woman. A good, beautiful, and wonderful woman who was bonding well with Mattie. She deserved more from him; both girls did. She had already proven herself many times over on being a great wife.

As if hearing his thoughts, Nora looked up and met his gaze. He could see the questions floating around in her mind.

She had caught him staring. Heat rushed up his neck into his face. Joe felt his heart skip a beat as he quickly looked away. He didn't know what to say. All he knew was that he had been a fool and he needed to make this right.

Tomorrow, he told himself. But right now, he was too embarrassed to say anything. He quickly left the room so Nora couldn't keep looking at him.

Tomorrow, Joe thought, he would do much better.

Chapter Seventeen

"May I join you?"

Nora looked up to find Joe rubbing his hands on his jeans. He offered her a hesitant smile before glancing over at Mattie, who sat nearby on the floor.

As for herself, Nora was perched on the settee while she worked on a quilt. Mattie was helping from one end while Nora worked on the other. As they had finished tying rags tightly together to create new rugs for the doorways, they'd discovered a partially finished quilt in the back closet that Nora thought should be completed.

"Sure. I mean, of course," Nora stammered.

She scooted further to the side to give Joe a spot on the seat. He slowly took his spot, shifting to get comfortable. He had set a book on the nearby table. Once seated, he picked it back up and fiddled with it.

If he made it home for the evening in time for supper, usually Joe ate and retired elsewhere. Sometimes, it was straight to bed, and other times he went off to hide in the office. They had been married two weeks and this was the first time he had strayed from his usual habits.

Nora wondered if this had happened for a reason.

Yet she could never quite tell what was on Joe's mind. The man was quiet and thoughtful. Though polite, he didn't volunteer a lot of information most of the time. She didn't always know what to say. All she did know was that lately, she was frequently noticing him looking her way.

"Thank you," Joe murmured. He fiddled with his book as he looked over the quilt.

Once completed, she supposed it would be eight feet by six. She was sewing the three layers of fabric together around the edges. As for Mattie, she was working her way through the middle to add knots of yarn through the layers. It would create texture around the flower designs and also keep the layers from slipping around needlessly. The fabric was a dark brown with small squares that created a colorful garden of purple and green flowers. Nora had found yellow yarn that Mattie was using now, and brown thread that she was using herself.

"It's a nice quilt," Joe volunteered.

Nora glanced at the young girl, who had ducked her head when Joe reached them. But she was still humming under her breath a hymn that Nora had taught her when they were trimming the blackberry bushes that afternoon. It was a lovely melody, tender and sweet, that always made her smile. Mattie liked it too, and she had quickly learned it.

Now, Nora turned her attention to Joe. "Thank you," she told him. "It is lovely, isn't it? This pattern was already created. We think it might have been something that Mattie's mother was sewing before... well, that she had begun. And we decided it was too lovely to leave packed away in the dark. I found some thick padding and this extra fabric in the attic and thought we might finish it. That way, Mattie has a brand-new quilt for winter."

"Oh," he said. She had seen the way his eyebrows raised and then lowered when he glanced down at the young girl. "Wow. That's... that's something. So, you're sewing the edges?"

She nodded and then showed him. "Just a simple stitch. I'll go around this again with a border fabric. But Mattie and I haven't decided on which color to use. Yellow, I think, or purple."

"Purple could be nice," he agreed.

Joe searched her eyes hesitantly. She could see something in them that made her straighten up. Nora opened her mouth to speak up, but she wasn't sure what she would say. Something was going on in Joe's mind. She just didn't know what it was. Still, something had to be going on for him to join the two of them like this. Could something be wrong?

"I..."

"I like purple, too," Mattie spoke up shyly. Nora closed her mouth as she looked at the young girl, who peered up at them with a piece of yarn in her hands. The seven-year-old offered a hesitant smile as she looked from Nora to Joe and back again.

Offering a smile, Nora nodded. "All right. We can do purple, then."

"Mattie," Joe ventured a moment later, "may I see what you are working on? It looks like difficult work."

The girl let out a short giggle before she quickly shook her head. She shook it so hard she nearly fell over. "No. It's not. It's fun. I like it. See?"

To their surprise, Mattie jumped up to her feet. The quilt piled around her shoulders and arms as she lifted it up to show her uncle. With one free hand, she pointed out the yarn that she had worked with by that point. It was nearly half the quilt.

"I did this one. And this one, and this one, too. All of the yellow. See that?"

"I do," Joe confirmed. "Wow. You did all of that? That's amazing, Mattie. You're very good at this."

Nora felt a lump growing in her throat as Mattie looked up at him with a beaming smile. She wasn't sure that she had ever seen anything so sweet.

Her heart felt so full as she watched the two of them begin to talk. They had practically spoken only through her since her arrival. Mattie would mumble things that she wanted or needed, and Nora would make sure it went on their shopping list. Then, Joe would ask her how his niece was doing, instead of going to Mattie herself.

And now, there they were, talking and smiling.

She swallowed the lump as she relaxed in her seat to listen to them. There was something terribly precious about Joe's cautious smiles and Mattie's hopeful words. Both of them were shy, whether they knew it or not.

If only they could see how important they were to each other.

Nora was only there because of both of them. She had stayed because she couldn't bear the thought of them suffering alone. And it turned out that perhaps they didn't need her much, after all. Finding herself simply glad to witness the conversation, Nora relaxed with a quiet sigh.

"Did you know my mother?" Mattie asked Joe while she clutched the quilt up to her chest.

"I did."

She watched closely as Joe looked away for a moment. There was a shadow in his eyes that didn't look familiar. What could it have been? Nora's eyes followed the crease in his lips as they tightened when he offered a nod to the young girl.

"Sophia was a lovely woman," he added after a second. "And a happy mother. She loved you very much."

"That's what Nora said," Mattie gasped. "Even though she never met my mother."

A flush crept up Nora's cheeks as Joe glanced over at her. Yet again, there was an unreadable look in his eyes. But she didn't look away first. Instead, it was him as he turned his attention back to the child.

"Nora is a very smart woman," Joe said at last. His voice grew soft as he fumbled with his hands. "Your mother loved you more than anything. Trust me, Mattie. She wanted to give you the world."

There was something in his tone that caught Nora's attention. It was the heaviness of sorrow. That was what she had seen in his eyes, too. She shifted as she looked at Joe. Though she hadn't thought much of it before, she realized that he must have known his brother's wife, as well. So, Joe had lost his parents, his sister-in-law, and now his brother. The poor man had suffered greatly.

A giggle from Mattie pulled Nora from her thoughts. The young girl plopped back down on the floor before shaking her head. "That's silly. She couldn't give me the world. It's too big. And it would just be dirt."

Nora found herself smiling as well. She shook her head. "That would be silly, wouldn't it?"

Mattie nodded so hard her little body wobbled. Then she ducked her head down to grab another piece of yarn that was waiting to be tied onto the quilt. She seemed to be satisfied with the conversation as she began to hum again. Nora watched her for a moment, glad to see that the child was coming out of her shell a little more every day.

The conversation ended, bringing in a comfortable silence.

While Mattie worked with the yarn, Nora sewed, and Joe just sat there watching them work on the quilt. The book was useless in his grasp.

He glanced over at her fingers once again, and Nora decided to speak up. They hadn't talked much lately, or really ever, but Nora wanted to change that. And perhaps he did, too, since he had come over to join her there.

"You know, my mother is the one who taught me to sew," she volunteered out loud.

Joe cocked his head when he looked at her. "Oh? She did a fine job, Nora."

That made her smile. She hadn't thought about her mother for some time. It used to be all she thought about as a child, for she missed that tender influence that she saw all around her and she no longer had. Her father tried, but he struggled in being a father just as he struggled to hold down a job and work.

Yes, she liked to think that her mother had been a fine woman who had done her best to prepare Nora for the life ahead of her.

Nora shrugged and then explained, "I was never very good at it when she was around. I'm afraid she passed without knowing I could even cross stitch. But when I was young, I enjoyed spending time with my mother. It was hard, but I liked it. Every stitch was an adventure."

"I never thought of it like that," he admitted.

She bit her lip. "It wasn't always like that. I found a job sewing at a factory in town. It was simple work. I sewed drapes, you see, for windows. I fixed the edges and put them together and everything. Oh, I must have poked myself a thousand times while I was there. No matter how good you get at sewing, there is always the risk of poking yourself."

"That sounds less exciting," Joe said with one corner of his mouth quirked up.

Nora chuckled. "Exactly. The work was menial and the same day after day. I grew very bored of it, for it was hard to enjoy doing the same thing over and over again. But... I think I'm finding my passion again. It's nice to be working on something that I want to work on. Does that make sense?"

"It does," he assured her. Then, he inhaled deeply. "I'm afraid that's been me and the ranch. I've been so desperate to learn everything that I've been having a hard time enjoying the labor lately. It's tiresome and hard. But there is something satisfying about it, all the same." Joe smiled at her. "Though I wish my mother could have taught me."

That was a joke.

It was unexpected, catching Nora by surprise. She laughed before she knew what she was doing, and her cheeks heated up as she did. Setting down her needle and thread, Nora shook her head.

She didn't know what happened, but it felt as though a wall had been broken down between them. Joe gave her a grin and Nora couldn't wipe the smile off her face if she tried.

Only she didn't care to try, because she liked wearing it.

Seated beside her husband and near her adopted daughter, Nora found herself relaxing in the evening as they made light conversation. She shared about the work that she'd done in her old factory, and Joe shared about the work that he was getting done on the ranch. There was so much going on that she had no idea about. It was impressive how much Joe did every day. No wonder he came home so exhausted.

As they talked, she found herself wondering if this is what a real family was like. Hers had been broken for so long that Nora could hardly remember. But there was such a warmth in her chest that she knew something wonderful was happening for the three of them.

Chapter Eighteen

Joe woke up feeling more rested than he had in a long time.

He laid in bed for a moment, hands on his stomach, as he stared up at the ceiling. It had been a while since he'd slept so heavily through the night. Taking a deep breath, he wondered if it could have been because of the night before.

It had gone so easily, spending time with his wife and niece.

The idea was strange. But sitting with them before the fireplace had brought a sense of ease he hadn't known before. He'd thought it would require more work, but it had not been nearly as difficult or uncomfortable as he had feared.

Being with them felt right.

His heart had been full when they'd retired for the evening. They had talked about light subjects, for the most part. He had made Nora laugh. Even Mattie was talking to him, at one point.

A smile started to spread across his face before he remembered his niece mentioning her mother.

Joe sat up. Sophia was immediately back on his mind, a bitter taste on his tongue as he tried to push her away. He couldn't feel hurt over her decision anymore. It had been so many years ago. She had picked his brother, and he had accepted her choice. He wouldn't have stopped her if he'd wanted to.

So, really, she had never been his. No matter how much his heart ached, Sophia belonged with his brother.

And now, the two of them were gone.

Sighing, Joe stood up and started to dress for the day. After his boots were on, he ran a hand through his thick hair and noted he would need to get a trim soon. Then, he was about to head out of the room when he heard rustling.

He turned to see Nora shifting under the covers. She was still fast asleep, her chest rising and falling steadily.

Her shoulder-length blonde hair curled around her chin as the young woman slightly faced him. She had plump pink lips that looked more inviting than he had ever realized. One hand was slipped under her pillow, the other hand rested comfortably over her abdomen. A stretch of morning light crossed the window to touch her cheek, and for a moment, he was tempted to wake her up just so he could see those hazel green eyes. They lay hidden below her thin arched eyebrows and above those fine cheekbones.

She was a lovely woman, one he couldn't help but be a little surprised at being a mail-order bride. Part of Joe had always assumed it was only women who had no looks and no money who pursued that avenue of finding a partner.

But Nora certainly had looks.

Swallowing, Joe forced himself to turn away. He didn't want to risk waking her when she needed the rest. And it would be rather odd for her to wake up and find him staring down at her from across the room.

So, he made his way out of the house.

Fresh air usually helped to clear his mind, and that would be best. As he stepped outside onto the porch, he reminded himself of the agreement he had made with Nora.

They had a marriage of convenience, or something like it. She had needed a husband out west, and he felt obligated to step up for his late brother.

He leaned against the nearby post at the steps down into the yard as he looked around. The sun was rising brightly, shades of pink and orange lighting up the sky. This was a beautiful view, and he couldn't take his eyes off it.

And while he watched, he wondered if he had explicitly said that their marriage was just that, one of duty and necessity. They hardly knew each other; just last night had taught him a lot about her. Joe wondered if they had been very clear about the boundaries of their relationship. Had they left anything open?

Though he told himself to be reasonable, there was a beating in his heart that he couldn't ignore.

It was impossible for him to also ignore the fact that his wife was a beautiful woman.

Nora was lovely, kind, and patient. His chest grew tight just thinking about her. Though he tried to push these thoughts to the back of his mind, there was something special about her that he could no longer deny.

If he spent more time away from the house, perhaps, then he would think less about her.

But Joe hesitated. He didn't want to be gone from the house so often. There was a family that needed him, and he wanted to do his duty. And he had a strong feeling that no matter how long he stayed away, he would still come home and see the remnants of Nora's day and her touch all over the home.

This was clear in the food she prepared, the gardening she tended, and how she took good care of the home. She had a strong character he was beginning to learn more about, that quiet strength and tenderness. On top of that was her obvious work ethic and the way she took such good care of Mattie.

He realized that ignoring Nora wouldn't even be enough. His eyes were opened to what a fine woman she truly was, and that wasn't something he could forget.

"Joe?"

The voice came from behind him. Not having heard any warning sounds like a door opening or footsteps, he startled easily. He nearly fell off the porch, grabbing the post to catch his balance as he turned around.

Nora took a step forward and reached out her hand, but she paused when he steadied himself. Her cheeks flushed while she looked at him.

His eyes grew wide as he wondered if she had known he was thinking about her. She couldn't. Could she?

"I'm so sorry," she murmured. Her eyes ran over him as though to make sure he was all right. "I... I didn't mean to startle you. I could have sworn you heard the door open. Are you all right?"

"Yes," he answered her quickly. "Yes, I'm fine. I just didn't expect you."

Clearing his throat, he straightened up and fixed the wrinkles in his shirt. Then he managed to give her a polite smile. Looking her over, he saw that she looked tired still, but there was a warmth in her eyes that held him captive.

"I'm sorry," repeated Nora hesitantly. "I just wanted to let you know I started to prepare some coffee. It's nearly ready. Would you like some?"

Joe scratched his head as he wondered how long he had been standing there. Either she had risen right after him to get to the kitchen, or he'd wasted daylight thinking about his wife.

"Yes," he told her. "Yes, that sounds great. Thank you."

She beamed, nodding before disappearing back inside. Once alone again, Joe inhaled deeply in relief.

Nora really was a lovely woman. If only he knew what to do with her or around her. His emotions were all in a tangle and he wasn't sure how to cut through them. Joe took a moment to collect himself before he went inside to join his wife.

"Here you are." She brought a mug over to him as he entered the kitchen. "A bit of milk, just the way you like it."

He accepted the mug, wondering how she had time to remember something so simple. "Thank you, Nora. I appreciate it."

Slowly, he sank into his seat to enjoy the drink. He knew that he was usually out of the house by that point, working hard on the ranch. There was still a lot for him to learn and even more to remember. But Joe couldn't convince himself to get back up. He wanted to sit there a moment. It was nice to have a quiet morning.

Especially with Nora there.

She poured a mug for herself, adding a fair amount of cream and sugar before sitting across the table from him. The young woman offered him a small smile before taking a sip of her drink.

Even when they didn't say a word, she made for fine company.

The two of them drank their coffee in the quiet morning, enjoying the peace. Joe couldn't think of anything better than this. There was a smile on his face by the time Mattie came staggering out of bed. The child had rumpled clothes on, with some of her hair sticking up. When she saw her, Nora chucked and helped Mattie into a chair before bringing her milk and a muffin from the other day.

"It's a fine morning," Nora spoke softly in the quiet room. "There's so much potential out in the world right now. Don't you think?"

Mattie shrugged.

As for Joe, he gave her a nod. "Certainly. A sunny day is an invitation to do just about anything. That means a day like this should not be wasted." He paused to drain the last of his drink before looking curiously at the two ladies. "Say, we shouldn't waste it. How about the two of you join me out on the ranch today?"

His niece glanced up at him and then at Nora, who cocked her head. "Oh? We won't be in the way, would we? I would hate for that to happen."

Joe shook his head. "Certainly not. I can leave most of the work to Moody and the men, and I'm sure they'll be happy to see the two of you. We can hitch up some horses and go for a ride. Like you said, it's too nice of a day to waste."

The two girls looked at each other. Mattie still looked rather groggy. But Nora smiled, ruffled the younger girl's hair, and gave Joe a nod. "That sounds splendid."

She finished cleaning up the kitchen while he went out to saddle horses for them as promised. As he did, he told himself that he was just doing it for them as a family. Not to impress Nora or anything. But he still hoped that she might be further impressed with the ranch, and with what he was doing.

Mattie hurried out of the house as Nora closed the door behind her. He could see them at the top of the small hill, and then grinned as his niece ran down the path as fast as she could. She reached him and looked around before finding her horse there.

"Thank you, Uncle!" Mattie ran to her small horse and hugged her nose.

The child had been riding ever since she was three, and he had seen proof of that when he had visited years ago. Sometimes, her father couldn't get her to leave the barn or corral.

Joe had thought about having her ride with himself or Nora before remembering this. She hadn't been riding since he had been there, which gave him a feeling that she might not have been riding since her father's death.

"Come here, you." Joe walked over to her to help her into the saddle. "All right, are you settled?"

She giggled before looking away. "Yes, Uncle."

"Look at you," Nora announced as she reached them at the barn entrance. "Mattie, you're so tall. I didn't know you can ride by yourself."

"I can," Mattie beamed.

"She can," Joe added assuredly. "I remember seeing her ride alone on a horse four years ago. Thought she would fall right off. But her father kept me out of the corral and told me to just watch. She was fine the whole time."

"All right, I believe you. I trust you both," Nora assured them. "Though I'm afraid you're both probably much better riders than myself."

Joe came over to help her into her saddle, as well. She had ridden once so far since she had been there, he noted, but otherwise usually used the wagon. He wondered how much she had gone riding back in the city, doubting that it had been very often.

"Don't worry, we'll go easy on you," he said with a wink. "Right, Mattie?"

He heard another giggle behind him as he gave the reins to Nora. She accepted them with an apprehensive smile. Her eyes fell on his while he took a step back. There was something in her face that seemed different today, he noted. Whether it was the beginning of freckles forming on her nose or something else, he didn't know. Nor did he mind. She looked beautiful, no matter what.

Joe felt his stomach churning on his way to his horse. It used to be Billy's favorite horse since the creature was smart and a comfortable runner. But now the animal was his, along with everything else.

He reminded himself of his promise to his brother to take good care of everything.

So, he did his best, keeping a smile on his face as he enjoyed the morning with his family. They met up with Ezra Moody, who pointed out some changes that were being made on the ranch. Mattie recognized him and Nora was happy to meet him.

Then, they continued on. Joe pointed out everything he could think of to show Nora, even if he was just naming a few of the trees so that Mattie could learn more about them. The three of them talked, rode, and bonded as they explored the ranch.

All the while, Joe kept glancing back at Nora. He tried not to, but part of him kept hoping that something might be said that could hint at something more between the two of them.

His heart was full as he spent the day with the two of them. Joe could tell why Billy had been so happy here. Everything felt a little perfect with his family, a large ranch, and a world of possibilities.

Chapter Nineteen

It was a rather tall horse.

Nora watched Joe help Mattie down onto the ground from her own mare. The young girl wore a shy smile as she clutched the reins of her horse. She was looking much more awake than she had been that morning, and even appeared happier than usual.

Then, Nora glanced at her own horse, wondering how she was supposed to get down. Joe made it look so easy. But he wasn't wearing skirts and he had to be quite used to riding for a longer period of time.

As for Nora, this was her fifth time on a horse. That was all the fingers she had on one hand, Mattie had sagely pointed out, which was not very many.

Going out riding for the day had caused Nora a bit of concern. Her stomach had been in knots for hours. But now that they had returned to the barn, she felt more comfortable on the ranch as well as on the horse. It was an easy-going mare who had followed after Joe and his horse the entire time. She hadn't felt like she needed to do very much in the way of guidance.

But now, they were done, and it was time for her to get down.

Nora glanced over both sides as she wondered which one would be best for her to get down off of. She bit her lip, considering her options. Her heart pattered. Though she tried to tell herself it would be easy enough to do it on her own, a few doubts in her head shouted otherwise.

"Nora? May I help you?"

Joe walked over to her with an open expression on his face. His hooded blue eyes studied her softly without judgment. She saw a faint sign of a smile, but he said nothing of the reason why he smiled at her as he reached her side and put a hand on her saddle pommel.

"If you don't mind, then, I could... Yes," she admitted at last. A flush crept up her cheeks as she looked down at him. "I'm afraid I'm not quite certain... of what to do."

He merely nodded.

The man was good at not judging her, and for this Nora was grateful. She had ended up with a good man, even if he wasn't the one she had first come out to marry. But she didn't mind. After Joe had left to saddle the horses after breakfast, she had found herself wondering if she was meant to marry him all along.

Billy had written very kind letters. He'd been serious and hopeful for the future. There was nothing wrong with the man, she thought. But from the way Joe talked about him, his own brother, she wondered. There was something about Joe that she felt herself drawn to. They had not been married for long, but there were moments where it didn't seem possible for her to have lived any other way.

"Here, I'll just take your waist," Joe said as he inhaled deeply. "You'll swing your leg over this way. Hold onto the pommel. Don't worry, the horse won't move."

She had immediately forgotten the horse when her husband reached up to touch her waist. It took all her strength not to react. Still, she bit her lip and dodged his gaze. His hands were firm and warm around her. Though Nora told herself this meant nothing, she couldn't stop a small shiver of delight from running up her spine.

"All right," she mumbled.

Clutching the pommel, she did as he had told her. She leaned forward and shifted, lifting up her leg over the side. It was hard to remember how she had ever managed this before. Her knuckles were white as she held on tight and then began to lean back. The ground had to be around there somewhere.

At the last moment, she lost her grip. "Oh!"

"Whoa," Joe called out right in her ear.

He stumbled back as her weight fell on him. To her surprise, his hands wrapped entirely around her waist. She grabbed hold of his hands before knocking her boots against the hard ground. Though she wavered a moment, Joe didn't let go and he didn't fall over. She felt his warm breath on her neck as the two of them suddenly stopped.

She could feel her heart stop. This had only taken them a second. But, already, her heart was pounding, and Nora felt quite dazed.

For a moment, the two of them just stood there. They inhaled and exhaled. By the third breath, she realized she was doing this in sync with Joe behind her. They were close, too. Very close. Nora glanced down to find her hands tightly gripping his.

It was Mattie who sprang them apart. Or, rather, the young girl walked over to peer at them with a concerned look on her face.

That jerked both Nora and Joe into action. She let go of him and then he did the same. "I'm all right," Nora called out. Her voice was rather loud, so she cleared her throat and tried again. "I mean, I'm fine. I'm sorry about that," she added, turning around to see Joe. Biting her lip, she fiddled with her hands.

His eyes were bright. A smile made it onto his face. The man took a step forward and looked her up and down. She supposed it was to make sure she wasn't injured, but she wasn't certain. She was mostly just curious about what he was thinking.

"Are you sure?"

"Yes," she told him, and hastily added, "I mean, you did save me. Thank you for that, Joe. It was my fault for being so clumsy. I didn't mean to let go so soon."

To her surprise, a small chuckle escaped his lips. Joe took another step forward; now he was within arm's reach of her. Nora tried not to think about that as he said, "I don't mind. I don't blame you. Horses can be a lot, I know."

When he licked his lips, she couldn't help but stare.

He was a handsome man, that was a constant reminder whenever he was around. On top of that, he made for a good husband and father. She couldn't help but think about the way he had been trying lately to be there around her and Mattie. Knowing that his heart was soft and his cheekbones were sharp was enough to make her feel very strongly about Joe.

She didn't know how to put it into words.

But Nora didn't like to think that she was a fool. There was something about her husband that intrigued her, made her want to spend every minute with him for the rest of their lives. She hesitated to call it love. After all, what was love? She hardly knew. All she did know was that she was married to Joe and she couldn't think of having anyone else.

Her eyes gazed into his for a good minute without anyone speaking up.

What was he really thinking when he looked at her? She felt her heart thumping loudly in her chest. All she wanted was to know what was in his head at that very moment.

"I'm hungry," said Mattie in a small voice.

Nora was pulled from her thoughts. So was Joe, as he took a step back. The moment ended. As she looked at the girl, Joe moved further away to tend to the horses. She wondered if he did this to be of help or because he couldn't stand another second of looking her in the eye.

Trying to focus on the child before her, Nora cleared her throat. "Right, yes. It is time to eat, isn't it? Let's return to the house and find something to prepare. What do you think about cornbread?"

Mattie nodded eagerly as she offered her hand. Smiling, Nora accepted it and led the way up the path to the house. The two of them walked hand in hand through the door and over to the kitchen. Only then did Mattie let go so she could drag out the cornmeal for them to use. The two of them started preparing a meal for the day, talking and laughing as they went.

But, in the back of her mind, Nora thought of Joe.

She looked out the kitchen window whenever she had a spare chance. Though she couldn't see him, she kept trying. She told herself that she was being ridiculous, but all the excuses she had were not good or helpful.

Perhaps she had imagined that moment with Joe.

Doubt flooded into her mind whenever they were apart. She lost her confidence and questioned herself about what she really felt about him. Perhaps she couldn't describe those feelings inside her because they weren't real. Anything seemed possible.

They hadn't kissed or held hands or exchanged tender words, though they were married.

That must mean something, she told herself. She was probably just imagining those looks he gave her. He had only been doing her a polite service when he'd helped her on and off the horse.

After all, he had made it clear with his marriage offer.

It was one of convenience, he had explained to her in a slow, deliberate tone. A marriage of convenience, because they could both use each other to survive. And mostly because Mattie needed them.

She slowed in stirring the pot as she scolded herself for entertaining any such thoughts. Joe had made it clear often enough that he was there for the ranch and she was there for Mattie. They were not in that house for each other.

A small pang of sorrow swept over her.

The ranch was a beautiful place, as Joe had shown her. Beautiful with so much potential. On their ride that morning, he had pointed out so many things along the way. He knew so much about the land and the animals. It was very impressive.

So, now, the ranch would be faring quite well. It made for a peaceful and lovely home. Even spending most of her time in the house didn't detract from that truth. Nora didn't mind either way.

"Nora?"

"Hmm, dear?" Nora blinked as she looked at Mattie kneeling on a chair. "Careful, there."

Mattie nodded and then promptly asked, "Do you like Uncle Joe?"

She opened her mouth to tell the girl that wasn't her business. But then she wondered how that could have happened. Pressing her lips together, she tried to think of something to say to Mattie. She hardly understood her own feelings, so how could she say them out loud?

"Joe is a good man," Nora said at last. "I do like him. Don't you?"

The young girl hesitated before shrugging. "I don't know."

Then she started talking about the cattle that they had seen, trying to imagine one as a pet. Nora smiled but said nothing more as her thoughts continued to wander.

Joe was a good man, but he would never be anything more than a simple husband to her. And part of her hesitated to call him that because of how little it meant. They were married and even shared a bed. But nothing more happened, or likely ever would.

After all, he had married her out of duty. He had told her that, letting her know that he didn't want to have to send her away if she didn't want to leave. He wanted to honor his brother and ensure a motherly figure for his niece.

It had all felt so simple when she accepted his offer. But now, she wasn't so sure.

The marriage of convenience and splitting of duties was all he had offered to her in the beginning. She shouldn't expect any more than that, Nora knew, no matter what she wanted. So, she pushed the feelings away with a shake of her head.

"Let's bake that cornbread, shall we?" she invited Mattie with a smile.

Chapter Twenty

Though Joe wanted to join the ladies in the house, he knew there was more work to be done.

While on their morning ride, they had stopped by where a few of the men were filling a dirt hole to see how everything was going. One of the men, Pete, had mentioned they intended to fill three more holes before the day was out.

A few hours had passed since then. But Joe wanted to see about that work—to see if it was completed and, if not, see how he could be of service.

The sun shone brightly down on him as he climbed back onto his horse. The creature had received some oats and a bucket of water, and so was comfortable and ready to be moving about again. The two mares the girls had ridden were set in the corral for now. He put his hat on his head, riding out into the fields.

"Just one is left," Ezra answered when Joe asked about their progress. The man shrugged and gestured to his left. "Pete is grabbing another shovel and then he'll be heading over to it. If you want to wait, you can join him in a moment."

Joe nodded. "Thank you. I would appreciate it."

He didn't have to explain himself any longer about trying to be there for any new projects. His foreman knew what he was doing and was usually helpful in letting him know if anything new was about to be worked on. They didn't discuss it much in detail unless Joe was asking questions and Moody was answering them.

"You've been here what, five years?" Joe asked Ezra after a moment. "But you said you've been in town for longer than that. What took Billy so long to bring you on here at the ranch?"

The man chewed on licorice tobacco as he looked around. He leaned against his horse, sharpening his knife. For a minute, Joe thought he hadn't heard or had chosen to ignore him. But, eventually, Ezra answered him.

"I've been here for most of my life. I care about the work that I do. I worked on another ranch for some years, you see, for Kane."

The name sounded familiar. Joe frowned, trying to think of who that might be. He couldn't quite put a face to the name. Though he had tried to meet a few folks so far, and the Camerons had told him quite a bit, he knew he was still missing a good bit of information.

As questions filled his head, he asked, "How did you come to work here?"

"It was best that Kane and I parted ways."

"Ah."

There was something about Ezra's gruff tone that kept Joe from saying anything more. Though he felt that Ezra always spoke roughly, he could have sworn that he heard some bitterness slipping off the man's tongue.

Joe waited another minute to try and remember who Kane might be. Still nothing more came to mind. He was about to ask his foreman about this stranger when Pete arrived.

He had work to do.

Brushing his questions away, Joe gave his foreman a nod before heading over to follow Pete. His question was forgotten as they started to deal with the large hole. Pete explained that they thought it first came from a fox or a gopher, some creature that burrowed into the ground. But then the animal had left, leaving behind a hole that grew over time. If they didn't tend to it, then it could cause a lot of problems.

The two of them worked together, taking care of the earth around the hole and then carefully sealing it up so that it couldn't turn up or be a problem again.

Besides that, nothing much was going on. He ate with his men at the chuck wagon and listened to them joke about the labor and about their lives. Most of the men were friendly with one another, laughing as they ate. But he noticed two of them, Ryan and Pete, didn't say much. He wondered if everything was all right with them.

Maybe he should talk with them sometime, Joe thought. He wanted to make sure his ranch hands were happy with their work.

But they were among the first few back out in the field. Joe tucked that thought away for later as he gave the men a nod and then started back to the house. He could finish tending to the horses and then retire early for the evening to spend more time with his family.

It was still a strange thought. His family. After spending years cooped up in the city, he was now surrounded by a family and the great wide open.

"Truly a marvel," he muttered to himself as he pulled up at the barn.

Joe climbed out of the saddle before leading his horse forward to brush the animal down. He checked on the horse's shoes and mouth and then let the animal loose in the oval corral. After cleaning and putting away all the gear, he returned to the three horses out there to see how they were doing.

He filled their trough with more water and was just returning the bucket to the barn when he noticed a small figure making her way down the trail.

It wasn't a very sharp incline, but Mattie walked carefully on the edge of the trail. She looked to be concentrating very hard. Joe stopped moving to watch the girl move cautiously toward him. At least, that was what he assumed she was doing. Looking around him, he wondered if she was off on some chore. But he wasn't sure, and she didn't wave to him to say anything.

He stood there and waited until Mattie reached him.

The young girl held her hands clasped behind her back. Her blonde hair fell softly over her shoulders, fluttering lightly in the wind.

Joe supposed she was there to give him a message. But what could it be about? It wasn't time for supper yet. If something was wrong, he felt that Mattie would have hastened over to him instead of taking her time. He considered a few ideas, but none of them made enough sense to potentially be real.

Shifting his grip on the large bucket, he spoke up. "Hello, Mattie. Is something wrong?'

The young girl hesitated before shaking her head. Her hair swept all around her.

Joe suddenly remembered about the moment he'd heard about when his brother's wife was expecting. Billy and Sophia had really wanted a child. Then, they had given birth to a precious little girl who they had adored. Mattie now stood without them, but as a strong reminder of how stunning her mother had been. Joe found himself wishing that Mattie had memories of the woman. Sophia deserved to be remembered.

Yet he also couldn't resist the thought that if he had been able to marry her, then Mattie would have been his.

Joe's stomach tightened at the thought.

In a way, she was his now. The idea left a bitter taste in his mouth. He didn't want what his brother had at such a cost. It pained him every morning to wander the house knowing that Billy should have been there. But now Joe had a claim over everything, including Billy's daughter. He supposed that Mattie was like his own newly-adopted daughter.

"Mattie?" Joe asked when she didn't say anything. "Are you all right? Are you well?"

The young girl hesitated and then nodded. She bit her lip and peered up at him. There was a strange look in her eyes.

He decided to set the basket down. He could worry about that later. As for her, he looked around and pointed to the nearby fields. "It's a lovely day outside and it shouldn't be wasted. I think a stroll out here on the trail without a horse would be perfect to enjoy on this fine afternoon. Would you care to join me? Don't worry, it will be short," he added when she appeared rather apprehensive.

She thought about it for a minute and then nodded. "Yes," she said softly.

Joe gave her a smile, nodding back. "All right. A walk it is."

There was clearly something on her mind. He had no idea what it could be, but he wasn't about to ignore her. Joe worried about Mattie now, whether or not they were together. He didn't know how it had happened, only that he had no idea how to stop. His heart went out to the troubled child as the two of them started down the road. It was a little rocky and uneven, but he took slow steps to give Mattie time to walk alongside him.

Once they were a few dozen yards away from the corral, Joe looked over his shoulder. He had expected something to be said by that point. But then, he decided not to say anything. Instead, he glanced down at Mattie, whose bottom lip was trembling.

His heart nearly burst. "Mattie? What is it? What's wrong?"

"I miss my Pa."

Mattie looked up at him through eyes that were beginning to mist up. She stopped and craned her neck up to get a better look.

He stopped, as well. Though he supposed part of him should have expected that, he hadn't. Joe watched a tear trickle down Mattie's face. His heart began to break even more as he tried to gather his thoughts and emotions.

She had been so strong. Stronger than he had expected any child to ever be. But this was harder for her than he could ever comprehend. Though disappointed that it had taken a while for them to talk, Joe didn't blame her. He couldn't. Mattie had only been doing what she could, both when he had arrived and now.

A lump formed in his throat as he looked at the poor child.

"I know." Joe swallowed. "I miss him, too. It's very hard, isn't it?"

Mattie pressed her lips together in a tight line before nodding. She dropped her gaze to look at her hands, then turned back to him. She took a small step toward him, sniffling. "And my ma. I miss them both a lot."

He thought about taking her up in his arms, but he didn't know how well she might react to such a hug. Joe didn't want to upset her any more than she already was. Her voice cracked and it was obvious that she was struggling to stay clear-eyed.

"I think about him a lot," Mattie continued eventually. "It doesn't feel real. I want him to come through that door. But he's not coming back, is he? He's gone forever. My ma and my pa."

Joe set a hand tenderly on her shoulder. "Oh, Mattie. They may not be here in person, but they will always be with you in your heart. Just like they are in my heart, too. And I think we can see them more clearly when we talk about them. What do you think?"

The young girl hesitated and then nodded. "Okay."

He had no idea where any of this had come from. Joe glanced toward the house, wondering why Mattie had come to him instead of Nora. Did Nora know that Mattie had left the house? But as he questioned himself, he scolded his thoughts for straying away from Mattie. He blinked several times and diverted all of his attention to her.

"Remember that?" Joe asked Mattie. "Even though people leave us, they can still stay inside our hearts. It will make us sad, but it will also bring us joy, I believe."

"Yes," she said as she inhaled deeply. "Yes, I think so. I can't see them. But they are here."

Joe nodded to her. "Exactly. And I think it's good that we're here. It's where your parents were happy, right? We can see that within the house. Your parents wanted you to be happy and safe here. Hopefully, with time, we can make that happen."

His eyes wandered over her head to admire the land around them. It really was a beautiful place. The sky went on forever without a single cloud.

"Yes. Thank you, Uncle Joe," she blurted suddenly.

Looking back down, he hesitated to see that there more were tears falling down Mattie's face. He thought about what they had just talked about. What had he said to upset her? He hadn't meant to offend her.

"I didn't want to leave the ranch," Mattie choked out as she clasped her hands to her damp cheeks. "It's my home. I didn't want to go anywhere else. Thank you for staying here."

He could feel his heart fracturing inside his chest.

Stunned, Joe quickly knelt down. Tears were falling faster now, surprising him. There was a somber air resting about them as he reached out and pulled her in his arms. The poor child. She would have been terrified to leave the only life she knew once her parents were gone. Joe wondered how she could be so strong for someone so young. Mattie snuggled into his arms, her mouth right by his collarbone. He could feel her warm breath tickling his skin.

She had been through so much, Joe thought. Too much, really. It killed him to think how long Mattie had been holding in these emotions. She didn't deserve to be so upset and hurt. No one did.

"I'm sorry," she sniffed in his ear.

But Joe just shook his head. "You don't need to apologize for crying. Or for any of this. I'm sorry, Mattie, you deserve so much better. It's all right. And it will be, I promise."

"Okay."

It took her a minute to collect herself. The girl clung to his neck with all her might as she sniffled, then began to hiccup from containing any cries. Joe pressed a kiss to her forehead.

He didn't know why, but it felt right. She needed comfort, and he would do anything he could to provide that to her.

As Mattie took a small step back, Joe looked her in the eye and put his hands on her shoulders. He gave her a sympathetic smile and a quick squeeze.

"Mattie, I promise. The pain will always be there, but it will get easier. We will laugh and we will cry. And I am always going to be here for you. This is your home. We're family, so you can always come to me. To talk, to cry, to ask for anything, you can talk to me. And I will listen."

The pain on her face softened. Rubbing her eyes, she nodded.

Joe felt something warm flood through his chest; it was a comforting sensation that he had never known before. He looked at Mattie, his niece, his adopted daughter, whoever she might be. She was a precious child, and he would do whatever it took to give her the best life possible.

The two of them spent a few more minutes there. Once she was collected, Joe brought her back to the corrals and invited her to stay and help him tend to the creatures. Mattie eagerly stepped up to brush the horses and then locked the gate behind them when they were done. The two of them started up to the house. As they did, she slipped her hand in his.

Was this what parenting was like? He felt like his heart might burst.

Chapter Twenty-One

It was earlier that afternoon that the two girls were talking in the kitchen.

"I miss my ma."

Shortly after she'd finished eating with Mattie, Nora had paused to listen to what she had just said. She put down her dishes and turned to the child. Though Mattie had agreed to sweep, she was just clinging to the broom now.

"Oh, Mattie," Nora breathed softly. She put the plate back into the bucket. Then, wiping her hands, she crossed the room to the girl. After crouching down to be eye level, she offered a bittersweet smile. "I'm sorry. I'm sure you do. I miss my mother, too."

"You don't have one, either. Or a pa?" Mattie clarified.

Nora shook her head. "Neither. It's very sad, I know. We never stop missing them, I think. Which is why I like to think that my parents are always nearby, watching over me."

The girl's eyes widened. "Do you think mine are here?"

Sighing, Nora tapped the girl's heart. "That's up to you, Mattie. What do you feel?"

Mattie screwed her face up in concentration. She turned her head from one side to the next before letting out a deep breath. It sounded as if she had been holding it all in. "I don't feel anything," she replied morosely.

"It may take time," Nora assured her. "Maybe you will feel them and maybe you won't. But you have the choice to believe that, if you want. Do you want to believe it?"

The young girl didn't bother hesitating. Nora held back a bittersweet smile as Mattie nodded vehemently. "Yes. Yes, I do."

Nora searched the girl's face thoughtfully, wishing she had all the answers for her. The young girl deserved the chance to feel secure in her life. She didn't need the fear of losing everyone she loved, just as she didn't need to experience being so alone. Nora's heart felt heavy for Mattie, wishing she could wrap the girl in her arms and keep her happy like that forever.

"Then think about it. Like at church," Nora added after a moment. "You go there to feel close to God. Your parents? They should be everywhere. It's up to you to find them. And even if you don't, that's all right. They won't be mad. Sometimes, it happens. But you know what else you can do?"

A tear escaped Mattie's hopeful face. She hurriedly scrubbed it away. "What?"

"You can talk to your Uncle Joe. He will listen. He knows this pain that you are going through, too. He lost his brother and his sister, remember? I think that he will want to hear about your sadness. He's sad, too."

The young girl looked at her through wide eyes. "Uncle Joe is sad?"

"He hides it," Nora admitted, "but I can see it."

Only a few minutes later, she had convinced Mattie that she should talk to her uncle. Though Nora would have been willing to sit there on the kitchen floor for the rest of the day, she had the strongest feeling that Mattie needed to be saying this to Joe. They needed to be talking about it. Both of them had lost so much, and they could hopefully find peace together. Nora knew their pain and wanted to help out. In doing this, she wanted to make sure she didn't put a wedge between them.

They needed each other, she thought, whether they knew it or not.

So, Mattie had grudgingly put away the broom and slowly made her way out of the house. Nora watched from the window. She stayed down, but looked up just enough to see outside. It was a beautiful day even with the sober mood in the house. Biting her lip, she said a prayer as she watched Mattie tentatively make her way down to where she could see Joe working in the corral.

Mattie reached him. Unable to look away, Nora glanced between the two of them. She leaned forward on the windowsill to see Joe put his bucket away. Then, he started walking with Mattie down the path.

She thought about trying to listen or watch, but she quickly scolded herself and put it out of her mind. This wasn't her business anymore, at least not for the time being. It was theirs, because it was their pain. All she was doing was trying to make sure that they were fed, clean, safe, and a little happier.

But even as she turned away, Nora glanced around the house. She wasn't sure how she would be able to concentrate on anything, knowing that a very important conversation was happening. So, she tried to distract herself.

She pulled out her late sister-in-law's recipes to find a simple cobbler. Thinking of all the blackberries she had recently plucked with Mattie's help, Nora decided to make a special treat for when she and Joe arrived back at the house.

After mixing the dough, she laid it out on the table to carefully knead. Her thoughts wandered as she worked.

Nora still remembered the way Joe had helped her get off the horse. They had been so close that she could feel his heartbeat. His hands around her waist had left a tingling sensation running up and down her spine. Though she told herself to lock the memory away, she couldn't help but wonder if he had felt something then, as well.

"Oh, Lauren," she murmured to the empty kitchen. "If only you were here to talk to."

Mixed feelings flooded through her bones as she tried to let go of the yearning that had begun to cling to her. It was frustrating to feel so alone in this.

It had only been two months since her arrival. Two months was not supposed to be enough to love anything. But she adored her home and her family dearly. They accepted her when most of the world had not.

Perhaps part of what she loved here was that everything was going smoothly, for the most part. Mattie was a sweetheart who needed love and kindness and compassion. It was easy for Nora to care for her, trying to do whatever she could to help the child. The home was beautiful, nicer than any of her past homes. She wanted to do right by it, just like she wanted to do right as Joe's wife.

The man could have married anyone, with his good looks and charm. Whenever he spoke about living in the city, it confused her to think that there was no one there waiting for him. But he had moved his life out there, and he had included her in it. He had treated her with nothing but respect.

Even when she had confessed her past to him.

There were moments where she expected him to change his mind. She waited for him to mention something about her terrible behavior, or to kick her out of the house. But those doubts were unfounded, and, in her heart, she knew that. Joe was too good of a man to treat anyone disrespectfully, no matter their past.

Nora finished kneading the dough and began rolling it out. Once it was a perfect eighth of an inch thick, judging by her fingernail, it was good to go in the pan.

She paused to look out the window to see how Mattie and Joe might be faring.

"Oh," she breathed softly when she saw the two of them hugging. Joe was down on his knees, and Mattie had buried her face in his shoulder. They were far down the lane so she couldn't see exactly what was going on, but the image of them hugging warmed her heart.

"Please, Lord, bless them through their pain," she murmured before glancing up at the ceiling. Her father had not been a church man, so she didn't grow up thinking much about a God.

But there had been Lauren, and Lauren believed in a higher power. She went to church every Sunday and read her Bible every day. Nora couldn't count how many times she had been invited to church. A few times, she had gone, but usually she was busy working by that point. Luckily, Lauren had loaned her a Bible, which Nora had read eagerly.

She paused after setting the crust into the pan, nudging it into position.

There were a lot of books in this house, Nora realized. Certainly, there would be a Bible somewhere. She tucked that idea away for another time, when she was ready to ask Joe or look for herself.

In the meantime, there was a pie to work on.

Her thoughts strayed to Victor Rawls, and she pursed her lips in irritation. That was a man who had never treated her like a human being. He had treated her as something else that she didn't quite have the words for. Just thinking about the way he would talk to her made her shudder.

But he was gone. He had no idea where she was, thanks to Lauren.

Nora took a moment to breathe while she leaned on the counter to keep her up. Recalling her friend's letter had brought back the fear and paranoia she had felt when she'd first left town. She stood there at the table, inhaling and exhaling, trying to collect her thoughts. All of those horrible doubts needed to be closed off. She was safe now, safe and married and happy.

"Nora?"

She jerked up. Opening her eyes, she put on a smile and turned to see Mattie and Joe standing there.

She flushed. She hadn't realized that the two of them were headed back, let alone already arrived. Nora fiddled with her apron as she gave them a smile. "There you two are! I'm making pie for dessert tonight. I hope you're hungry."

"Are you all right?" Mattie ignored her words to ask her a question.

It caught Nora by surprise. She blinked several times as she tried to think. Sometimes, the girl was remarkably shy and had nothing to say. But, as she slowly came out of her shell, it was clear that she was very attentive to the world around her and wanted to understand it.

"Yes," Nora responded quickly. "Yes, of course."

Mattie studied her for a moment before coming to the table. She looked around to see what was being done. As she did, Nora noticed a few dried streaks on her cheeks. The child had cried, but she looked happy again. Hopefully, that was a good sign.

"It looks like we need some fruit for the pies?" Joe asked casually as he stepped over.

For some reason, she expected something else from him. She thought he might say something about Mattie or about returning to work. This was the earliest he had returned home so far, Nora felt certain.

Her heart hammered. Trying not to show how flustered she felt, Nora nodded. "Right, yes. Blackberries. They're in the cellar."

She was just about to add that she would go get them when Joe tapped Mattie on the shoulder. "Do you mind helping Nora out with the blackberries?"

"No," the girl chirped. Then, she disappeared out of the room.

Joe moved quickly around the table. Nora looked down to clear out the flour. But before she could move away, he put a hand on her elbow. It was a light grip, just enough for her to notice and stop moving.

"Are you?"

She furrowed her brow in confusion. "I'm sorry?"

"Are you all right?" Joe repeated his question more clearly with a furrowed brow. "You looked, well, stressed when we stepped inside. Or sick."

Swallowing, she quickly shook her head. "Oh, no. No, I'm not sick. I was just thinking. About the past," Nora added hurriedly with a grimace. "That's all."

"Oh?"

The question was inviting. Joe took a small step forward so their shoes were practically touching. He cocked his head to the side, giving her his full attention. Something about him seemed lighter, she thought, and wondered what had happened.

But she had a question to answer first.

"It's really nothing," she assured him. "I just didn't want to think about it. It's nice being here, where I can leave it behind."

"Indeed," he said, his voice dropping an octave in a softer tone. Joe looked at her straight on, a flicker of light in his eyes.

It seemed to mean something, but she wasn't quite sure. Nora could feel her heart beginning to beat faster with Joe right in front of her. She met his gaze and wondered what he was thinking. His grip was warm and comfortable. It was just on her forearm, but she was inclined to lean into it, if she let it happen.

"Nora," Joe started to say, "there's something that I—"

But then the door burst open as Mattie returned. Both of them jumped in surprise, having been caught up in the moment. If they could call it that. Nora gulped, feeling Joe let go of her.

Was that moment supposed to mean something? She wasn't certain. But her heart was still beating quickly.

He said nothing, so she walked over to Mattie with the jar of blackberries. "Perfect," Nora exclaimed. "These are perfect, thank you. Do you want to help me with the pie, Mattie?"

The girl nodded eagerly, following right behind her as they walked around the kitchen. There was a child's apron to put on, and then they needed to dump the berries into the pie pan.

Joe offered to clean up the table mess and worked around Nora and Mattie as they prepared the cobbler. Whatever he was going to say was gone, she supposed. But part of her didn't mind. It was just the three of them in the house together, chatting about their ride that morning and other things.

All the while, though, Nora couldn't help cheating glances over at Joe.

Chapter Twenty-Two

The mood brightened around the kitchen as the three of them worked.

Joe shifted his gaze between the two girls, unable to hold back a smile. Both of them were covered with flour from working with their dough. They giggled, poking each other as they kneaded.

They were happy.

He thought about this as he helped them out. Though the kitchen wasn't completely familiar to him, he'd had some experience as a bachelor in the city. Even coming here, he had spent some time tending to the room. But the large space had never felt quite comfortable to be in until now, as he worked alongside Nora and Mattie.

Seeing their smiles, his stomach flip-flopped.

This was what it was supposed to be like, he realized. This was how a family should be when they were all together. He marveled over this as he slowly swept around the room.

As always, his eyes returned to Nora.

She had looked stressed when he'd arrived with Mattie. Seeing her taking deep breaths with her eyes closed while she leaned against the counter had worried him for a moment. He wanted to believe her when she'd said that nothing was of concern. He didn't want to think that she might be upset or miserable and trying to hide it from everyone. Especially him.

When Mattie had stepped out, he tried to invite her to talk.

There was so much that Joe wanted to talk to her about. A weight had settled on his shoulders, making him realize that he couldn't keep putting this off. His muscles grew tense. Though he enjoyed watching Nora with Mattie, the words hung on the tip of his lips, tempting him to speak up.

She had a right to know his heart.

Joe had considered this on his way up to the house with Mattie. Though he had been thinking about it for some time, that afternoon had sealed the deal. His niece had come to share her fears and pain, opening her heart to him. Joe would always be grateful to her for that.

And now, he needed to do the same with Nora.

Being friendly and around in person wasn't enough, though he had thought it might be. But now, his fingers gripped the broom so tightly that his knuckles turned white. He could hardly concentrate as he listened to Nora tell Mattie a funny story about cooking back in Delaware with a friend of hers.

He paused, watching her eyes light up. Her hands were covered in flour and oil and blackberries, but she still waved them around in effect as she relayed her tale.

She needed to know the truth.

Joe tried to tell himself that it wasn't a big deal. That the past was the past and it wouldn't matter what happened. But a doubt slipped into his mind, and he began to worry. What would Nora say? They had talked about being honest with one another. He had said they needed to have no secrets between them.

And there he was, finally ready to confess his own.

A lump formed in his throat, and Joe stopped in his tracks to lean on the broom and watch Nora there. She moved around confidently with her head held high. Though she had flour on her cheeks and her apron was a mess, she didn't mind. It only added to her charm, he thought. This was her home, and she knew what to do there.

"Nora?"

She looked up from closing the stove in the corner. Wiping her hands on her apron, she straightened and gave him a faint smile.

He hesitated. When he said nothing, she asked him, "Yes, Joe?"

Mattie was in between them, drawing shapes in the flour that was still in a small heap on the table. He had a feeling that the flour would always be somewhere it didn't belong in the kitchen. But he didn't mind. That wasn't the reason why his stomach was churning.

His hands grew moist. Setting the broom against the wall, he dried his hands on his pants and gave Nora a hesitant smile. At least, he tried.

"Can I talk to you?"

She opened her mouth and then closed it before turning to look at the stove and fireplace. They were using both to prepare their food quickly and at the same time. Everything was inside and all there was left to do now was finishing cleaning up. Nora appeared to think about it for a minute before she nodded.

"Of course, Joe," she said agreeably before turning to Mattie. "Do you think you can finish cleaning up, dear?"

Mattie nodded quickly.

Nora turned back to Joe with an expectant look. She was waiting on him, now, to tell her where he wanted to talk with her.

He glanced around, for he hadn't gotten that far. Inhaling deeply, he weighed their options for a moment before he gestured for her to follow him to the back door. She obeyed, a strange look crossing over her features as she walked with him quietly out of the house.

Joe had thought that the moment they were alone, he would be able to talk about everything.

But even as he could feel the anxiety rising in his throat, Joe couldn't find the words. He wanted them to be just perfect so that Nora couldn't misunderstand him. Hopefully, she wouldn't judge him, either. Now that they were alone, however, he wasn't so certain. An awkward tension rose between them as Nora clasped her hands in front of herself and waited.

He glanced over at his wife and then off the porch to see the sun beginning to set.

The sky above them was beginning to grow darker, with swirls of pink and yellow among the clouds. It made for a beautiful view. The world out here was more dazzling than he had expected upon his arrival. Though he loved New York, with its impressive architecture and all the crowded streets, there was something particularly pleasant about the quiet view of nature.

"Joe? Is something wrong?" Nora asked when the silence stretched on.

He cleared his throat as he realized he was reaching for distractions. Scolding himself for being rude to Nora, Joe forced himself to straighten his shoulders and talk to her.

"No. Not really," he assured her. But then he hesitated and scratched the back of his neck. He hoped this didn't mean there was a problem, but he wasn't entirely sure. He supposed that would depend on Nora and her reaction. "I just wanted to talk with you."

A faint smile graced her lips. "Well, I'm here. As are you. Shall we talk now?"

Chuckling, he shook his head. Joe put his hands on his hips as he took a deep breath and said, "Yes. Yes, we should talk now."

"All right." Nora offered him a kind smile, though she did look a little nervous. She cocked her head at him and shrugged. "What would you like to talk about?"

Joe tried to think of where to begin. There was so much he wanted her to know, to understand. But he struggled with finding the right words to explain himself.

"I... well, Mattie. I mean... she came and talked to me," he explained. Maybe starting with her would help. "She came outside. Though I'm sure you know where she was. But... we talked about how sad she has been and how much she misses her parents. There was so much she hasn't said until now. I didn't think she would ever open her heart to me like that, but she did. We talked about everything. It broke my heart to know she had been suffering alone."

Nora took a small step forward. "She has been through a lot. I'm glad she talked to you. She needs love from both of us."

"And she'll get it," Joe assured her. He cleared his throat. "After talking with her, though, I realized that there are a few things that I still need to tell you."

"Oh?" Nora's eyes widened slightly.

Joe glanced toward the house, hoping Mattie wasn't around to overhear. She was a sweet kid, but he didn't know how she would take hearing something like this at her age after everything she had been through. "I said we would be honest with one another, didn't I?" He gave her a pained smile. "I need to keep that promise."

She nodded slowly. "I see. All right, Joe. I'm listening." Then, Nora pressed her lips together, as though holding back a grimace.

He felt the same way.

"My past is... a little complicated. I hadn't planned to stay out here, you know. Not when my brother asked me four years ago and not when he passed away. I was going to bring Mattie to the city. But then you showed up and I realized a few things... but there is still something that weighs on me.

"I knew Sophia well, my brother's wife. She passed away from a sickness just four years ago and I didn't want to... There's just so much..."

Nora's gaze softened as he stammered away like a fool. "Why don't we sit down?" she suggested.

He glanced at the bench and then nodded, following her to the seat and sitting beside her. But then he stared at how close their knees were to touching and wasn't sure how long he could stay still. Even now, his left leg started to bounce from his nerves.

"I loved Sophia."

The words spilled out of his mouth. Joe looked up to see Nora staring at him. He couldn't read her expression and wondered if that was a good thing. He opened his mouth to say more, but struggled with what to say.

Standing up, he started to pace. "I loved her as much as Billy did, I think. We adored her back in Pennsylvania. She was beautiful and sweet and kind. Already, we were talking about marriage, you know. But then she met my brother and that changed everything."

Nora watched him pace. "That must have been hard."

"It was," he admitted. Swallowing hard, Joe inhaled deeply. "As you may imagine, it didn't feel good when she picked him over me. It felt like I had lost a game I didn't know I was playing. Billy had won, and I'd never felt so ashamed. He was married and I was left there alone, feeling less than nothing.

"So, I left. That's why I went to the city, you know. There was a lot of potential in New York and I needed a distraction. I got a job and worked hard. I had a good reputation and frequented many social circles. I had money, influence, and whatever else I wanted in the city for seven years."

Her eyes were still on him as he walked. Joe kept pausing in case she had a remark to share, but Nora said nothing. She sat with her hands in her lap, watching him thoughtfully.

So, he continued. "I let my anger and pain cloud my judgment. I was jealous and upset, and I let that dictate my life. Even when I was miserable with my success, I couldn't admit to it. Not until I came here this second time.

"The first time I came, when Sophia passed, Billy invited me to stay. He said I could move out and should work on the ranch with him." Joe felt his throat close up. "If I had, everything would be different. He would probably still be alive, you know."

That's when Nora talked. "Oh, Joe," she breathed softly.

He forced himself to keep talking, no matter how much it hurt. "If I hadn't gone back as a selfish man, my brother could still be alive and Mattie would still have a father. I should have said yes. Then, when Billy passed, I... I knew I couldn't choose my empty city life any longer. Not over my family. It was a lesson I learned too late."

Shaking her head, Nora said, "Joe, you can't blame yourself. You're here now, and that's what is important. I'm sure Billy would think the same thing."

"That's what the Camerons said," he admitted. "They said he never blamed me. But part of me still clings to that. It would make me feel better for... for all the ill will I've harbored all this time. In my heart, I know it's not Billy's fault Sophia chose him. And I don't hate her for it, I don't. But... it was never an easy decision to accept."

Part of him felt like he was talking to himself as he paced. He walked from one end of the porch to the other, only occasionally glancing at Nora.

Joe turned away from the house and back toward her to find her standing. He stopped in his tracks.

The pain that welled up in his chest softened when he saw her face. Nora wore a sad smile with a tender gaze. There was no hurt there, no judgment. Joe tried to take in a deep breath. He had never felt so vulnerable before in all his life.

She reached out and took his hand in both of hers. His breath caught as she squeezed his hand and then tugged him close.

Nora's arms wrapped tightly around him before he realized what had happened.

Joe closed his eyes as he slowly relaxed. This hug felt different, like she was telling him something. He rested his chin on her shoulder and let out a sigh. It released a lot of the hurt within him.

"None of this was your fault," Nora murmured. "Don't hurt yourself like that. There have been tragedies here, but that's just the way life is."

"I know," he choked out. "I think I know. But…"

She pulled away. Holding his hands, Nora gave him a tender look. "But nothing, Joe. I'm sorry for all the pain you've been through. But you can let it go. It's not too late to find peace for your troubled heart. And you're not alone anymore. I'm here, and so is Mattie. We're all here for one another."

A lump formed in his throat.

Joe wasn't sure what he had expected from Nora, but it wasn't this. He'd thought she would be at least partially upset about him hiding an old love from her. But, as he looked into her open expression, he knew that wouldn't happen. She had too much goodness within her to do that.

He knew then that the feelings he had for her were true. Nora was a wonderful person, and he couldn't help but wish he hadn't told her it was a marriage of convenience. He wanted so much more with her at that moment, but he didn't know what to say.

So, he didn't say anything. Nora gave his hands a squeeze and they returned inside, a weight lifted off his shoulders.

Chapter Twenty-Three

"Our barn needs a new roof, and we need a reason to celebrate," Audrey told them when she stopped by that evening.

Nora shared a look with Joe before nodding. "That sounds lovely, Audrey. We'll certainly be there tomorrow."

It was late notice for a barn dance, but she didn't mind. Already, her mind was racing about how she could make another pie for the event. Then she could wear her nicest dress. It wasn't beautiful or the height of fashion by any means, but she loved it and tried to only wear it on special occasions. This had to be one of them.

"Will I go?" Mattie asked from the hallway once Audrey left.

"Of course," Joe answered before Nora could. "It wouldn't be a party without you there. We can all finish up our work early tomorrow and go straight over."

The young girl cheered before running back to the kitchen where they were just finishing up supper. Apparently, Audrey and Dan had spent most of the day in town inviting folks for the event and wanted them to attend, as well.

"What exactly does a barn dance involve?" Nora asked as they sat back down around the table. She shared a hesitant smile as she added, "We didn't have those in Delaware. In fact, we never had any dances."

Joe looked at her in open surprise. "Truly? Well, that is a shame. It's a social gathering where the Camerons can receive some help in raising the roof on their barn. That's a heavy load and requires several hands. Then, there is music and food and dancing."

"I like to dance," Mattie put in.

The adults looked over at her with a smile. Nora nodded as she considered it. "That sounds like it's going to be wonderful. I've always wanted to go to a dance, after all."

Ever since they had come inside from their serious conversation, Joe had seemed more confident and more, well, Joe. His smile widened as he told her, "Trust me, you'll have the time of your life. Mattie and I will make sure of that."

Nora chuckled as Mattie agreed.

The three of them enjoyed the rest of their supper before cleaning up together. She was amazed again at how well they all worked in unison. It was as if they had always been a family. This brought peace into her heart as they piled together into one room to read before eventually retiring for the night.

As Joe said, they handled their chores early for the day, and he even gave his men the rest of the day off. Nora found time to make two pies for the event, and then made sure Mattie got a bath before they changed for the evening.

"What beautiful girls," Joe cheered as the two of them stepped out onto the porch.

It was nothing, but she blushed all the same.

Nora clutched Mattie's hand as they made it down the steps and over to the wagon that Joe had set up. He had blankets and the pies in there already, along with a few tools in case they were needed for the barn roof.

The sun was still high in the sky, warming their backs as they crossed the property line onto the Camerons' land. Mattie was singing a hymn under her breath and Joe concentrated on leading the horses. Nora's mind wandered as they moved along, imagining what the evening would be like. Her heart pattered with excitement at something disrupting their normal schedule.

And it was a *dance*.

Lauren had been to plenty in her lifetime, though Nora didn't know where or how or why. Most folks had been so focused on their work that there were hardly any celebrations set up around town. But even if there had been some, she knew, she wouldn't have gone. She had spent so much time working; and if she wasn't working, she was sleeping.

A small thrill ran up her spine as they reached the house and barn.

Several other wagons were parked nearby, most of the horses set in the nearby corral. Lanterns lit the path to the barn and tables had been set up all over the place. And people were everywhere.

"Here." She looked down as Joe appeared with an outstretched hand.

Smiling, she took him up on his offer and was helped down from the wagon onto the ground. Mattie was right there, as well. Joe stepped away to tend to the horses for a moment, leaving Nora to admire the view before them.

"It's beautiful, isn't it?" she asked Mattie.

The young girl nodded as she held Nora's hand, standing close.

A few of the faces in the crowd looked familiar, though Nora couldn't be certain. She hadn't spent much time in town and had only been to church three times since she'd arrived. Her heart hammered at the thought of being surrounded by so many strangers.

But then, someone started playing a fiddle and her concerns were swept away by the sound of cheery music. Mattie let out a giggle just as Joe returned to their side, carrying the two pies in his hands. Smiling, he gave her a nod and then led them down the path.

"There you are!"

Audrey Cameron came racing over to them with outstretched arms. She cheered as Mattie reached out to her. Sweeping the girl into her arms, Audrey kissed the child on the cheek twice before setting her back down. Then she hugged Nora and gave Joe a hearty handshake.

"I was getting worried," Audrey admitted breathlessly. "Dan said you would be here and there was plenty of time still. We've really only just begun. But I was very much hoping you three would join us." Beaming, she gave them all a good look. "Well, shall we enjoy this party?"

Nora and Mattie nodded.

"We brought pie," Joe reminded them with an easy smile. "Where should these be put?"

Putting a hand over her heart, Audrey gave Nora a look. "That is much too kind of you. They smell incredible. Let's put them right over here, shall we? Oh, I could eat them right up. Mattie, you helped make these, didn't you? I can tell. They have your touch. Oh, Nora, you're too sweet. Come, you three, join the fun. Dan is over with the men since they're nearly ready to raise the roof."

Chuckling, Joe nodded. He gave Nora and Mattie a short wave. "I must attend to my duties, then. Save some fun for me."

Mattie tugged on Nora's skirt. "Can I go with Audrey?"

"Of course," Nora assured her as the young girl watched Audrey start talking to other people around the nearby table. There were more pies, it looked like, so she hoped hers weren't a problem. Her eyes followed Mattie as the girl stumbled over to their neighbor and clung to her skirts. Audrey beamed down at the girl and resumed her conversation.

That gave Nora a moment to herself.

Breathlessly, she looked about the place. Though she had been over to the ranch several times, it had never looked quite so magical as this.

Everyone looked so happy. Everywhere Nora looked, someone seemed to be laughing. The air was warm and buzzing with excitement. She tugged self-consciously on her dress and wondered if she should have pinned her hair up. It wasn't very long, but she noticed how many other women had tucked their hair up in braids and the like on top of their heads.

Then she thought back to how Joe had said she looked beautiful.

She shrugged off the concern and went to watch with the ladies who were calling out their support to the men working on the roof. When Joe looked up and saw her among them, she gave him a wink.

They clapped with every bit of progress that the men made. One of them told her, though she forgot his name, that it helped the men work faster. And the faster they were done working, the faster everyone got to enjoy the barn dance. Nora didn't mind and cheered along in true excitement as she saw the roof added to the barn. She had never seen that happen before and knew she would never forget it.

"Not too bad, is it?" Joe wiped his hands as he came over to join her when it was all done.

Nora beamed at him. "It's wonderful. Perhaps we should fix the roof on our barn just so that we can do this again."

That made him chuckle. "I'll consider it." Then, he glanced around and asked her, "Where's Mattie? With Audrey?"

She nodded. "They were headed back to the house for more towels, last I checked. She should be back soon." Twisting her hands, Nora glanced around as if she might see their little girl somewhere nearby.

But Joe didn't seem too concerned. "She'll be all right. As long as the Camerons are around, she'll be just fine. And if she's busy, then I believe there is something I must do." Confused, Nora looked up at him as he offered her his elbow. "May I have this dance?"

"Oh." Her face warmed. "I'm not sure I know how to dance."

"Neither do I," he assured her. "Let's go."

It was impossible for her to resist Joe like that. He was smiling and she felt warm and excited. She slipped her arm through his, trying to ignore the thrill that spread through her body. Nora let Joe redirect her to inside the barn, where the music played loudly—a happy tune that she couldn't quite name. But she didn't let it stop her as Joe led her onto the dance floor with the other couples.

They were not the best dancers, Nora learned, but at least they had fun.

She spun and she clapped and she hurried around to keep up with the beat. Joe did the same thing, both of them grinning as they tried to figure out just what to do. It felt rather absurd and she couldn't help but laugh.

And their evening continued.

Nora couldn't ever remember having this much fun. She spent the time right beside Joe. Mattie appeared on occasion, only to run off again. But she kept them informed of where she was going, and they knew they could trust her. They were both just happy that she wasn't hiding or upset.

They ate, they talked with others, and they danced. Nora enjoyed the revelry with all her heart, wishing the night could go on forever.

"Oh," she managed as she clasped a hand over her abdomen once they'd finished a polka together. "I think it's time for a break. I can't breathe."

Joe chuckled, nodding. He took her by the hand and led her outside. She noticed he was breathing hard, as well, his chest heaving as they walked around the barn to where no one was around. Then they leaned against the wall, inhaling deeply.

She glanced over at her husband.

Her heart pounded as she thought of him holding her again like he had for a few of the dances. She still felt her entire body buzzing with light. It was hard to focus on anything if it wasn't part of Joe. Her husband had a droplet of sweat trickling down his forehead and his hair was flopping around his brow.

"I've never done so much dancing in all my life." Joe took a deep breath and then leaned against the wall. "I don't know if I can walk."

A small laugh escaped her lips before she shook her head at him. "Oh, you'll be fine. You just need another piece of pie."

"After the three I've had?" he pointed out with a chuckle. "I'm not sure that's a good idea." Sighing deeply, Joe leaned his head back against the wall. He closed his eyes. "I wish we could stay here forever. Life would be much easier."

Nora's smile faded at the grudging tone he used. Was something wrong?

"It would be," she said after a moment. "But you would miss the ranch, I think. We all would miss our homes."

He wiped his forehead with his arm. "I don't know." Then, he noticed she was watching him, and Joe offered a sheepish smile. "I'm sorry, I don't mean it. I think. I was just thinking about the ranch. It's a lot of work."

She nodded. "It is. I can't imagine all that you deal with every day."

"I have a hard time imagining it, too," Joe noted. The light in his eyes dimmed as he frowned. "It's just been a lot of work lately. There are endless problems to remedy. I thought that by now, it would get easier. I just..." he trailed off, not seeming to want to say anything more.

But she could hear the frustration within him.

Clearly, Joe was trying not to say too much, but she could see that he was tired of the hard work that he had signed up for with the ranch. Nora wished she could fix his problems and the ranch all at once. It would make everything better for them.

All she could do was reach out and take his hand. She watched his eyes widen and then look at her.

"It's hard, but you can do this," Nora assured him in a low voice. "You're not alone anymore. I'm here and I believe you can do this. You can do anything, Joe."

Something in his eyes changed with those last words. She couldn't describe it, but her heart skipped a beat when she saw it happen. Her chest was still heaving, just like his. He squeezed her hand and then tugged.

Caught by surprise, she stumbled right into him. Nora grabbed his vest to catch her balance. But before she had time to do that, Joe wrapped his other hand around her neck and pulled her in. She saw his bright eyes just before he kissed her.

Immediately, she felt her body soften, as though she were melting in the sun.

Joe tasted like berries and sweat. His lips were warm and inviting, making her want to stay put for the rest of time. The world disappeared as she lost herself in the moment. She had been wondering for so long now what it would be like to kiss Joe.

Though Nora had had some ideas, none of them were nearly as good as the real thing.

Chapter Twenty-Four

"Do what you have to do."

Victor Rawls didn't care to give his men any more directions about what he wanted them to do. He wanted to leave it open to interpretation in case they needed to get creative. And on the off-chance that they were caught, he could deny that he had meant anything illegal by it.

And then, he waited.

His two men, Joseph and Ricardo, were some of the best lockpickers in all of Delaware. They were wanted for crimes in Chicago and had come here to live out their lives quietly. But men who were used to a life of crime always had a hard time getting out.

So, it had been convenient when he'd met them a few weeks back.

"A letter?" Joseph had asked when Victor said he wanted to hire them. The man had shared a look with Ricardo and then shrugged. "That's it? No money or jewelry?"

Victor pressed his lips tightly together as he could see the men plotting some ideas. If left unrestrained, troublemakers would continue to make all sorts of trouble. But he couldn't have that. If that happened, there were no guarantees as to what would come from it.

"A letter only. That, or a telegram," he charged them. "It will be a piece of paper kept safely away somewhere. I'm looking for the address of one Nora Gilmore, and this woman will have it. Wherever she's hiding, I have to find her. Go to this home when no one is around. This needs to be a careful and quiet job—no one can find out. Do you hear me? If they catch a whiff of you two coming around, then you get nothing."

That garnered a scoff from Ricardo. "You don't know us very well. We can do that just fine. But the payment had better be worth it."

It would be.

He discussed the final terms with the two thieves before offering one final reminder for them to be quiet and not leave any clue of what they had done. Victor thought of going with them to make sure they did the job right, but he didn't have the time. There was too much for him to do. So, he'd left the men, giving them one week to complete the job he had tasked them with.

Five days later, Joseph and Ricardo showed up on the back steps of his office.

"What are you doing out here in broad daylight?" Victor demanded. "Get in here."

"You said you wanted the news fast," Ricardo reminded him. "If you like, we can just leave."

"No, that won't be necessary."

Joseph scoffed as he slumped into a chair. Victor's chair, not one on the other side of the desk. The move annoyed Victor immediately and he glared at the man. But the sandy-haired thief did nothing but slouch further in his seat.

As for Ricardo, the man fumbled with his pockets before finding something inside his coat. It was a warm day, but he appeared dressed for winter. He scratched his goatee and then slapped a crumpled envelope onto the table.

"Perfect," Victor breathed as he snatched it up. It was just like Christmas. He ripped the envelope open and pulled out the piece of paper. There was a small water stain in the corner, but it didn't detract.

He skimmed the message before checking the bottom signature. It was her handwriting and her signature.

"At last," he growled.

"Right, so we found it. Now, about the last half of our payment?" Joseph reminded him. The man started tugging open the drawers on the desk, shuffling through everything.

Victor put the letter and envelope in his pocket before slamming shut the drawer that had just been opened. He gave the thief a stern look before he pulled out the dollar bills that had been requested in payment. Carefully counting them out, he waved them in the air and handed them over to Ricardo to handle. He was too annoyed with Joseph's impertinent behavior to give it to him.

The men muttered their gratitude and shuffled out. Finally, they were out of his hair. Chuckling, Victor wiped down his seat and relaxed into it. He even put up his feet as he pulled the envelope back out.

Nora's handwriting was small and curvy, just like her.

He hungrily read the words, letting them all sink in. Pride flooded his chest when he saw that she'd mentioned him, telling her friend to be careful. Such foolish women, he thought; they had no idea what was in store.

It had been nearly four months now.

Four months since Nora Gilmore had disappeared. Victor had exhausted his resources in trying to find her. For weeks, he'd set people to following anyone that she knew around town, looking through boarding houses and hospitals. He had even traveled outside of town to a few other places to look for her, and he had contacted some sheriffs around Delaware.

His game of cat and mouse with her had gone on long enough.

And it was time for him to win.

To his frustration, however, it seemed that Nora had gone away farther than he'd expected. He had never heard of Fairwell, but he knew Nebraska was a good distance away.

So, he bought a train ticket and started to pack.

She'd mentioned having a husband now, and there was a kid in the picture. None of that made sense to Victor. He reasoned that it was a trick, in case he found the letter. But even if it was the truth, he told himself, that other man had no right or claim to her.

Nora was his.

Besides, he had to make an example out of her. If anyone else found out that running away could set them free from the debts they owed him, then he would never get any of his money back. That couldn't happen.

One way or another, she was coming back with him and would pay off that debt.

There were no excuses that would work now. Within two days, Victor closed up business. Once his bags were packed, he climbed onto the train and headed west. It was a long journey, and one that he didn't consider very enjoyable. When he finally arrived, he couldn't have been any more relieved.

Victor stepped into Fairwell and immediately searched out a saloon.

He needed a drink. His throat was dry, and he needed to learn about the folks in town. One never knew how they might react to a stranger. Especially in such a small town as this. He wrinkled his nose and made it into the town's only bar.

Once he had his whiskey, the man glanced around the room to study the folks there. Maybe eight were in the saloon at the moment, even with the sun still high in the sky. He studied them carefully before turning back to the counter.

"I'm looking for help," he told the bartender. "A special sort of help. Someone who has influence here in these parts."

The bartender raised an eyebrow. "You mean Harlan Kane? He's over in the corner."

That had gone a lot more smoothly than he'd expected. Victor drained his glass before looking across the room to see who this Harlan Kane character might be. The man had black hair and a scruffy beard. His hat sat on the table next to him.

He didn't look like much, Victor noticed. But perhaps he was all one could get in a town like this.

Victor fixed his suit jacket and then walked over. He stood at the front of the table and gave Harlan a second to look up at him.

"Haven't seen you here before," Harlan noted through squinting eyes. "What's your business here?"

Victor brought out the folded note that he had stolen from Lauren's home, showing it to the man. He tapped on the name before taking a seat. "Her. I need her."

The man peered down before suddenly chuckling. "Ah, the Bowmans, hm?"

Nora Gilmore Bowman. The name didn't matter much to him. Victor narrowed his eyes and waited for the man to finish chortling. When he did, Victor asked, "I've got some trouble with them and I hear you can help."

Harlan snickered. "I certainly can."

The man started to share a story. At first, Victor wasn't interested, but he found himself quickly drawn in.

Harlan talked about how Billy Bowman owned the nicest ranch around and had hired his former foreman, Ezra Moody. This caused a serious threat to his own cattle operation, which Harlan didn't want. So, he'd been easily able to have two of his men ride with Bowman for a roundup, which they had nudged into a stampede.

"I should have bought it then," Harlan growled in frustration. "But the man's brother from the East came out here. Nearly got it from him, too, but the man decided to stay. Thinks he can suddenly run a ranch. Obstinate fool. Then he married himself a girl and has his brother's daughter. He's more stubborn than I gave him credit for. But I won't underestimate him again."

Something about his tone caught Victor's attention.

Drumming his hands on the table, he thought for a good minute about how this could play into his own situation. He wanted to get Nora back, and he wanted that money. If he could do that, then Harlan Kane could probably do whatever he wanted.

Smirking, he barked a laugh of his own. "Well, it's a good thing I'm here."

It only took the two men the rest of the afternoon to come up with a plot that would work out for both of them.

Victor could easily break up this happy little family that was doomed to fail anyway. Once this was done, there was no reason Joe Bowman would want to stay. The man would flee back East, desperate to sell.

Once Harlan had what he wanted as well, he could double the amount Victor felt he was owed.

This all seemed almost too perfect to be true. But he knew he could make this happen. Victor rented out a room and began to prepare. He was finally going to see Nora again.

Chapter Twenty-Five

Nora hefted the basket in her arms.

Perhaps she was purchasing too many spices. She glanced at the jars hesitantly, even though she had already paid for them. They needed a few more, she knew, and she couldn't resist trying a few new ones. She couldn't remember the last time she had basil and dearly wished to use it again.

And she did have the money, she knew.

When Audrey came by that morning and invited her and Mattie to join her on a trip into town, Nora couldn't resist. She went out to the barn to tell Joe, who told her how much she could take with her. The amount was double what she'd thought he might agree to.

"Are you sure?" she had asked him in surprise.

He had been oiling a saddle that needed some work, leaving streaks up his forearms since he'd pulled his sleeves up. She had tried not to stare too much before looking at his face. Then, he'd looked up, and she'd flushed.

"Of course," Joe had told her. "Get whatever you need. If you could grab a few nails from the blacksmith, that would be helpful. I could use some more three-inch ones; however many he has available at the moment."

She could tell he was studying her face as he talked. Nora nodded slowly, reluctant to leave. Though she tried to think of something more to say to stay longer, she couldn't.

"Nora!" Audrey had called. "Are you ready?"

The loud noise had made Nora jump. Joe had hidden a grin, but she'd still been able to see it from the way his eyes shined. A hot blush had spread across her face as she'd thanked him and hurried off. She had slipped inside for the money and her hat before joining Audrey and Mattie on the small cart.

Now, in the mercantile, Nora tried to tell herself that she could make this purchase and not get in trouble.

They had the money. They always needed more spices for food. It was a reasonable move for her to make. But it was hard to recover from the guilt of buying something extra like this. She had never been able to afford so much in all her life, and it was hard to adjust to.

"Is everything all right?" Audrey asked.

Nora looked up and nodded. She gave her friend a sheepish smile. "Yes, it's fine. I'm fine. I've just never bought so many spices before. I don't think Joe will mind, do you?"

"You know him better than I do," Audrey pointed out. "I'm sure it'll be fine. Your basket looks heavy. Do you want to set it in the cart? I'm afraid I'll be another minute."

"Yes." Nora then remembered what Joe had told her. "And I'll visit the blacksmith. His forge is just down the next street, is it not?" Audrey gave her a nod. Nora smiled and then looked for Mattie, who was browsing the selection of candies. "Mattie? I'll be right back. Keep an eye on Audrey. And here's a nickel," she added after a moment.

The girl's mouth dropped open as the coin was placed in her open palm. "Really?"

"If I can spoil myself with a good purchase today, then so can you," Nora assured her with a light chuckle. "Stay with Audrey and I'll return soon."

Humming quietly to herself, Nora headed outside. She hefted her basket into the cart and moved a few items around so that nothing would fall over once they started moving again. Once satisfied with that, Nora straightened up and began walking down the lane to find the blacksmith.

She turned the corner and stopped.

Any joy in her heart immediately disappeared as Victor Rawls stepped into her path.

The world turned cold as she gaped, wondering if she was dreaming. This had to be a nightmare. He couldn't really be there. Nora blinked in the hopes that he might go away. But he was still there, walking toward her with that wicked grin of his. She could see his polished shoes, the shining cufflinks, and a fierce glittering in his gaze.

Nora tried to breathe, even though it felt like she was underwater.

She tried to move, to run away, but she couldn't. Then, alarm shot painfully through her body as she thought about Audrey and Mattie. They were still in the shop. If Victor had learned she was here, what else did he know?

And how?

Her thoughts scrambled desperately to understand what was going on. None of this seemed possible. Bile rose in her throat, but she swallowed it down.

Victor approached her. "It's been a while, Nora."

Instinctively, she took a step back. But he followed, taking a larger step forward. Nora inhaled shakily as she took her head. "You… you can't be here."

He spread out his arms. "I'm afraid that's not the case, my sweet. I am here. I had to come for you, didn't I?"

A shudder ran through her body. Life was finally beginning to make sense to her. She was happy with her family and the future ahead of her.

Joe had even kissed her the other week at the barn dance. Handsome Joe, with his wise eyes and sincere nature. They hadn't talked about that kiss, but she noticed that he found excuses to brush past her in the hall or touch her hand with his. She knew they would talk soon, and she felt inside her chest that something was budding between them.

But all that joy disappeared with Victor Rawls before her.

She had forgotten what he was like. There was the exorbitant amount of sour oil he used to slick back his hair. He had that thin-lipped grin that made her think of toothy demons in a child's imagination. And there was that way he looked at her, as if he wanted to swallow her whole.

"You… I left… how?" stammered Nora. She could hardly get her tongue to work. Most of her body felt numb. Even now, her legs were weak, and it took all her strength to remain upright.

Her question garnered a deep-throated chuckle from him.

"We must credit that good friend of yours. Lauren might not have been willing to share your whereabouts, but that wouldn't stop me. Your own correspondence did you in, my dear. Your letters to her led me straight here."

"No," she breathed.

Victor leaned forward, towering over her as his smirk changed into something much darker. "I told you I wouldn't let you go," he growled. "You made a very grave mistake when you tried to get away from me. I told you not to try and leave."

Her legs were stiff, but she managed to pick up one and take a staggering step back. Shaking her head, Nora tried to think. Desperation clawed at her throat. "I... Fine. I'm sorry, Victor. I'll get your money. I'm married now, all right? I have a husband. He'll pay you. I'll go home right now and talk to him."

Maybe Joe would pay. No, she felt certain that he would.

She thought of his compassion when she'd told him about the debt and what had happened. He was reasonable and would help her with this. Then she would find some way to pay him back. It was the only way.

But before she could say anything more, Victor snarled at her. "You think you can run off with more excuses? No, it's too late. I know where your ranch is, Nora. I don't care about that or your husband or your child. You've tested my patience enough. You're coming back to Wilmington with me one way or another. There, you will work off your debts until I am satisfied!"

"No," she choked out. "No, that's not fair. You can't just... I'm married!" Nora swallowed the hysterics that threatened to rise up. "I belong here. You can't kidnap me, Victor. Please, give me a chance."

He raised his fist and she flinched, waiting for the blow. But he just kept it there, staring her down. "You've had your chances. And if you run again, if you try to fight this, then I can't guarantee the safety of your husband and child."

Fear crept up her body like tiny painful pinpricks.

Nora gaped at him. That had to be a lie. No, he wouldn't hurt anyone. Would he? She didn't know.

Thinking quickly, she grasped for excuses. "But... even if I did go, I'm a married woman. No one would... it's not decent!"

The man straightened up with a rather nonplussed expression. But she still saw the twinkling in his eyes as he told her, "You wouldn't be the first unhappy wife to run away from her husband."

Nora shook her head in disbelief. She covered her mouth with her hands in hopes of keeping the tears at bay. Her chest heaved as she wondered how this could have happened.

She was supposed to be safe. She had gotten far away from Delaware and she had gotten married. She had a family now. Nora thought that would have been enough to deter anyone from bothering her, like Victor Rawls coming all this way after her.

But if he was willing to come all this way, she realized with dread, then he wasn't about to back down.

"I want to see you here in two days' time," Victor ordered her. "Two days! Pack your bags, because you're coming with me."

Nora felt her knees buckle. She heard a short laugh overhead, and then he was gone. Staring at the ground she knelt on, Nora tried to understand her fate.

But already she knew her trouble. As long as Victor Rawls was around, she would never be safe. He would drag her, kicking and screaming, all the way back to Delaware. And, there, she would spend the rest of her poor, miserable life doing whatever he wanted.

A shudder rippled through her and she wrapped her arms around herself for comfort.

"Nora?" a faint voice called out. "Nora!"

It took only a few moments for Audrey and Mattie to race to her side. She must not have been hard to find, sitting there in the street. Nora thought numbly of the blacksmith and his forge, but she could no longer recall why she needed to go there.

She couldn't remember a lot of things at that moment. All she knew was that she didn't want to be there.

"What's wrong?" Audrey asked as she crouched down. "Nora? What is it? What happened?"

"He came for me," Nora managed to say before taking a deep breath. She tried to think clearly. Vaguely noticing Mattie and Audrey there, she hiccupped. "I have to tell Joe. Joe has to know."

It was all she could think about. She had to tell Joe what had happened. Then she would have to tell him that she had to leave him forever. A lump formed in her throat as Audrey helped her to her feet.

"Let's get you home," Audrey murmured. The woman didn't ask any more questions as she guided them to the cart and drove them back to the ranch.

That ranch had become the best home Nora had ever had. She thought of that vaguely when they arrived at the house. Her eyes wandered as she let the view around her sink in. This would be one of the last things she ever saw in Nebraska. Soon, it would be all gone.

What was she supposed to do?

Chapter Twenty-Six

Nora was paler than he had ever seen a person.

He paced around the kitchen in frustration once she had told him what happened. That, in itself, had taken a good while. She had been clearly shaken when Audrey had brought her and Mattie home.

Audrey had called out to him as they pulled into the yard. At first, he'd thought it was just to help bring in the supplies. He had walked over, trying to get the last of the grease off his hands with an old rag. Mattie had hopped down off the cart and he'd been just about to tell her a joke when Audrey had raced down and around the other side of the cart to help Nora.

It was the way she'd held herself that told him something was wrong.

He was immediately alarmed at the way she slouched. Joe had raced over to Audrey's side and helped his wife down. Her hands were shaking. He had quickly looked her over for injuries before the confusion spread.

"What happened?" he demanded as he wrapped his arms around Nora, whose breathing sounded rough. She looked so ill that he wasn't sure she could walk. But then she leaned into him and he guided her up to the house.

"I don't know," Audrey had admitted. "I'm sorry. She left the mercantile before us. We went to go find her and she was on the ground. Nora has hardly said a word since. I think she's in shock."

They brought her into the kitchen and led her to a seat. She felt rather chilly, so he asked Mattie, "Can you please fetch her shawl? The one by the door."

She nodded and dutifully obeyed. Once Mattie returned with the garment, Joe wrapped it around Nora's shoulders. She gulped before closing her eyes. That reaction worried him. But at least it was something, he told himself. He had never seen her look so stunned. Her eyes looked haunted as she stared down at the table.

"I'll make some tea," Audrey announced. "That always helps."

Their neighbor bustled about the kitchen, inviting Mattie over to help. Once the water was heating up, the girls stepped out and brought in the purchases they had made in town. He hardly gave them a glance as he sat with Nora, hoping she might say something.

She didn't until she'd had a few sips of tea. "I'm all right," she managed faintly.

That just made him frown. She clearly wasn't doing well and there was no need to lie.

Audrey kissed Nora's cheek and then Mattie's before going to the door. "I don't think this is my business. Come fetch me if there's anything I can do for any of you. I'm sorry if I caused any trouble."

"Not at all," Joe assured her quickly. "Thank you for your help."

She managed to share a tight smile with him before she ducked out the door. They listened to her horses start moving as she headed out of their yard.

In the remaining silence, Nora suddenly inhaled sharply, her chest heaving. She blinked and looked around, as if she had just now realized that she was at home. Tears were threatening to fall from her eyes. He watched her blink furiously as though to try and stop herself.

Then Joe remembered Mattie was there.

His niece was moving slowly and quietly around the kitchen. She tiptoed as she put away the purchases that had been made, without making a noise.

It was kind of her to try and help. But, worried about what Nora might say, he decided it would be best if Mattie weren't around to hear.

"Mattie? I saw a few weeds by the sunflowers. Do you think you could go pull them up? Please?"

The young girl turned to look at them cautiously. She seemed to consider it for a minute before she nodded her head and quietly left the room without another word.

Joe hoped that she wasn't upset by his request. He just wanted to give Nora the space she needed and didn't want to worry Mattie. Once this was all sorted out, he told himself, then he would talk to her.

She was gone now, and it was just him and Nora.

He brushed a strand of her hair off her forehead before peering into her eyes. His wife turned to look at him with a tearful look. "Nora?" he asked softly. "What is it? Did something happen in town?"

Nora inhaled sharply and then buried her face in her hands.

He took that as an affirmative.

"It was him," she managed to choke out at last. A shudder rippled across her shoulders, and he put a hand on her in the hopes that would help. "Victor Rawls is here." For a minute, Joe couldn't think of anyone who would have distressed his wife so much. "The man I'm in debt to."

That brought everything back into focus.

Joe thought quickly, remembering that night Nora had confessed about her past and her troubles. He remembered some faint annoyance, which had quickly been washed away when he'd realized how worried she was. She was afraid of this man and whatever he might do to her. It made sense now just why she was so rattled.

But it didn't make sense how this man had found her.

"But… I didn't think you told him you came here," Joe said hesitantly. "Did you?"

"No!" Nora spoke so vehemently that her entire body shook. "I didn't! I would never do anything like that. He's a dangerous man, Joe."

She proceeded to tell him just what had happened to her in town. Nora struggled with her words, but slowly, her body loosened up and she was able to breathe more calmly. It was nothing that he had expected her to say, Joe acknowledged, but he didn't doubt her words for a second.

Nora was honest, after all. She had a pure heart filled with love.

And he had the pleasure of seeing that on a daily basis. Every day, she amazed him. Whenever he thought of his wife, all he wanted to do was wrap her up in his arms.

Like when he thought about that kiss.

Joe didn't regret that for a moment. He could still remember how sweet she tasted. But they had said nothing after the kiss, instead moving back into the party to get drinks. Nora had blushed as deeply as he had and nothing more was said that night or since.

Of course, he kept meaning to talk to her about it. Especially late at night, when he could tell that she had yet to fall asleep. Joe wanted dearly to know what she thought of him, if her feelings had changed in any way. But he didn't know how to say those words—and even if he did, he was too nervous to try.

His heart was filled with love for her. If only he knew how to tell her.

There were hundreds of other occasions where all he wanted to do was kiss Nora. But he didn't know if he should, worried about how she really felt toward him.

And now, there was no time for kissing or anything else.

Nora finished up her story and Joe started to pace. He marched around the room in frustration, wishing for a miracle.

What could they do? The sheriff was out of town at the moment, dealing with a case in the next territory over. He had left right after the barn dance and no one knew when he might return. No one would be around to keep law and order in the town.

But what could the sheriff do, anyway? He couldn't do anything to Victor Rawls just for threats. They would have to wait until something happened. And by the time it did, it could be much too late.

He felt the anger explode in his chest.

As his hands tightened into fists, he knew what he wanted to do right then. He had done some wrestling and boxing before and wouldn't mind going a few rounds with this criminal. Joe just needed one chance with the man.

"He can't do that!" he snapped angrily to no one in particular. "You're my wife and I'm your husband. That's not legal. There's no way he could refuse to let you go once that so-called debt is paid off. If it's even real."

"If?" Nora asked in confusion. She stood up, the shawl slipping off her shoulders. "Joe, I don't know what you mean by that. But no matter the debt, he says he's going to take me away."

Her voice cracked when she spoke. It broke his heart. Joe ran forward and embraced Nora tightly. He hushed her softly before kissing her forehead. "No. No, he won't, Nora. I promise he won't get you."

She clung to him tightly. "But he threatened you. And Mattie!"

"I promise," he interrupted before she could grow any more upset, "no harm will come to you or Mattie. None of us will get hurt, all right? I promise, Nora." He ran a hand through her hair, holding her there until her breathing calmed down.

Even then, the two of them stayed put for a few minutes in the kitchen. The room was quiet, and they were free from the rest of the world. Nora would be free, too. She had to be. He closed his eyes as he rested his cheek on top of her head. They stood there, quietly breathing and thinking.

He would do something. He had to.

Eventually, he led Nora to their bed so she could rest for a little while. She said she didn't need to, but the circles under her eyes told him otherwise. Joe told her to stay put for at least an hour. Then, he excused himself.

After spending a few minutes talking with Mattie in the garden, he continued making his way across the ranch. He climbed into the saddle and moved quickly to find a few of his men gathered by the fence.

"Call the others," Joe charged their cook. The man's cowbell would bring them all over. So, the cook did, nodding before pulling out his triangle. It *dinged* several times, and then there was silence. His heart hammered as he waited for the other men to arrive.

Ezra Moody was with the last party. "What's going on?" he demanded, seeing that everyone else was as confused as himself.

Inhaling sharply, Joe stepped forward. "I have a quick announcement and I wanted you all here for it." He narrowed his eyes almost imperceptibly. "There's trouble in town and so all of you need to keep an eye out. A threat has been made to my family, and I'm asking all of you to help out. If they are threatening me, then they are threatening this ranch."

"What?" the men cried out.

His foreman took a step closer to Joe. "Are you sure about this?"

"I am," Joe told him. "A man by the name of Victor Rawls has come into town. He knows my wife from back in Delaware." He provided a quick description of the man before continuing. "The only folks I'm allowing on this ranch right now are people I personally know. That includes all of you. Nobody else. Do you hear me? Nobody else. I want all of you to be keeping an out for any strangers showing up here at the ranch. And until Mr. Rawls has left town, I want a night watch."

A few of the men groaned, but that was a natural response.

Joe went on to lay out his plan. He explained the details carefully. And with Ezra's help, they organized a list of men for the next week on how they would be managing the night watch. He wanted to think it was completely unnecessary, but Joe wasn't interested in taking risks. Not when it came to his family.

Once told, the ranch hands returned to their duties.

Ezra Moody remained, glancing up toward the house before walking over a little closer. "You know, it might be best to tackle the problem at the root. It's a good plan you have. But maybe there's a more direct approach?"

Nodding, Joe said, "I'm glad you think that way. I was hoping to get some support. Two days from now, I know where he'll be. If you're willing, I'd like you to come with me."

His foreman was indeed willing.

The next two days were very stressful. Even Mattie could sense it in the air and hardly said a word. Nora's hands shook at every sound. Joe spent the nights talking with her to let her know that she was safe and that he was going to stop Victor Rawls.

And then, it was time to head into town.

First dropping Nora and Mattie over at the Cameron ranch, Joe and Ezra started toward Fairwell. They wore pistols strapped to their sides in case the trouble grew worse. Joe had five hundred dollars in his pockets on top of that, in case Rawls wanted to do some negotiation. Whatever the situation, he wanted to be prepared.

"Are you sure it was today?" Ezra asked him when they reached the train station.

At first, the two of them hid back in the shadows, looking for anyone who might fit the description that Nora had given them. But no one there looked like the man Nora had described. Ezra and Joe wandered the street, keeping their eyes open.

"Yeah. He said two days from two days ago," Joe told him with a grimace. Something didn't set right with him. Looking around, though, there was nothing out of the ordinary.

Joe believed Nora. No one could fake the shock and fear he'd seen in her eyes. She wouldn't lie to him like this, he knew, and there was no reason for her to do it. No one gained anything by making up this story. Victor Rawls existed.

But even as they spent another two hours in town, no one showed up.

Chapter Twenty-Six

Dread had made a home in Nora's stomach.

Three days had passed since she had come back from town after seeing Victor Rawls. His face still haunted her at night. She found herself looking over her shoulder constantly in case he turned up at her home.

"You're safe here."

She looked up as Joe appeared from the back door and rested a hand on her shoulder. A flush spread across her face while he studied her with a worried expression.

"I wasn't..." But she couldn't bring herself to say anything that wasn't true. Shaking her head, Nora tried to clear her mind. "I'll be fine. You don't need to keep coming over to check on me. I know you have a lot of work to do."

Their morning had been slow thus far. She had tidied up the kitchen for a while with Mattie, who was now playing on the front porch with her hoop. Now she was preparing a midday meal. Joe had been there for every meal since she had told him what had happened in town. Though Nora loved having him at the house, guilt was prodding her in the back since she knew he had a ranch to manage.

"It can wait," he decided with a shake of his head. "What are you cooking? I can help."

He took a step back to look her over before offering a reassuring smile. For a minute, she could forget about her fears with him.

Nodding, Nora grudgingly allowed her husband to help out. He made her smile with his jokes and they talked about what she might prepare for supper that evening. She could forget that there was any trouble when they were together.

But before they could sit down and eat, there was a hurried knocking against the door.

"Joe? Joe, we need you," Ezra Moody's voice called out. "Now!"

Nora jumped at how hard he knocked. Joe started out of his seat and hurried to the back door before she could stand. Nora quickly followed.

"Rustlers," the foreman announced before either of them could say a word. "I had my suspicions before, but Ryan caught one in the act. We're chasing after them now. Three of them are crossing onto the Cameron ranch."

"What?" Nora couldn't help but spout. "How?"

Joe shook his head as he gave her arm a squeeze. Too soon, he let go to grab his coat and hat hanging up beside them. "It doesn't matter. I thought our count was off last week. Stay here, Nora. Everything will be fine. Keep an eye on Mattie."

And then they were gone.

Nora swallowed as she watched the men hurry over to their horses; Moody had brought Joe's animal over so they could move faster. They ignored the paths and cut across the land. She bit her lip while she watched them, hoping they would be safe. There wasn't much she knew about rustlers, but they were thieves and that was more than enough trouble for anyone.

As she returned inside, Nora said a silent prayer. She pulled her apron off while looking at the table. It was set perfectly for a family three to sit down and eat together. Perhaps she would keep it this way until supper time.

"He will be back," she assured herself as she thought of her husband. "He will be."

"Nora?"

Inhaling sharply, she wiped the concern from her face to put on a smile for Mattie, who had finally come inside. The child had been playing outside long enough to bring some color to those cheeks of hers. But as Mattie made her way into the kitchen, Nora noticed her hoop was missing. In place of it, there was a piece of folded paper in her hands.

"There you are, Mattie. What do you have there?" she asked. The dread swam around in her stomach like it was a warning.

"A letter. He said it's for you." The girl skipped over to hand it to her.

Nora didn't understand. "A... from who?"

Mattie thought about it and then shrugged, eyeing the food on the table. "I don't know. He didn't say. The man said I needed to give this to you."

There was nothing on the outside of the letter. Nora felt her heart clench as she gingerly picked it up. It had to be from someone on the ranch, she decided. Or someone in town that Mattie already knew. No one else would dare come so close. Her throat dried up as she read the note.

Nora, you don't belong here, and you know it. You are coming back to New York with me, whether you come voluntarily or I drag you. Three days. I'll be waiting and I'll find you when you're at the train station. Don't try anything stupid. Victor.

"Oh..." She clasped a hand over her mouth to keep from crying out in alarm.

Victor had been there. Or he had paid someone to be there. She didn't know, and it didn't matter. He was showing her that he could get to her no matter where she was. Nora was never going to be safe from him.

Her legs grew weak, so she hurriedly took a seat at the table. With a shaky breath, Nora read the letter again in the hopes that she had been imagining everything. But all the words were still there. Victor Rawls wanted her, and nothing would make this stop until she went with him. Only then would Joe and Mattie be safe.

This realization brought tears to her eyes.

"Nora? What's wrong?" Mattie had been looking over their meal, eyeing the jam in particular. But then she looked to Nora and hurried over to stand before her. "Nora?"

She couldn't explain what was going on. Mattie was too young to understand such horrors, to know how dangerous people could be. Shaking her head, she tried to keep herself from falling apart. At least not in front of Mattie.

"I'm fine," Nora managed to choke out with a watery smile.

It would be best if she left now, Nora realized. Joe would convince her to stay if he knew. Maybe she could drop Mattie off with Audrey before walking to town. She couldn't take a horse or the buckboard. Yes, it would be best if she went now and disappeared before anything grew worse.

"You should... you should eat," Nora stammered as she gestured to the food. "I'll be back in a minute."

She ran off to her room to start packing. But she could hardly see straight and couldn't recall where she had placed the bag that she had brought out west on her journey there. Sniffling, Nora rubbed her eyes with the palms of her hands. She grabbed two of her dresses and put them on the bed, ready to roll them up. Except her arms felt heavy and she worried she was going to throw up.

A knock at the door made her jump.

"Nora?" Mattie's squeaky voice called out to her.

Sitting on the edge of the bed, Nora looked around and wiped the couple of tears that had managed to spill over her cheeks. Telling herself she had to pull herself together, she stumbled to the door.

"Yes, Mattie?"

The young girl bit her lip as some of her hair fell in her face. "I tried to clean the jam but... I made a mess."

Nora's shoulders slouched. "Oh. Oh, that's all right, Mattie." She sniffled again as she reined in her emotions. "Let's go clean it up."

As she followed the meek child into the kitchen, she found that most of the jam had made it onto the table instead of onto food or in its jar. There was a trail leading onto the floor with a crumpled towel next to it. The mess was hardly anything, especially compared to the fears bouncing around in Nora's head.

She forced herself to put on a smile. "All right. Let's get a spoon to save some of this jam, shall we?"

They cleaned and, while they did, Nora tried to think of a way to tell Mattie that she wouldn't be there any longer. That she would leave. Could she do that? Nora's tongue felt thick at the very idea. There was no good way to tell this to anyone, especially since she didn't want to go. She didn't want to leave the one place where she felt like she was home.

Nora was pulling her thoughts together as they tidied up. The day was warm, so she opened a kitchen window. Then, she went to the sink and started scrubbing out the jam from a cloth. But then she noticed something. Distracted, she looked around. All thoughts of Victor Rawls disappeared. Something was off. But what was it?

The bitter taste in the wind caught her attention.

Nora jerked her head up to look toward the open window. The sun was beginning to set in the distance, creating for long shadows and vibrant colors in the sky. But, as she sniffed the air, she knew something was wrong.

It seemed as though the fear in her heart would never truly fade.

She scrambled over to the door, yanking it open to see where the scent could be coming from. Her eyes widened—she could see it, as well. There was smoke pluming high in the air, ash-gray clouds that were too thick and heavy to be safe.

A gasp escaped her lips as she looked below the smoke.

There was no way to deny the red haze of flames far off in the distance. Nora scrambled out onto the back porch, her mouth gaping as her heart sunk. There was a fire. And it had to be large for her to see so much.

It wasn't on her ranch. But any comfort she might have felt from that discovery was immediately weakened when she realized it was coming from next door. Their neighbors.

"No," Nora breathed in horror.

She could taste the bitter ashes once more. They were stronger now, and she had an inkling that it would only grow worse.

There was no time to hide nor hesitate. Nora's heart hammered as she ran back into the house. She breathed deeply as she hurried about to grab the one thing that mattered: Mattie. Little Mattie was still at the table.

"Nora?"

"We have to go at once," Nora said. It took all of her strength not to collapse in a state of panic. But there was no time. They had to move quickly. She scooped the child out of her seat and put her on her feet. Grabbing the girl's hand firmly, she started moving them back toward the door. "Now. Run, Mattie!"

The little girl grunted but obeyed. Her grip tightened on Nora's hand as they ran out the door. She didn't even turn around to lock it, let alone close it behind them.

Every minute mattered.

"Up you go," she said breathily as she heaved Mattie onto the buckboard seat. "Stay there!" Then she ran to the nearest stall, quickly readying a horse that could guide them. Even though it took a minute to prepare the animal, this would still be faster than if she ran. Nora prepared the horse, wiped her brow, and hurriedly joined the girl.

Then, they were off.

She gasped for breath as they went. Her chest heaved from moving around so quickly, as well as from the horror they were riding into. Nora prayed as they went, asking the Lord to help them and protect their neighbors.

"Don't be dead," she whispered under her breath. "Don't be dead, please, don't be dead."

She had lost too many people.

Just the thought of losing her neighbors made her eyes sting. But Nora didn't have time to brush away any tears at the moment. She had to keep her eyes open to be prepared. There was no time to dawdle.

A small ounce of relief filled her heart when the house came into view. It was not on fire. The house was safe, at least for the time being.

It was a different story for the barn, covered pen, and shed. All three were blazing. They were close to one another, within a couple dozen yards. Nora stopped for a minute to watch everything. Hundreds of thoughts ran through her mind.

Three buildings on fire was not an accident. It couldn't be.

But the idea that these were intentional fires sent a rippling fear throughout her body. Nora felt her stomach roll uneasily. She forced herself to climb down. Helping Mattie onto the ground, as well, she held the child close for safety.

Mattie clung to her tightly. "What's happening?" she asked tearfully.

Nora's heart pounded as she shook her head. "I don't know," she murmured.

She tried to comprehend the view before her, but she knew they didn't have time. Her eyes looked over the buildings with horror. The roof of the shed had caved in already, and the others were on their way.

Were there animals inside any of those buildings? People?

They had to find out. They had to stop this monstrous fire before it grew and swallowed everything. Nora coughed as she tasted the smoke on her lips. Something was terribly wrong, and she wasn't sure how they could fix it.

Chapter Twenty-Seven

Joe didn't understand.

Everything in his life had been fine—until, suddenly, it wasn't. And after that, everything had continued to grow harder and harder. Just as he was beginning to find peace and happiness in this new life he had started out west, something terrible had happened.

"Are you sure they went this way?" he demanded of Taggert while he looked around.

They had crossed over onto the Cameron farm earlier in search of ten missing cattle. One of the Camerons' ranch hands, Lyle, had caught up with them to see what was going on. Joe explained why they were trespassing and wanted to know if they had seen anything or dealt with any trouble.

"Yeah," Lyle had said with a wince. "I thought they were your men, so I let them go along. That's what they said. They had your cattle and everything. But I did think it was odd."

Joe furrowed his brow. "Odd?"

Lyle nodded as he fixed the hat on his head. "Yeah, odd. They weren't very friendly. Hard-pressed to be on the way, it seemed. I'm afraid it makes sense, now, why they were on the move. Should have known—Moody here won't stand for anything but the best. They went that way, veering toward the canyons," he added. "If you ride hard, you might be able to catch up to them."

"Thank you," Moody jumped in. Turning to Joe, the foreman nodded. "Three of us should go. Taggert, with us. The rest of you stay in case you see them or anyone else causing trouble. Joe?"

He had heard of posses going after men for their crimes out west, where there seemed to be no law. It had sounded more like fiction up until this moment. The day was hot as he looked around, sweat dripping down his brow. He brushed his forehead with the back of his arm and then nodded.

"Let's go," he ordered.

The three of them started off. Taggert had unclipped his gun from his belt and Moody had his rifle already resting on his lap. The glinting metal repeatedly caught Joe's eye, reminding him of the pistol that he was wearing, as well. It weighed heavily on him, both physically and mentally at the thought of using it on someone. He had always thought that one was only used for sport or animals. Yet this didn't feel like either situation.

But he rode on all the same.

Galloping alongside his ranch hand and foreman, Joe hardly had time to think about anything else. He directed the horse along as they crossed the river at its lowest point. Water splashed around them, even getting his knees wet. It just helped to cool him down as they brushed past a grove of trees and started down a faint trail between two grassy hills.

He had missed ten cows just the other week.

Now, they were missing another ten. There was no chance that this was a coincidence or accident.

Someone was stealing from his ranch. But who? And how? Suspicions ran through his mind, but none felt right.

He knew it wasn't Dan Cameron or his men. These rustlers were just using their land to move the animals around. They were moving toward the edge of the property as it was, and would soon be off it. Joe wasn't sure if anyone owned the land behind them. He doubted it, for he had seen no sign of any settlement.

Then who?

Victor Rawls was a ridiculous thought. Joe considered it for a moment as he ducked a few branches. The man had to be in town somewhere. But, if he was from the city, he wouldn't know anything about ranches—just like Joe had known nothing upon his arrival. Rawls would be found out and stopped, but it was very unlikely that he was the rustler.

This made Joe wonder if perhaps the rustlers were strangers who were just looking for the right opportunity. Ten head of cattle would bring in over a hundred dollars, which would be a lot to someone unwilling to work.

He didn't know of anyone else losing their cattle to rustlers lately.

It wasn't something he had talked to anyone about, since it hadn't been a problem. There had been too much going on with his family and the ranch for him to consider that anything else might go wrong.

And now, it was.

Joe felt as though the troubles of the world were weighing down on him. Life had never been this confusing or difficult until he came out west. Pursing his lips, he narrowed his gaze on the path ahead of him as he tried to think about how this would end. They would get the cattle back, stop the rustlers, and send them to the sheriff. Then, he had to go back home to Nora and reassure her that all was well. It would be. He would protect his family.

"There!" Taggert shouted as he gestured up ahead to their left.

Movement beyond the bushes, something big and brown. Joe's heart quickened as he and his men started over in that direction. He took the reins in one hand to tug out his gun. Though he didn't want to use it, he knew that living in the west was different. And he couldn't risk anything happening to him or his employees.

Seeing Moody starting to slow down, Joe commanded the same of his horse. They turned off the dirt path and moved through the trees before they suddenly came to a clearing.

"Eight head," Taggert announced.

The foreman nodded as he went around the clearing on his horse, gun directed toward the trees. Moody didn't look their way as he searched for any sign of someone else around them.

But there wasn't. Ten of the eight cattle were standing there, grazing as if nothing had ever happened. There was a slight sheen to their coats to show that they had moved quickly under the afternoon sun. And nothing more.

It didn't make sense, he thought, stealing cattle and then deserting them. Or, rather, all but two of them. Why would they leave two behind? His stomach clenched; he knew little about rustling, but this just didn't make sense. It didn't feel right.

"Moody?" Joe asked his foreman apprehensively.

The man returned to their side as Taggert slid out of his saddle to see to the animals. Moody had set the rifle back in his lap, looking around with narrowed eyes. He pursed his lips, and it was then Joe knew that his instincts weren't off by far.

"Something is up," the man said in a gruff tone. "I don't like it."

"Any sign of the other two?" Taggert asked them.

"Any sign here can't be followed or trusted. Too many animals around and there's a lot of hoof prints here, cattle and horses. It's like they were teasing us."

Joe frowned. "Teasing us? That doesn't make any sense. We have most of the cattle. What good is having two? It's not worth the theft, surely."

His foreman shifted in his seat as he considered it. "They could still make a few dollars with two horns, anywhere from five dollars to eighty. Just depends on how far they are willing to take the creatures. But you're right, it's hardly worth the effort. There was no sign of them slowing down with any trouble. If I were a rustler, I would have kept going. But these horns? It's like they were meant to be found."

"For us," Joe added as he nodded to Ezra. Then he glanced at Taggert, who was mounting his horse now. "It's like they wanted us to find them all the way out here."

That was when an alarm bell went off in his head. His eyes widened as he stared at his men, who seemed to have the same realization all at the same time.

"Something's off at the ranch."

It was clear to all of them now; they had been pulled away from the ranch, led off on a merry chase. If they didn't start questioning what was going on, then they would keep going forward to find the other two missing cattle. They would keep going, farther and farther from the ranch.

Yet they had some of his cattle.

Joe couldn't help but hesitate. Part of him doubted anyone had created a plan so elaborate. What would they gain from this? There were still people on the ranch working and keeping an eye out for trouble.

He looked over his shoulder back toward the ranch and then glanced at the cattle.

"It doesn't make sense," Joe repeated.

"I'll stay back," Moody decided. "I can keep looking for the other two. You and Taggert can return the cattle to their herd. All we have is a suspicion without proof. Go back and if there has been no trouble, then come back and join me on the trail."

Joe didn't like the idea of leaving a man behind. But as they talked, he knew Moody had a good point. The man was experienced, through years of hardships, and knew how to watch for signs of danger. While Taggert was also smart, he was younger and softer. Less experienced, just like himself.

"All right. Any signs of danger and you come right back," Joe added with a warning. "I'd rather keep my foreman than two cows."

Moody gave him a tip of the hat and then turned toward the trees.

This left Joe with Taggert to round up the animals and get them back to the ranch. The two of them worked well together, quickly guiding their small herd down the trail. Though annoyed, the cattle moved willingly, and soon they were rounding the corner of the last hill. Just beyond a grove of trees would be the sight of the Camerons' house.

Before that, however, he caught something else in the wind.

He frowned and looked around. It smelled like smoke. And smoke meant fire, which was usually deadly on a ranch. Joe glanced over to Taggert, who had his nose up in the air as he had smelled it, also.

"Do you think..." the ranch hand started to say.

Joe glanced around before he decided to make his way to the cattle. "Keep pushing forward for home. If it's not on our land, then keep the cattle directed toward home. I'll go take a look around."

Then, he started off down the road. He could swear that the clouds building nearby were too dark to be normal clouds in the sky. Joe felt his body tense as he made it around the grove of trees.

And there it was.

Straight ahead were the Camerons' buildings. Their home was nearly a mile away. But even that distance made it obvious to see the flames shooting up from several of the structures. Plumes of black smoke curled above them, turning pale as they reached for the skies. Joe stared in disbelief for several seconds before he nudged his horse to start moving.

He headed straight for the fire.

They would need help fighting it, he thought, and they had to put it out soon. Or else the buildings would be useless completely and the fire might spread to the land.

It could spread to his ranch, too. To his cattle and his home and his family.

Joe couldn't let that happen.

He rode his horse hard all the way across the open land. It didn't take long for his eyes to start watering. The smoke grew thicker. Feeling the wind brush through his hair, he hoped it died down or everything could quickly take a turn for the worse. His eyes burned when he squinted, looking for anyone around.

There they were. He found them by the barn on the other side.

Dan and his ranch hands looked as if they had just arrived. They were covered in sweat, but it was only the women who were covered in soot. It was Audrey and Nora, he realized. His heart constricted, watching her drag water from the well and dump it around the shed. The roof was drenched in flames, the door thrown open. Tools and the like had been tossed out of there in case it couldn't be saved.

Jumping off his horse, Joe raced around to help. His eyes and throat burned, but he forced himself to keep moving. He helped the men get the last of everything out of the barn. Anything with metal was hot to the touch, but he didn't let it stop him.

"Nora," he called worriedly when he saw her pause, bending over to catch her breath. Joe ran over and put a hand on her back. Nora crouched on the ground as she coughed loudly. "You need to get back. You've done enough."

She shook her head. "The barn is still…" But she gagged before she could say more.

He turned away from the fire to give her a stern look. His wife's entire body shook from exertion. She had done so much already, outdoing the men with her hard work. Her hands were black and red as she brushed her mouth with the back of her hand.

"I want you to stay back," Joe told her firmly. "I'll make you if I have to. Please, Nora."

That got her attention. Pulling her head up, Nora looked up at him. He could tell she was considering this, thinking carefully about it.

But then her expression changed to one of horror. She suddenly let out a loud scream, nearly deafening him. Nora touched his shoulder and then ran off. She ran right into the barn before Joe realized what she had done.

"No!" he cried out. A loud crash sounded in the barn. The roof was falling apart, he realized. He squinted to look for his wife, struggling to see past the fire that had reached the doors.

It took him a minute, but he found her. Nora was helping a fallen figure beneath a large wooden beam that had fallen.

Joe cursed as she disappeared again. The fear of losing her was all too real. And they had only started to get to know one another. He moved forward to run inside, but someone grabbed his arms to stop him.

"It's too hot," they shouted in his ears.

"My wife," he started to cry out loud, desperate to get to her. He couldn't lose Nora, not now.

Then he froze as she suddenly appeared. She was hunched over as she carried Audrey on her back. The other woman had been in the barn and must have fallen under the beam. She was unconscious, and Nora was making sure she got out.

He reached her at the same time as Dan.

"Put this fire out!" Dan shouted to the men. "Now! Joe, can you help me?"

"Of course," he assured him. "To the house."

He helped Dan with his wife up to their ranch house with Nora close behind. The rest of the men continued working through the sunset until, at last, the fire was out. The shed would need a new roof, the foreman told them, and the barn would need to be rebuilt. There was a lot of work that would need to be taken care of.

But first, they had to see to Audrey Cameron.

Chapter Twenty-Eight

Nora dumped her useless hands in her lap.

There was nothing she could do with them to help Audrey. She wasn't a doctor, and she knew nothing of head wounds. Besides, the majority of her fingers and palms had been wrapped up with a soothing salve from all the burns she had ended up with during yesterday's fire.

She shuddered at the memory.

It had been so terrifying that she hadn't been able to sleep. Instead, she had curled up on the couch with Mattie on her lap. Neither she nor Joe had insisted that anyone retire to their beds. In fact, he'd ended up joining them on the couch beside her after bringing them blankets. She had fallen asleep with her head resting on his shoulder.

Though she knew she must have slept, it was midmorning now and she still felt horribly groggy.

Audrey laid in her bed and reached out a hand to Nora.

"It's all right," the woman said in a soft tone. "Really. The doctor said last night that I will be just fine."

A concussion. That was what the doctor had said just an hour ago after stopping by. One of the Camerons' ranch hands had gone to call on him last night, but Dr. Heger had been busy tending to a sick baby. He'd come when he could, which had been an hour after sunrise.

Nora and Mattie were already there.

Little Mattie sat on the edge of the bed, clutching a pillow close to her chest. Her legs dangled over the edge, bouncing slightly from her nerves. The young girl had been particularly quiet all morning.

She looked over to Audrey now, cushioned so she was nearly sitting up in her bed. There was a tight bandage wrapped around her head and she had dark circles under her eyes. Other than that, there was no sign that she'd been hurt.

"But..." Nora bit her lip, not wanting to think about anything growing worse. There were so many horrible thoughts in her mind.

"Don't," Audrey instructed her kindly. "No matter what, it will all be fine. Now then, I'm worried about your hands. Those are awfully big bandages, Nora. I should have given you my gloves yesterday."

Quickly shaking her head, Nora forced a small smile on her face. "No, I am well. The doctor gave me some salve. They should be good as new in a couple of days, he thinks. It's nothing serious. I can still get up and do whatever it is that I need to. But, with you here, I just... is there anything I can do? How can I help you? Are you hungry?"

Her foot bounced off the floor anxiously as she tried to stop thinking about herself.

"No, not right now. But thank you. I do appreciate the companionship," Audrey added. "From both of you lovely ladies. It would be so dull to be left here alone."

"Then we won't leave your side," Nora said with a smile.

So, the women talked. They recounted all that had happened and what had been going through their heads the entire time. It only took a second to bring Nora back into a state of fear with her shuddering and dry mouth. They tried to find something to laugh about after that, and Mattie brought them some water.

It was nearing midday when the girls heard footsteps around the house. Sitting up, they looked at the partially open door until Dan and Joe showed up.

The former stepped through into the room, while Joe just peeked his head in. Nora's heart skipped a beat. There were no words to explain the hope that spread through her soul when he was around. Just remembering his arm wrapped around her the night before made her forget about the throbbing in her hands.

"Audrey," Dan asked, "how are you doing?"

The woman smiled. "Well, my head aches, but I'm not tired. Have you come to sit with us? I'm sure we would love the company." Audrey sent Nora a wink that made her flush.

"Just stopping by," he answered with a shake of his head.

"We wanted to check on you," Joe chipped in before looking at Nora. "All of you."

Nora bit her lip to keep the smile from growing so wide. Her body ached from all the hard work she had done the day before with the fire, but it meant little now.

"We're cleaning up the mess," Dan announced. "Only a few things were lost because of all you ladies did to save, well, everything. All signs of the fire should be gone by nightfall, I think. Everyone is doing a great job at cleaning up."

That was a relief. Nora wanted to put this behind her as quickly as possible.

"What happened?" Mattie piped up. Everyone looked to her, surprised she had been bold enough to speak up. She quickly ducked her head. Nora leaned over to pat her hand comfortingly, offering a small smile.

"It was…" Dan glanced at her and then looked at the women. He turned to Joe, who gave a short nod. Their expressions had sobered up, so Nora listened closely. "We found burned circles in each building. Looks like gasoline spills started everything up. All the men smelled it when we started this morning."

Gasoline spills? In three different structures?"

"That doesn't make sense," Audrey said slowly as she put a hand up to her head. Nora was thinking the same thing. "Dan, why would… It's too much of a coincidence."

Everyone looked to Dan, who turned to Joe and gave him a small nudge.

It didn't comfort Nora. She frowned, watching him hesitate and straighten up. He took a small step into the bedroom before speaking up. "We don't think it was. We think it was deliberate. That, and the rustlers."

Nora had forgotten about the rustlers. Her eyes widened in surprise as she tried to understand what he was saying. She glanced at Audrey, who looked even more confused.

"The rustlers? I don't… what do you mean?" Nora forced herself to ask.

"We couldn't find anyone," Joe explained slowly. "About a mile and a half away were eight of the cows. Moody found the rest just a few hundred yards further along. They were left alone, without anyone around. Though they had time to get away with the animals and didn't appear to have faced any problems, whoever stole the cattle changed their mind. Or they didn't want them in the first place. I believe it was a ploy to get me away from the ranch."

Dan nodded. "And?" "And… a few of the men on our ranch said they saw someone on our property after I left. A few of my ranch hands stayed behind after seeing the fire. They stayed put near the cattle and barn, which must have scared them off. I think whoever started the fire here may have tried to start one on our land, as well."

Nora gasped as she suddenly remembered the note that she had received the other morning. Clasping a hand over her mouth, she looked around the room in disbelief. She had been in so much shock the day before that she'd forgotten about her intentions of leaving her family behind and about telling Joe anything.

Her eyes fell on Audrey.

"Oh no," Nora moaned as she moved closer to her friend on the bed. "Oh, Audrey."

The woman glanced at the men and nodded. They left without another word, taking Mattie with them. Nora thought about calling them back, because she knew she should talk to them as well. But there was so much emotion caught up in her throat that she could hardly string two words together.

"It's all right," Audrey assured her before giving her hands a squeeze. "We're safe now."

"No, you don't understand," Nora choked out. A hot tear trickled down her face. "This is my fault. I did this."

Audrey cocked her head. She looked so terribly tired. And the bandage on her head just reminded Nora of what had happened. "No, you didn't. Don't say that."

"But it is," Nora responded before closing her eyes. "If I had left like he wanted, then you wouldn't have been hurt and your barn would still be intact. I should have gone with him. He said I had to go. He said there was no other way."

The young woman shook her head. "Nora, it's all right."

"No, listen," Nora begged of her. Tearfully, she launched into her story about what had happened when her father passed away. Telling Audrey about Victor Rawls, the man who had haunted her steadily for so long, was a painful task. But she forced herself to do it all the same. "I thought I was free of him. I didn't think he would find me. But he did. He came here and I saw him."

Audrey's eyes had grown wide. She gripped Nora tightly. "You're married, Nora. He can't possibly do anything now."

"But he will," Nora responded. More tears trickled down her cheeks. She stopped bothering with them, knowing she couldn't control them. "That's what the rustling and the fire were all about. I just know it. I can't prove it, but he did it. He's trying to make me go with him, Audrey. And he's risking everyone's lives to make me go. It's all my fault. I never should have tried to run from him. I shouldn't have stayed, I… I should have gone when he told me to. If it weren't for me, none of this would have happened."

Her friend shook her head. "Don't say that," Audrey told her fiercely. "This is not your fault. If it was this Victor Rawls, then it sits on his shoulders. I meant it, Nora. Don't you dare think that you had anything to do with this. No one forced him to act. This was his choice, and he must be stopped. Have you talked to Joe?"

A hiccup escaped her lips before Nora shook her head. The last twenty-four hours had been a strange blur.

"Then tell him," Audrey said in a soft tone. "Please. He needs to know."

She was right. Though Nora feared that it could still be blamed on her whether or not it was her fault, she knew in her heart that Joe had a right to know. If she left, she could not do so without sharing the truth.

After a few more moments with Audrey, she dried her tears and left to let her friend get some rest. Nora's hands were shaking as she stepped out into the front room, where the men and Mattie were seated.

Joe stood up the moment he saw her. She had a feeling that he could see the tear stains on her cheeks and how much her eyes were beginning to swell.

Swallowing, she struggled to give him and Mattie a smile. "Can we go home, please?"

He nodded. After sharing a short farewell with Dan and assuring him that he would return soon to help, Joe led them out of the house. They were quiet as they piled into the buckboard and started for home. She felt the stares on her, but Nora was too busy trying to find the right words to tell Joe.

"Mattie?" Joe asked as they stepped inside their own house. "Why don't you go to the cellar and bring out some more jam."

Nora sniffled as the child looked up at her and disappeared without another word.

At last, she was alone with her husband. She thought that she would feel better with him there. Part of her did, but she couldn't get Victor Rawls off her mind.

"Nora?" Joe asked her.

She inhaled sharply and then hurried from the room without a word. The letter, she thought, he had to read the letter. Then he would understand how serious this matter was. He would see that she had to leave them. It was for their own safety. Nora heard Joe calling after her as he trailed behind her to their bedroom.

It only took her a moment to find the letter. Then, she shoved it into his hands.

"What is this?" he asked in confusion.

"Read it," she whispered hoarsely. Nora licked her lips while watching him scan the lines. The furrow in his brow seemed to grow deeper. "It was him. The cattle, the fire? I know it was him. He had to be behind it. Joe, he's not going to stop." Tears sprang to her eyes once again. "Rawls won't leave us alone until I go with him. I have to, Joe. It's the only way to keep you and Mattie safe."

He jerked his head up. "What?" he asked sharply. "No, you're not going with him. Nora, don't be ridiculous. If this was him, then it's only further proof to stay far away from him. He's dangerous!"

"I know," Nora choked out. "But I can't let him hurt you. After Audrey—"

"Then we'll stop him," her husband said decisively. He dropped the letter to step forward and hold her steady by the shoulders. "Somehow. One way or another. No matter how long it takes, Nora. But you're not going with him. Never."

She blinked back the tears to clear her vision. Nora dearly wanted to believe him. His grasp was warm and firm, a reminder of what a good and protective man he was. Joe was too good for her, she thought.

She looked at him through her watery gaze and wondered how she had grown so fortunate. But she worried now that her luck was up.

Chapter Twenty-Nine

He couldn't let this happen to Nora.

The young woman stood before him with tears in her eyes. He could see the guilt hanging heavily on her, weighing her down. It wasn't something that she deserved after all that they had just been through.

She glanced down at her hands, bandaged after her valiant efforts in protecting their friends' property. Nora continuously proved to everyone, especially to him, how vital she was. How perfect she was. And he wasn't about to let her go just because they were scared.

It wasn't something he wanted to admit, because he was mostly mad. Anger coursed through his body at the thought of someone causing Nora so much pain and fear. Joe had to work hard to swallow down ideas of harm.

"But..." She bit her lip.

He shook his head. "No, Nora. I don't want you even entertaining the idea of going with him. All right? Your place is here. With us. With me."

The words slipped out before he realized what he was saying or even knew what they meant. But as his wife widened her eyes in surprise, Joe understood his meaning perfectly. It hadn't quite dawned on him before, but this life was all he wanted.

Never again would he entertain the idea of going back East. This was the life he wanted and needed. Nora and Mattie were all that mattered to him. Wealth and influence meant nothing if he didn't have his family beside him. It was still new, but he knew what was important. There was no reason to ever think about leaving or changing anything.

Gazing up at Nora, he realized that he needed her to know.

"It's been hard, I know," Joe assured her. His heart thumped loudly in his chest as he held her there. "Coming here, I didn't know what to expect. I've been out of my depth since I arrived. The ranch has faced problem after problem. For a while, I thought about grabbing Mattie and taking her back to the city. When you came, I considered the same. I know the city and I know what to expect. No surprises. There would be comfort and ease and fewer worries."

She blinked, her eyelashes fluttering. "Really? But... you didn't say anything."

"I didn't," he agreed with a slight nod. "Because my life isn't in New York City any longer. The life I had there is over. It was empty and... and meaningless. Nothing would be the same if I went back. And I don't want that."

Nora shakily wiped her tears with the back of her hand. "But... you had so much there, Joe. Are we... if you wanted to, then...?"

"That's what I'm trying to tell you," he said softly. "If nothing. We are staying here. This is where we belong, Nora. You, me, and Mattie. This life is all that matters to me now. And I mean it when I tell you that I will never, never allow Victor Rawls or anyone else to take you away from me."

Her eyes widened as she studied him. It seemed to take her a moment to understand what he was saying, to know that his words were true. Joe looked at her steadily to give her no doubt that this was the truth. He wouldn't lie to her. This was their life, and no one was going to stop them.

No one would hurt Nora or Mattie ever again so long as he was around.

Thinking back to the day that he'd first seen Nora at the train station, Joe knew he was a fool for having taken so long for this to register within his heart. He had seen in an instant how beautiful she was; it had only taken a few minutes to realize how lovely her soul was, as well. He just hadn't recognized the feelings growing within him until now.

They could be ignored no longer. He couldn't leave them on the shelf. Though his heart pounded, and it took all his strength to keep his eyes on Nora, Joe believed this with all his might.

"I... I never..." Nora stammered as she searched his gaze. When she couldn't find the words, she stepped forward to wrap her arms around him.

He inhaled sharply at the embrace before quickly doing the same for her. Nora hid her face in the crook of his neck; she smelled like their morning meal with a touch of smoke. Joe closed his eyes as he tried to remember the last time he had appreciated such a hug. The two of them stood there for several moments, breathing deeply.

At last, Nora let out a soft sigh. He took that as a sign that she was feeling better. When he pulled back, she rubbed her eyes with the uninjured parts of her palms. There was a hesitant smile on her face, along with pink cheeks.

"All right," she said at last. "I believe you. This is my home, too. You're my home. But I don't know what we're to do, Joe. How are we supposed to make him go away?"

He felt the lightest feeling soar into his chest at her first words. Joe tucked the emotion away into his heart for later as he considered her question. Seeing Nora bite her lip, he attempted to think of a solution.

"I don't know," he confessed after a minute. "Not yet. But I will. We'll figure it out. We're not going to give up on this.

Victor Rawls will be out of our lives one way or another. Just give me some time to think, all right?"

"I trust you," Nora assured him with a softness in her gaze that made him forget any and all weaknesses.

Joe felt as if he could accomplish anything when she looked at him like that. He could take on giants, trouble, and the entire world if that was what she desired. Lost in her eyes, he didn't think he could look away if he wanted to. And he didn't, not when she was seeing the best of him.

He gave her arm a squeeze and then stepped back. Though he liked the idea of staying with her in their room for the rest of the day, or longer, he recalled that there was still work for them to do. On top of that was Mattie. They couldn't hide from her like this when she needed them. They all needed each other, especially now.

So, Joe headed back out into the kitchen with Nora beside him. They walked comfortably side by side, arms brushing against one another.

Mattie was at the table with bread and jam. The kitchen was clean, all except for the spattering of dark red jam on her plate and chin. She smiled up at them as they entered, and he grinned back at her with a small chuckle.

"Did you save some for us?" he joked.

"I did!" Mattie assured them with a long nod. She gestured to the two plates beside her. Two pieces of bread were on each of them, slathered with butter and jam.

Nora sat down across from Mattie and beside Joe. "Why, thank you, Mattie. That was very sweet of you. Hungry?"

"Not anymore," the child said.

The three of them ate and talked around the table for a while, trying to move on from all that had happened over the last two days. Joe knew he needed to see to the ranch, but he put it off for as long as he could. Until, at last, he grudgingly stood up to go.

"You two should get some rest," he said decidedly. "No hard work. I already have Taggert helping out with the cows and everything for the rest of the week. Just until your hands are better," he added to Nora. "Maybe tomorrow I can take the three of you back to visit Audrey."

Mattie straightened up. "I want to see Audrey."

"It's a good plan," Nora murmured. She bit her lip as though thinking about something serious. But she said nothing as she turned to look at Joe. "Don't stay out too late. Please?"

"Of course not," he promised. Joe patted her shoulder and ruffled Mattie's hair as he made his way out of the house.

He didn't concentrate on much work as he tended to a patch of poisonous weeds and spoke with his ranch hands. A few of them had seen what was going on the day before, and Moody wasn't much of a talker about what had gone down. Joe kept his answers to their questions short before calling it a day.

Nora and Mattie had prepared some hot potatoes for supper. It was a light and easy meal, and they enjoyed eating together quietly as night set in. Joe read to them in the next room before the young girl started to nod off. Though the sun had just set, he thought it best for everyone to retire to bed early.

"Joe?" Nora had prepared herself for bed quietly. But now, in the dark, lying side by side, she turned to face him and whispered in the dark, "Are you awake?"

Shifting to face her, he squinted. "I am. Is something wrong?"

"No. I don't think so," she amended. "But I think we need help. If… if we want to stop Victor Rawls. Perhaps Dan would know something. He and Audrey might have some ideas. Or is that too dangerous? Joe, I don't want anyone to get hurt."

He was quiet for a minute as he considered what she was saying. Weighing the options in his head, slowly he nodded. "I know. But more help might be good. And they should know who tried to hurt them."

They talked for a few more minutes before Nora's words began to slur with sleep. He promised her they could continue the conversation in the morning.

And they did. Once everyone was dressed and had eaten, he prepared the buckboard. Mattie brought a basket filled with some jam and bread to share with the Camerons as the three of them made their way across the conjoining ranchland.

It only took a few minutes for pleasantries. Joe could see Nora nearly bursting with the thoughts on their conversation the night before. Her leg bounced and she couldn't focus on anything that was happening.

"We have to talk," said Joe as he watched Mattie settle on the edge of the bed by Audrey. "Dan, did Audrey tell you about what Nora said yesterday? About Victor Rawls?"

The other couple exchanged a troubled look before Dan guiltily nodded. "Yes. I'm sorry, Nora."

She shook her head. "It's all right. It's better that you know." Nora glanced up at Joe. "We want to talk to you two about this. I think we need help to make Victor Rawls leave me alone. Leave us all alone."

A long conversation ensued.

No one wanted to take drastic action. After discussing their boundaries, everyone came to the decision that Rawls had to be arrested and held accountable to the law.

"The only way that could happen," Nora said slowly, "is for him to confess. I don't think he will say anything about the loans. The numbers may be... complicated. But perhaps I can make him confess to burning down the barn and shed."

Joe nodded. "And he has to admit that in front of a judge. That won't be easy. Nor will getting to him. Moody and I went to town to deal with him," he explained, "but he never showed. I think he knew we were there, and was watching us. Or he could even have other men watching for him. He might not be alone."

Hearing that, he saw Nora shudder. He stepped closer to set a comforting hand on her shoulder.

"You think we could flush him out?" asked Dan.

That's when Nora cleared her throat. "I think I have an idea."

She went on to explain the rough plan she had begun to build up in her mind. Dread filled his stomach, but Joe forced himself to keep listening. As she spoke, Dan and Audrey began to nod along. They even filled the gaps to her plan to make sure it would work out. Once it was all explained, Nora looked at them hopefully.

"Well?"

"I don't like it," Joe admitted as they all looked at him. "It's dangerous." His eyes settled on Nora's sweet face. "But... I don't have any other ideas. Let's go ahead with your plan, Nora."

No one quite relaxed after this, but there was an eagerness in everyone's gaze as they began to sort out the fine details. Joe's stomach clenched uneasily, though he didn't know what else could be done. So, he stayed with them and prayed, hoping for the best.

Chapter Thirty

They said patience was a virtue. And Victor despised that with all his heart.

Patience, virtue, all those ideals were only in the way for him. They would have hindered his progress in making the money he had spent so long to earn. The world didn't just wait to create the moment. No, people had to create the perfect moment. He worked hard to make the world bend to his will, and he wasn't about to stop now.

Yet somehow there were still forces against him, trying his limits.

He sat in the restaurant, watching the window. Shifting in his seat, he couldn't seem to sit still.

Whatever patience he had was beginning to wane.

What had he been thinking to give Nora Gilmore three days? It had been two days and he wasn't sure that he would make it to tomorrow. Already, he was planning their trip back to New York City. All of his bags were packed, ready for him to pick up at any moment.

Victor Rawls couldn't wait to get out of this dusty, filthy nightmare that these people called home. His lips curled. He saw folks smiling and didn't understand how or why they would do that. Clearly, they had never been to a properly civilized city.

He reminded himself that it wouldn't be long.

Twenty-four hours, and then he could get out of this place. Victor would be on the next train back to New York with Nora by his side. They would be able to put all of this past them and he would finally return to his normal life.

Glancing down at his plate of food, he held back a groan. The food was greasy and overcooked if it wasn't plain and too crunchy. No one knew how to prepare meals out here. Nor did they eat decent cuisine, like clams. What he would give for a clam dish. Or even any other seafood.

But this place didn't even provide menus.

Victor looked around the small restaurant that held only eleven tables. The windows were partially open to let in the light; this only served to point out the grime on the walls and dirt on the floor. People around him talked cheerfully and loudly, whether they were customers or they were people working in the kitchens. There were so many conversations going on at the moment that he could hardly hear himself think.

They had the option of corned beef or ham for the day, and he was beginning to regret his choice of beef. The potato beside it was hardly cooked and lacked any seasoning. There was a side of greens, but he couldn't tell what they were since they had been cooked for so long.

So, he took a sip of coffee. It tasted like dirt, but it was preferred to anything on his plate. He drained it and then stood. There was no way he could spend another minute there. Perhaps he could swallow down the bitterness with a drink at the saloon. Once decided, Victor paid and then stepped outside onto the sidewalk.

He didn't even have a chance to cross the street when he heard his name called.

Immediately, he turned, an insult ready on his lips. But he held it back when he realized who had said his name.

There she was. His very own Nora. She held her skirts up slightly to help her move faster as she crossed the street to him. With the sun shining down right on her, it made it look as if she wore a halo.

And she was racing to him.

Victor couldn't resist standing up a little taller. He shifted his stance and waited for Nora to arrive.

When she did, she was breathless. Those plump pink lips of hers appeared so inviting that it was hard to convince himself not to move. The young woman fixed her skirts and then looked up at him. She looked nervous as a mouse, which made him grin. She was always so timid about everything.

"Well, well, well," he said. "I've been waiting for you, Nora."

She swallowed and looked over her shoulder before talking to him. "Victor. I… I'll go with you tomorrow."

It was impossible for him to hold back a chuckle. "Of course you will." He couldn't help but preen a little, glad he was wearing one of his finest suits. "I knew you would have to change your mind sooner or later. I know you better than you know yourself. I'm just surprised it took you this long."

Her cheeks blushed red. "I didn't…"

"Didn't what?"

She blinked before shaking her head. "Nothing," Nora stammered. "But I will. I mean it. I can't let this go on any longer. Please, Victor. I don't want my friends and family to get hurt anymore. You'll leave them alone, won't you?"

Family? As if she had anyone but him. The man and child she was pretending to play house with meant nothing and they both knew it. Eventually, Nora would realize this was the truth. Victor pursed his lips for a moment as he considered scolding her. But he changed his mind at the last moment.

Putting a smile on his face, he knew he would have plenty of time later to help her wash her thoughts free of all the people who didn't matter.

"If you come with me? Of course," he informed her with a tilt of the head. "Tomorrow morning at ten. Bring your bags or don't, I don't care. But I have our tickets and I expect you there, ready to go."

Nora bit her lip before giving him a jerky nod. "Fine. Yes, I'm coming. I told you."

The young lady almost sounded bitter.

He tutted. "You could sound a little more thrilled about this. I'm saving you from yourself, you know. Whoever would want to stay in a dump like this town is beyond me. Soon, you'll be back in civilization where you belong. Where we both belong."

She let out a shaky breath. "And you won't hurt Joe? Or Mattie?"

Those names sounded vaguely familiar, but Victor wasn't quite certain. He supposed they might be the names that her family was called. But they hardly mattered. He only grew annoyed as he stared her down, wondering why she cared so much. Those people meant nothing. But, again, he stopped himself, proud of his self-control. They were going to have a nice, long train ride together. That would give him plenty of time to correct Nora's ways.

"I told you I won't," he said, unable to keep the irritation out of his voice. Then he narrowed his eyes at her. "So long as you come with me, there's nothing to worry about. But if you do try anything, Nora dearest, then what happened to that ranch will just be the start."

Her eyes widened as though in surprise.

Did she not realize how serious he was about her? She was coming back with him one way or another. Victor was quite proud of himself for setting this up. He had worked with Harlan Kane to make that happen. Though his men had taken care of it, everything had been his idea.

"I understand," Nora stammered. Then she glanced around before fumbling with her hands.

There were small bandages wrapped around them, he noticed. What could have happened? Surely, she wasn't so stupid she had tried to help out with the fire. But it hardly bothered him. His heart thumped as he realized that Nora was really going to be there in the morning. Though he knew it was inevitable, there was a thrill at the thought of her being there with him. It was going to happen.

"I should go," she said after a moment. Then Nora ducked her head and started back from the way she came. It reminded him of how she used to walk in around him, as well as that last evening in the factory. Her shoulders were always hunched, as if she was trying to hide. As if someone could hide that beauty.

Victor's gaze lingered on Nora until she was gone.

His bad mood flitted away. A smirk lingered on his face as he made his way down the street. He took two turns and then found himself at the saloon. The taste of his lunch had since faded, and now he deserved the chance to treat himself with a rich drink.

Just as he sat down and placed his order, however, the seat beside him was suddenly filled. It was midday, so the saloon was mostly empty. He opened his mouth to make the stranger leave before realizing who it was.

"Harlan." He grinned. "You were right. All I needed was a drastic measure. Your men performed perfectly, you know. I just talked to Nora; she's coming with me."

The other man already had a drink in hand. He offered only a grim smile before shaking his head. Slouching to grow comfortable, he let out a throaty huff. He stared hard at Victor for a second, confusing him, before downing his drink.

"Maybe," Harlan said. "And maybe not. Remember Pete and Ryan? My men heard something."

Victor narrowed his gaze at the man before taking a small sip. "I'm listening."

Chapter Thirty-One

She was still shaking as she made it back home.

Nora could hardly believe she had been able to go to Victor Rawls like that. Just seeing him exit the restaurant had made her shudder. All she'd wanted to do in that moment was run away from him. But instead, she forced herself to go to the man.

And then she had told him what she would do. She said that she would go with him, back to New York City. A small bag had already been packed for her. It was just as she had planned with Joe, though the planning had been much easier to manage than actually executing any aspect of it.

She climbed down off the horse, making a face as she remembered Victor's wicked grin. He had eyed her as though he were ready to eat her up.

Nora hadn't thought it was possible to hate the man more. But she did. She feared him and hated him with all her heart. Quickly, she said a short prayer in the hopes of never having to see him again after this week.

Just as she led the horse over to the corral, Joe appeared.

"Here, let me," he said as he opened the padlock and swung the gate open. "How did it go, Nora?"

Joe had wanted to come to town with her. Truthfully, she had wanted him to be there as well. She felt stronger and more able with her husband beside her, or at least close by. But, worried that Victor Rawls had eyes around town, Audrey had pointed out that it might be best for Nora to do this first step alone.

It had taken Nora all morning to build up the courage.

She had taken a morning ride with Joe and Mattie, and then had meant to make her way right into town. But then she had found a few excuses to keep her busy. Joe had started to suggest that they change the plan; only then did Nora decide to go.

One way or another, she had to talk to Victor Rawls. And she had, though hard and disconcerting as it had been. Nora was just glad it was over.

Forcing a smile on her face, she gave Joe a nod. "I think he believes me. I mean, he... yes. Yes, I'm sure of it."

He paused from closing the gate behind her to reach out his hand. Nora put hers out as well, and relaxed as he gave her a comforting squeeze. She hadn't realized how tense she had felt until right then.

"I'm certain he did," Joe told her. "He had no reason not to. You did wonderful, Nora. Now just think that this is almost over. We have to deal with him tomorrow and then we're free of him. You're free of him."

That gave her hope.

Swallowing, she nodded. Her hand, though still wrapped in a thin bandage, felt cold as he let go of her. She watched him close the gate and then turn to her horse. The animal waited patiently for the saddle and bridle to be taken off before walking over to the water trough. Nora stood back and watched thoughtfully for a few minutes.

She had thought she was free of Victor Rawls before.

For the first four months of being here with Joe on the ranch, Nora had been convinced that nothing like this could happen. She'd thought that he couldn't find her. Even after her friend's letters, the two of them had assumed that the man would relent and leave her be. Her life had been complicated with her new family but so much better than before. She had just been settling in comfortably when he showed up and ruined everything.

That couldn't happen again. Nora told herself this over and over again. This time, things with Victor Rawls had to be done right so she would never have to even see his face or hear his voice. She was done with him and wanted to be free. She was tired of the sleepless nights, worried about the man coming after her.

She stayed out with Joe to brush down a few horses before she returned to the house. Her thoughts wandered as she worked. The doubts crept in even as she forced herself to keep hope.

Mattie was there, and so was Joe. They were her family. Nora knew this without a doubt, and she knew she would do what it took to protect them. She thought of this throughout supper and afterward as she slipped under the blankets beside Joe.

Though she thought about telling him some of her fears, she didn't know where to start. Her thoughts weighed her down and Nora drifted off into an uneasy sleep.

In the morning, it felt as though she hadn't even closed her eyes. She awoke with a heavy feeling in her stomach as she brushed her hair and dressed. Nora told herself she was doing this for a reason. She told herself that everything would work out. There was no reason to worry.

"Where are you going?"

Nora looked up from setting her bag down by the back door to find Mattie standing there. The young girl looked sleepy with her unbrushed hair and wrinkled dress.

"I… I am going on the train." A lump formed in her throat. "Do you remember what we talked about the other day? We went to talk with Dan and Audrey. I said I would get on a train and pretend to leave town with a very… with a man."

Her adopted daughter's eyes widened. "You're leaving?"

The broken words stabbed Nora in the heart. She hurried down the hall and knelt down to sweep Mattie into a tight hug. "No! Not really. Oh, Mattie. It's all right. Don't you cry. Tonight, everything will be fine. I'll be here. One way or another, my dear, I will be here."

"I don't want to lose another mother," Mattie said slowly, rubbing her eyes.

She hadn't called Nora that before. Her heart pounded as she held the child close. It took all of Nora's strength not to tear up, but her eyes itched, tempted. "You won't. I will be with you soon."

"Promise?"

"I promise," said Nora. "Everything is going to be okay. I have to do this. I must. It's the only way for us to be free as a family. Tonight, everything will be much better."

She spoke more confidently than she felt. But as she talked, the hope grew within her chest. This time, she was not alone in her struggles. Instead, she was surrounded by her family and friends. They were helping her and would make sure that everything worked out the way it should.

After giving Mattie one more squeeze, Nora kissed the girl's cheek and then helped her finish getting ready for the day.

Joe had already gone off to the ranch that morning, but he returned to join them to eat their porridge. The three of them sat together at the table, more subdued than usual, to enjoy their morning meal as a family.

And then it was time for them to go.

Her husband tied her traveling bag onto the saddle. "Don't forget to bring it with you," he instructed her in a low voice. "Or he'll know something is up. Just stay calm and try not to say too much. I believe in you, Nora. And I'll be with you all the way."

She inhaled deeply and nodded. "All right. I'll be fine."

"I want to come with you," Mattie said as she hugged her skirts. Nora lost her voice for a moment, touching Mattie's curls.

Then Joe was at her side, picking her up. "I'm sorry, dear. You're coming with me. Remember? You get to go sit with Audrey. She'll love the company, and you two will have some fun. Say goodbye to Nora now."

It was a tender farewell that made Nora's throat constrict. She ruffled Mattie's hair with a sad smile before forcing herself to step away. Then, she stiffly managed to mount the horse and directed him toward town. She glanced at Joe. They exchanged nods, not saying anything more, before she turned away. If she stayed any longer, she knew the tears would fall.

The nerves simply wouldn't go away.

Nora forced herself to review the plan before she started telling herself that it would work. This was a good plan, and everything would be fine. She wasn't alone and Victor Rawls wouldn't get away with this.

By the time she reached the train depot, she was feeling a little braver. She left the horse tied to a post before untying her bag and making her way up the steps. Nora took a deep breath as she said a quick prayer.

She felt his gaze on her before she found him.

Victor Rawls wore an ivory suit with stripes and a fancy hat as he stood by the steps of the train. It was already there, parked and ready to go. Her stomach tightened as the man gave her a nod.

Nora forced her legs to start moving. There was only a small crowd gathered around on the platform, ready to leave town or see someone off. Smoke filled the air. She wanted to cough, but she bit her tongue instead. Her nerves grew tightly wound. All she wanted to do was run away right then. But she didn't.

She steeled herself as she reached him.

"Don't you have anything nicer than that?" Victor Rawls asked after eyeing her dress. "Come on, then. Ladies first."

Biting her lip, Nora stayed quiet while she gave him a slight nod and then obeyed. She only had a small bandage on three of her fingers now, since they were healing so well. Clinging to the iron railing, she felt the large machine humming beneath her feet. She didn't remember that from her ride out west. But she didn't remember a lot about that ride.

The black locomotive held ten cars, she noticed, and three of them had their doors open for people to step on and make their way out of town. Nora stepped inside the car that Victor had stood beside and found herself in a tiny hallway with several separated compartments to her side. That meant he had paid a pretty penny to give them some more room for the journey.

"Sit down."

Nora gulped as she obeyed. The second compartment door had been opened, and that had to be theirs. There were two benches that faced each other with a window at the end. She glanced around it before gingerly sitting by the window.

"No need to look so excited," Victor said with a frown. He eyed her before taking a seat. To her relief, he chose to sit across from her and not right next to her.

But any hope faded as he set something on the small table that jutted out from the wall beneath the window. It was hardly big enough to set a plate down.

Victor didn't set a plate. Instead, he put a gun there.

She jerked back in surprise, blanching at the sight of something so dangerous. Dread filled her stomach as she turned to look up at the man, wondering what he was thinking. Surely, he wasn't going to kill her?

"Just a warning," he said in a casual tone. "I would hate for you to do anything rash."

Nora opened her mouth just as the train whistle rang out. Then, the train began to move, and she put a hand on the window to steady herself. The blood drained from her face when she glanced from Victor to the gun. "I... I wouldn't. I told you, I was coming with you. I just don't want anyone else to get hurt."

Looking up at him, something cold seemed to trickle down her neck in warning. She had done her best to convince him that she was coming. That was part of the plan. Though she had just begun to feel hopeful for their plan, now she realized they must have missed an important detail.

There was something wrong. She could feel it.

He was still glaring at her. "If you didn't want anyone to get hurt, then you wouldn't have that posse waiting for us around the hill."

The cold spread across her skin, turning her clammy. She felt the chill inside and out of her bones as she grasped what he had just said. Nora stared in disbelief at the man who gave her a harsh look with a particularly mean glint in his eye.

She had no idea how he knew. Unable to move, hardly thinking straight, she tried to make sense of it.

But Nora didn't understand. "No. I didn't..." Slowly, she sank into the back of her bench while she shook her head. "You... How?"

Victor Rawls let out a deep, dark chuckle that made her skin crawl. She sat pressed into her seat as much as possible to keep away from him. Especially as the man leaned forward to stare her down.

"You think you're the only one with folks helping? Tut, Nora. You should know better. I have a posse of my own. That man you call your husband isn't beloved by everyone. Harlan Kane was more than happy to help me out. Especially Kane's men who have been working for him all along. That's right—you've been sold out. Now, here's how it's going to happen: we will keep moving. Joe will die and leave Kane the ranch. And that leaves you with me."

Bile rose in her throat, though she swallowed it back down.

She thought quickly, fearful of the future that he had just presented to her. The thought of losing Joe hurt her heart. And what of Mattie? Victor had said nothing of the young girl who would be left to fend on her own.

That couldn't happen.

Something had to be done to alert Joe, Nora realized. He couldn't know what had happened. They would be taken by surprise and she couldn't let him get hurt. She stared at Victor blankly, thinking hard.

Just then, the train began to slow down. They were finishing their bend around the hill and would be moving further into the mountains soon. But ahead was an old station stop from long ago, where Joe would be waiting with the other men. They must have caught the attention of the conductor to slow it down.

A soft screech made her jerk her head up. The door opened to reveal the ticket taker. But before he could say a word, Nora jumped up and spun out of her seat to run right past the man in uniform. She slipped down the train aisle and started to sprint.

"Nora! Get back here!"

She gasped, but she didn't turn back. Her heart pounded in her chest as she could hear Victor scrambling after her. But she couldn't stop. Not now—not when her husband's life depended on her.

Chapter Thirty-Two

Joe sat with three men on their horses right beside the small platform. Moody and three other men were standing on the deck, waiting there. All of them were still, tense, and waiting.

The train was slowing down.

His heart pounded in his chest as he told himself to stay calm. It was a good plan, he reminded himself, and it was going to work out just how they had planned. They had covered their tracks and he felt certain about this plan.

The train would stop. They would bring Nora off and make Victor stay, threatening him to make sure he stayed away. Already, he had gone into town to have the telegram office alert the next several stops about the man who was told to stay aboard. If tried to disembark, the sheriffs were to arrest him and keep him from coming back.

It was simple and effective. That was what he'd thought.

But any confidence he had felt moments ago dissipated when he saw a figure tumble off the train. The locomotive was still moving toward them, screeching with its heavy brakes to park at where they were stopped. Joe frowned, trying to see clearly where someone had come off the train.

It had looked like a woman.

Joe told himself that this wasn't possible. There was no reason for someone to get off before the train stopped. Narrowing his gaze, he searched along the dip in the ground that created a moat. The summer had been dry so there was no water. Just grass and bushes and trees. It had been a nuisance to ride his horse over there since the earth was overgrown. No one came over here anymore.

Something was wrong.

Why else would someone jump off the train? He cursed himself for not having boarded as well. That had been his plan, the preference he'd suggested, but everyone said it could put Nora in danger if he was seen. Though he'd had no qualms about hiding in a compartment or paying for a ticket, Joe had grudgingly allowed himself to be talked out of the idea.

But now, he regretted it.

"Nora." Her name spilled off his lips as he saw the figure straighten up. Nearly half a mile away, he couldn't see her face or discerning features. There was no way for him to tell what particular shade of blue the dress was. But Joe was certain it was her.

She was on her feet and moving his way. She was running as if something was wrong, as if to get away from someone.

As proof, another figure proceeded to jump out of the train after her. Joe's grip tightened on the reins as he peered forward to try and see who it might be. Someone in pale-colored clothes, plus a hat that fell off. Yet the figure didn't go back for it.

It had to be him. That must be Victor Rawls.

Joe's heart sunk into his stomach as he realized that their plan was not foolproof. He ransacked his mind for what they had missed, but he had no idea. Everything had been set to go down once the train stopped; not like this. They had to do something. His mouth grew dry at the thought of losing Nora.

He couldn't let that happen.

Flexing his grip on the reins, Joe nudged his horse to face the running figures. She needed his help, and he wasn't going to leave her to fend for herself. They were a family now, a unit, and he would do whatever it took to be there for her.

A shrill whistle caught him off-guard. Looking around, he found Moody whistling loudly, waving an arm at him. Then, the man gestured to the other side of the platform. To Joe's disbelief, a large group of riders were coming straight toward them.

The hill shrank beyond the platform, creating a flat path that had been easy for them to climb. It had taken them a little longer to arrive at their hiding spot than he had liked, but it made the situation ideal for not letting anyone get away.

Except now they were about to be the ones trapped, with crowded brush and trees behind them and a gang headed straight their way.

Joe tried to think of who all those riders might be. Certainly, they were not with the law. They had left the sheriff in town. The man had considered coming to join them, but Moody had assured them they had it covered and didn't need any more manpower. It was better that there was someone to stay in town in case of other trouble.

Now, there was trouble coming from both directions.

Joe thought quickly before waving a hand to get Moody's attention. The man was preparing his gun and glanced up, giving Joe a questioning look. They didn't exactly have time to waste.

"Nora," Joe shouted and gestured behind him. "I have to get her."

The foreman glanced beyond his men in the saddle and then gave him a short nod. "Go, then. Riders, around the platform! You two, get in the saddles, as well. The rest of us will stay put in case of more guns."

He continued talking, but Joe didn't have the time to linger. Concentrating on Nora, he leaned down in the saddle and nudged his mount to start moving. The horse had noticed the tension as well, prancing nervously. But now the animal was ready to move. Joe felt the muscles bunch up beneath the saddle before his horse took off at a gallop.

Holding on tight, he focused his gaze on the rough path ahead.

Joe searched for Nora even as he heard the pistols cocking and guns shooting behind him. A gunfight had broken out. He said a quick prayer for his men's safety.

Part of him wanted to turn back to watch over the men. They didn't deserve to suffer or get hurt for this, let alone die. Though every man had been a volunteer, a bitter taste crept into his mouth at the idea of anyone dying.

He glanced over his shoulder but couldn't get a good look. The terrain before him was rough, so it was very bumpy on the ground beside the train.

The large machine was nearly to a stop. It was louder than anything he'd heard before, especially being so close. He flinched as they neared one another, but he pushed himself to keep going.

Gunshots continued, still loud though the voices had faded away. Joe reminded himself that he couldn't turn back. Not yet, not when Nora needed him.

They were growing closer. His heart hammered in his chest as he could see much more clearly now that it was her. It made his heart ache to see her wide, terrified eyes. She reached out for him at one point, even though they both knew he was too far away. Joe tried to tell his horse to go faster, but he seemed to be moving as fast as he could go.

Glancing over her shoulder, he could also better see Victor Rawls.

Joe had heard a lot about him, but this was the first time he had ever seen the man in person. A sickly feeling settled in his gut. Seeing the large man running after his wife infuriated Joe more than he thought possible. His body shook at the thought of Rawls ever touching his wife, even speaking to her.

That wouldn't happen ever again if he had any say.

All he could see in his mind's eye was how much Nora had been through because of this man. He had preyed on her and her father, when her father was still alive. The man had to be desperate to go to such a length to get to Nora. Though Joe could understand the desire to do that much and more for her, he knew with every fiber of his being that Rawls didn't deserve her. He never would. No, Nora deserved to be in a place where she felt happy and safe.

Which was what Joe wanted to provide for her.

But he couldn't do that unless she was safe. Grinding his teeth, Joe pushed his horse to keep moving. Even when the animal stumbled, they managed to stay upright.

Then he pulled the gun from his holster.

It was an old revolver that he had found in his brother's room the first day he had come to the ranch. Billy had a few of them, but this was the only one Joe felt comfortable keeping on his body. Which Ezra had made a point several times that he needed to do; one never knew when there might be trouble. Though it was an old Colt, he had cleaned it up and learned how to shoot it before Nora even arrived. He had already known how to use guns, thinking how arcane they were. But now he couldn't be more grateful to have the cool metal in his hand.

He straightened his arm and quickly realized that he couldn't get a good shot. Nora was right there, only a hundred yards away now. And Rawls was too close behind her for him to have any clear aim.

Joe forced himself to start slowing down. He was about to come upon them, not wanting to risk anyone getting hurt. A moment of panic gripped him tight. He hesitated, glancing at the two people he was about to run into.

That was when a shot rang out. It was too close for comfort, pinging loudly off the tracks by his head. Joe caught a glimpse of Rawls with a weapon in hand before it was pointed at him again. He inhaled sharply and then leapt off his horse.

There was little room, with all the brush, to turn around in the saddle. He made for too big of a target on the horse, something that Ezra had pointed out to him with the other riders only a short while earlier. So, Joe went flying. He somehow managed to keep a grip on his gun as he rolled on the ground and came to a stop.

He felt bruised all over, but he didn't let that stop him. Quickly, he hurried back onto his feet, ignoring how his head still spun. Joe wanted to sit down and throw up any food he had eaten that day. But he didn't, instead standing up to look for Rawls.

Just as he cocked the hammer, he froze.

There was Victor Rawls. The man had stopped running. He stood against the steep ravine by the tracks, directing a gun at Joe. But what bothered Joe most was how the man had an arm wrapped firmly around Nora's waist.

Chapter Thirty-Three

Nora's chest heaved.

She could hardly breathe. Her legs felt weak, shaking from running so much. It couldn't have been for very long, but to her it felt like hours. She had been trying so hard to get away from Victor.

She had run as fast as she could only to see Joe go flying off his horse. The sight had been so unreal, so startling that she couldn't help but stop and stare. Had he been hit? She brushed the hair from her face as she watched him roll over on the ground.

But before she could see if he was still alive, an arm wrapped around her midsection.

"No—" The word was cut off.

Victor's grip around her tightened, cutting off her air. She choked, grabbing desperately at his arm so that she could breathe again. Nora felt the blood rushing up into her face. Her vision blurred for a moment just as he lifted her off her feet to turn the two of them toward Joe.

"Shut up," Rawls hissed angrily in her ear.

She flinched at the sound of his voice. His breath smelled putrid. But she stopped fighting him, shakily moving her arms away from his. To her relief, his grasp on her loosened. Not a lot, but enough for her to start breathing again.

Nora gasped, seeing Victor raise his gun with his free hand. Just moments ago, she had heard it go off behind her. Nora had nearly fallen over then at the deafening noise. She had grabbed her side to see if she had been hit, but there was no blood. She was fine. Then, she had looked up to see Joe falling.

He was on his feet now.

Nora stared at him, chest heaving, as the last few seconds slowly came together in her mind. She blinked and then studied Joe. His sleeve was torn, and his hair looked like a crow's nest. But she didn't see any blood. The man raised his gun before spotting her there. Joe's eyes widened when they settled on her.

This was not good.

It was worse than anything she had been afraid of before this morning.

"No," she choked out in a whisper. "Victor, please."

She squeaked when he adjusted his hold, jostling her hard. Sweat poured down her forehead as she blinked and tried to think of something she could do. It wasn't like she could just stand there and let the men shoot each other. There had to be some way to fix this.

"Let her go," Joe called. "Now, Victor Rawls."

Nora couldn't help but flinch, seeing Rawls aim his gun clearly over at Joe. Rawls could shoot Joe if he wanted, she realized. There was nothing she could do. Dread filled her stomach. Just a few days ago, she had been worried that she might have to leave town with Victor. But in that fear, Joe had still been alive and well.

"You must be the so-called husband," Victor said with a chuckle. His chest rumbled, pressed against her back. Nora gritted her teeth but said nothing. "What a fool you must be. Pity, for you could have at least stayed to keep your ranch. But here you are, giving up what's left of your worthless life."

Blinking hard, she focused her gaze on Joe. She didn't want to see anything else. No matter what happened next, she didn't want to think about anything but her husband.

Nora's mind ran over the last five months. Had it really been such a short amount of time? It hardly seemed possible. She had gone through so much. And she wouldn't give up a single minute. Joe had been there every step of the way. Though it had been rough for them in the beginning, confused and uncertain, it had gradually begun to change.

They were a family now. He would always be her husband.

She panted as she tried to think of something to do to fix this mess that she had gotten them into. It was her fault, she realized, for letting Victor find her. She should have done something back in the city to make sure he never came looking her way. It was because of her that he was there, and so she had to come up with an idea to make him leave them alone for good. This plan might have failed, but she couldn't give up now.

Another deep breath in, and she gathered what was left of her courage.

"I mean it," Joe called. Gingerly, he took two steps forward. "Let her go. You take Nora now, and that's kidnapping. You've lost, all right? Just let her go and leave us in peace."

Victor cocked the hammer on his own pistol before shaking his head. "I don't think so. Now stand back, or I'll shoot. Don't think I would hesitate."

"It's fine," Nora croaked as she kept her eyes on Joe. "Please, Joe." Her throat constricted before she gave him the slightest nod. Her eyes flitted up to Victor, who didn't bother looking down at her. "I'll go with you, Victor. Just don't hurt him."

The man shifted his feet as Joe crept a little closer. He wasn't far away now. They couldn't be more than ten feet apart. She felt as though she could almost touch him. Her hands ached at the thought of holding his. Any minute, she told herself, and she could be in his arms. She just needed to wait for another opportunity. Once Victor was distracted, she could escape.

Standing still, she felt Victor's grip loosen slightly. He chuckled in her ear. Her nose twisted, but she kept her eyes focused on Joe. Did he give her a nod? She blinked several times. His gesture was so inconspicuous that she couldn't be certain she wasn't just imagining things.

"Oh, you're definitely coming with me," Victor growled in her ear. "But I don't think you have any say about what I do or don't do. Not after that stunt you pulled. Now, I just—"

Before he could say anything more, Nora took a small step to the side. It was hardly anything beyond a slight lean. But it gave her the momentum she needed to swing her arm backward, elbowing Victor as hard as she could.

He let out a loud grunt.

At the same time, his grip slackened enough for her to push him away from her. Nora broke loose and took full advantage of the chance. She knew she might not get another. Free of Victor's hold, she darted to the side. The ground was uneven, but she kept moving. Her heart hammered loudly in her chest, beating so hard that she felt as though she might fall right over.

Feeling that she was far enough out of his grasp, Nora whirled around.

A shot rang out.

She gasped, covering her mouth with her hands. Fearful of her husband's death, she turned to look at him in horror. She couldn't lose him. She couldn't. But before she could call out his name, she realized that he was still standing.

And he was running.

Her eyes widened as she watched Joe sprint over to Victor, who was staggering backwards against the upward slope. A red stain blossomed over his shoulder to signal that he hadn't been the one to shoot. The man began to slump. Already, his gun was in the dirt.

Joe swept forward, kicking the weapon away. His gun was held again with two hands that were directed once more at Victor.

"Don't move," her husband ordered the man. "Don't even think about it."

She stared, too stunned to do anything for several moments. Joe was fine, Nora realized, and he wasn't hurt. Instead, he had saved her.

"Nora?" Joe called to her without looking over his shoulder. "Nora? Are you there? Are you hurt?"

She moistened her lips and nodded before realizing her mistake. It took her a minute to find her voice. After clearing her throat, she tentatively answered, "I'm here."

Her voice sounded squeaky, but she didn't care. She took a small step forward, expecting Victor to climb up to his feet and start shouting at her. She expected something more. More trouble, more pain, more misery. There always seemed to be something worse around the corner.

But seeing that Victor remained lying down in the dirt, an ounce of hope spread through her chest. It settled her stomach and she nervously took another step forward. When still nothing bad happened, she took another and another.

Nora walked until she was standing just an arm's length from Victor's feet, very close to Joe. Her body shook and her arms wrapped around her chest. She glanced at Victor before swallowing the lump in her throat. He wasn't getting back up. Instead, the man was concentrating only on the wound he had sustained. It was as if she no longer existed.

"Nora?"

"I'm here, Joe." She watched as he fixed his grip on the gun. Then he put it in one hand and moved around Rawls until he could reach out a hand to her. It was a blind reach, but she immediately put her hand in his and stepped a little closer.

He gave her hand a squeeze. "Good." Joe gave her a quick look over, his gun still pointed at Victor on the ground. "It's all right, Nora. I'm okay. We're going to be okay."

Not until then did she realize that she had been crying. Tears trickled down her cheeks, cool against her flushed skin. Nora gulped in her breath and nodded before he turned away. They were both beginning to calm down when she heard a horse galloping over to them.

To her relief, it was Ezra.

He had two horses riding behind him, saddled but lacking riders. She looked up and caught his eye as he gave her a comforting nod.

"The masked gang was driven off," Ezra announced loudly. "We hit two of them but don't know how badly. Benson is the only one injured and he has headed back with three of our men. And I'm guessing this here is the man this is all about. You're a popular fellow."

Joe scoffed as their foreman climbed out of the saddle. "A very wanted sort of fellow, I would say. All we have to do is take him back for the sheriff to worry about. We have enough against him now. Right?"

Her eyes widened as he turned to her for a reply. Nora quickly remembered, however, and gave him a jerky nod. She swallowed hard as she recalled all that Victor had confessed to her. It would be helpful now in having him taken to court.

"Yes," she managed.

"The only thing I don't understand is how they knew we were ready for them," Ezra said after a second. He frowned down at Victor while pulling some rope out of his saddle bags. "It doesn't make any sense."

That was when she remembered what else Victor had shared with her. She hiccupped, making the men look her way.

"I know why." Nora swallowed before pursing her lips. "He had someone on the inside. Two men that worked for another man in town. Kane, he said the name was?"

An angry sound escaped Ezra's lips. "Kane? Harlan Kane? That blasted yellow-bellied fool! I should have known." He muttered a few words under his breath that Nora was glad not to hear. Then the man straightened up and gave Joe a look. "It was Pete and Ryan. They used to work for him. Sounds like they never really stopped. I thought they had changed their ways, but..."

Joe shook his head as the man trailed off. "I understand. They were hard workers, I thought. But it would also explain why so much was going wrong on the ranch. Even you said all those problems were too much for one summer."

"Well. Nothing more we can do here now," Ezra said, glaring at Victor. "Let's get this man in jail. I've already split the men up, Joe. Some will accompany myself and this fine gentleman into town and the others will take you two home. You don't mind sharing a horse, do you?"

Nora's grip on Joe tightened.

A minute later, she was seated in front of him in the saddle with his arms around her. Nora's heartbeat had finally begun to slow and she found herself relaxing against Joe as they left Victor behind and headed for home.

Nora could hardly believe it. She was finally free. And soon, she would be right back where she belonged—with her husband and daughter.

Epilogue

That nightmare by the train still kept Nora up some nights.

It had only been a week, so Joe was hopeful that it wouldn't last too long. She had been through so much already. All he wanted for his wife was peace and happiness.

Every time she woke up shaking in the middle of the night, he was there for her. He would wrap her up in his arms and tell her she was safe until her breathing grew calm again. During the day, they didn't really talk about it, but he could tell from the small touches as they brushed past one another that she appreciated him. For a few days, they could pretend there was nothing out there in the world, and certainly nothing that could hurt them.

And then, it was time to get back to real life.

Joe hitched up the wagon before Nora and Mattie made it outside. The three of them soberly clambered up into their seats to head into town. No one said a word as they arrived in front of the town hall.

There wasn't a real courtroom yet. Some folks were talking about the possibility, worried about how big the town continued to grow. But there weren't even blueprints yet for something like this, so for now the circuit judge brought forth each case at their town hall. The windows were too small to let in good light or decent air.

Joe wrinkled his nose as they stepped inside. Mattie clung to both him and Nora as he held hands with his wife.

Then, it was time.

Inside the town hall, they walked through the short hallway. The floors were clean and squeaky as he opened the door to the makeshift courtroom. There was a spattering of chairs around with a table set up for the judge, Mr. Fendleson.

He found three chairs waiting for him and his family up front. Joe felt his stomach churn as he led Mattie and Nora there.

Victor Rawls and Harlan Kane were finally going to stand trial for their misdeeds.

Joe took his seat beside Nora. Mattie sat on her other side, grudgingly letting go of the hem of his jacket. He leaned over to give her a reassuring smile.

Judge Fendleson appeared a few moments later, taking his seat without any recognition. The audience looked up at him, waiting to see what would happen.

"Welcome," Judge Fendleson announced in a deep baritone. "I see we have something of an audience today? I would like to get down to business, so we will begin this court hearing immediately. From what I can see, we have all the necessary witnesses and our lawyer here. The two plaintiffs have decided not to request their own help. Is that correct?"

Rawls and Kane were in the room. Joe craned his neck to spot the two men seated beside each other, up against the wall. Remembering all the rage he had felt over their misdeeds, he struggled to constrain himself.

The opening statement was given by the lawyer speaking on behalf of the law. Then, the two accused criminals were each given a chance to say something.

Both of them claimed to be innocent of any wrongdoing. Joe's hope sunk lower into his stomach. He wasn't sure if anyone would try to do that now.

"I would like to call Nora Bowman to the stand," the lawyer announced.

Nora jumped. She looked over to Joe worriedly, so he gave her a supportive smile before squeezing her hand. Then, he gave her a nod to further reassure her.

"You can do this, Nora," he murmured.

She bit her lip and nodded before moving to the front seat beside the judge. Joe didn't take his eyes off of her. Without her sitting with them, he saw Mattie switch seats to sit beside him. She grabbed hold of his arm.

Both of them watched Nora.

The lawyer walked over to her and said, "The truth comes down to you, Mrs. Bowman. You alone know what has been said between you and Victor Rawls. He met Harlan Kane because he came here to retrieve you. He says that you left behind your debt and broke a binding promise to marry him. Can you give us your statement?"

She nodded slowly as her gaze moved over to Joe. His heart pounded as he listened to her begin to tell her story.

Her voice shook at a few points. Whenever she needed to, she took a deep breath and thought about what she would say before slowly explaining herself.

Joe hated to hear everything that she had been through. No one deserved the pain and misery that Nora had endured. He couldn't be prouder of her for standing up to speak against such evil.

"No further questions," the lawyer announced. "Thank you, Mrs. Bowman. Now I'd like to call Victor Rawls up to the stand."

She hurried away from the chair back into the audience. Joe couldn't help but catch sight of her wiping off a tear from her cheek. But he said nothing as Nora smiled at Mattie for switching seats, and she took the open chair. Though Joe wanted to sit with his wife, he was complacent now to sit beside Mattie.

He turned his attention back to the court as Victor began to try twisting the truth within his version of the story. It made no sense, Joe thought. He looked around to see if anyone was believing him. Victor Rawls was talking about rescuing Nora and it made him sick to his stomach.

"When you first met Harlan Kane, what did the two of you talk about?"

Victor Rawls glowered at the lawyer and then at everyone in the room. The man mulled over his answer before slowly spitting out, "A few things. In fact, enough to warrant a reduced sentence."

A small gasp escaped Nora's lips and she stared ahead in confusion. Joe felt the same way as he turned to study the two defendants.

Harlan stood up, wrists in handcuffs, growling at Rawls. "What are you talking about? You don't know anything! Shut your face!"

The judge brought his hammer down hard on his desk. "Silence! This is my courtroom. Rawls, you were asked a question. Answer it or be held in contempt of this court. What do you have to say for yourself? Who said anything about a reduced sentence?"

Victor Rawls chuckled, an ugly sound that made Nora shudder so violently, Joe felt it from two seats away. He reached over to set a comforting hand on her shoulder.

"If you knew what I knew, then you wouldn't worry about it. Knowing how Billy Bowman really died would be worth something, I think."

Joe instinctively stood up at the sound of his brother's name. Victor Rawls shouldn't have known anything about Billy. That made no sense. He didn't understand. A cold sweat broke out across his brow. He felt Mattie tug at his jacket for him to sit down again, but he couldn't. Why had that man said Billy's name?

"What are you talking about?" he shouted. "What do you know about Billy?"

"He knows nothing!" Kane cried out.

But Rawls had started laughing. He threw his head back and then shook it before looking straight over at Joe. "What? Did you really think that stampede was an accident? Huh? A perfect accident, I would say."

Joe couldn't hear anything more that was said. He grew blinded with hatred and pain. His hands balled into fists as he started toward Kane. If what Rawls was saying was true, then that man had murdered his brother. And he had to be stopped. Yet before he could make his way over to the man, arms wrapped around him.

"Stay," Nora whispered. "Please, don't do it."

He fought with himself as the noise grew in the room. Everyone was shouting now. The judge was trying to call for order, the lawyer was trying to ask questions, and the convicted men were screaming at one another, confessing everything they knew about each other's misdeeds.

It quickly turned into a mess.

Especially since Pete and Ryan were already arrested and next door in their own jail cell. The two men were dragged into the room to share their stories, and finally, they confessed to the stampede. Joe sat down, stunned, and unable to move.

The trial continued for most of the afternoon. While it was clear that all four men would be convicted, there was still so much of the story to hash through and better understand. Joe thought for a minute that it might never end. Until, at last, the judge banged his gavel and glared at the room.

"It's been a very upsetting day," he announced in a hard voice. "And I shall be glad when it is over. The four men on trial have admitted to their guilt. This court also finds them guilty. I have no words to shame you or uplift you. Only this: you are all hereby sentenced to a lifetime in prison."

Could it really be over? They held hands as though they were one another's lifelines. Joe vaguely recalled clapping, the men being led back to jail, and everyone being dismissed. He made his way out of the town hall with his family beside him.

A few people made light conversation, congratulating them for putting away those horrible men. But it was all a fog until he was alone with Nora.

Mattie was just a few feet away with Audrey and Dan, who hugged her tightly. He glanced over at them and then back to his wife. Looking at her, he realized that they were truly free now. Nothing else was hanging over their heads like a dark cloud. There would be less trouble on the ranch now because no one else would be hindering his progress. And no one would be there to hurt Mattie or Nora.

It was time to tell her. Joe inhaled and turned to his wife.

"Nora?"

She looked up at him with wide eyes. Swallowing, she gave his hand a squeeze and offered a small smile. "Joe. Are you doing all right? Over what... About Billy?"

"I don't know," he admitted. His brother could have been alive right then; Joe's heart ached at the thought. "That will take some time. But there's something I want to tell you. I've been thinking lately..."

He worked hard to push everything down. The pain, the fear, and the uncertainty of the future.

"Yes, Joe?"

Something would come up again, one way or another. But he didn't have to let that control him any longer. Joe wanted a good life. And there, he hoped, Nora would be.

Joe had felt these words struggling to escape his lips for days now. He knew there was no right time, and he decided to go for it.

"I love you." The words spilled out. "You deserve to know the truth of my feelings, and that's how I feel about you. I have for a while. It's been hard trying to find a way to say, to tell you... but I do. You mean the world to me, Nora. I can't imagine wanting to be anywhere else but with you. This isn't a marriage of convenience to me anymore—at least, not in my heart. And I guess... I was hoping you might feel the same?"

Joe studied her hopefully, unable to look away from those big bright eyes of hers. They shined brightly in the sun as they studied him in return.

Then, he saw it. A small smile crept up onto Nora's lips and began to grow.

She stepped closer before nodding. "I do. I didn't think you would, after all that happened. But…. I love you, too. Honestly," she added with a shy grin.

His eyes widened, and he wondered if his luck was too good to be true. "Really?"

A short laugh escaped her lips. Nora stepped forward and threw her arms around his neck. He instinctively curled his own arms around her waist. Once there was nothing between them, not even air, Joe leaned forward to kiss her. She responded eagerly, smiling the entire time.

Joe didn't mind. He wouldn't trade a moment like this one for anything in all the world.

Extended Epilogue

Humming, Nora bustled about the kitchen.

There was corn to pop, oranges to dry, and so much more to make the holidays festive. It was her second year on the ranch with her family and she already had more ideas on how to make it even more wonderful than the first.

Never before had she had much time to celebrate Christmas. The holiday was two weeks away and she could hardly wait. Most years, during her childhood, her father had been too busy working to make time to do anything. And then, when she'd worked, well, Nora didn't have the time to spare or even anyone to celebrate with.

But now she did.

"Momma!"

She turned around to find Mattie standing in the doorway, victoriously holding up a spool of thread. The eight-year-old beamed at her before bringing it over to the counter.

"You found it!" Nora cheered. "Perfect." She hurried over to check it out. It was the very spool that she had spent all of yesterday looking for. They would need it for their decorations. The item had been checked off on the last trip Joe took into town for errands, and she recalled having held it at one point. But beyond that, Nora had no idea where it had been. "Wherever did you find it?"

A giggle escaped Mattie's lips as she leaned forward on the counter. "I went outside and found it on top of the chicken coop."

Nora's mouth dropped open. Face flushing, she stared at the young girl before glancing out toward the window. "What?

No. That doesn't sound right. You're not playing with me, are you, Mattie?"

She was still giggling as she shook her head. "Nope!"

Thinking quickly, Nora tried to place the memory of when this must have happened. A sheepish grin spread across her face. She couldn't remember even going outside since it had grown cold and slippery out there with the recent snowfall. But that was how life had been for Nora over the last couple of months. There were gaps in her memory and her thoughts were all over the place.

She gave a chuckle and then ruffled Mattie's hair. "Well, thank you. We can prepare the popped corn this evening while your father reads to us. How does that sound?"

Mattie nodded. "I like that! What are you doing now?"

"I am…" Nora looked around hesitantly while she rubbed her belly. It was a habit she had picked up recently and now she couldn't seem to stop. "Oh, right. Supper. I was going to make us a casserole. Do you want to join me?"

"Yes," the child replied automatically. Then, after a pause, she added, "Papa says I can't leave you alone in the kitchen anymore."

Nora had just started to try bending down to pick up a pot that hung low on the wall. But she stopped, leaning against the wall with one hand, to frown at the child. Mattie looked at her earnestly with a clean face and bright eyes. "Did you tell him he was being ridiculous? I'm just *pregnant*, Mattie. I'm not dangerous."

A small giggle escaped the girl before she clapped a hand loudly over her mouth. She scrunched up her nose to make a face and then, between her fingers, she said, "I know. Do you need help?"

Nora's fingers were so close to grabbing the pot that she wanted to use for boiling the potatoes. A few months ago, this had not been a problem for her. Nora wanted to say no. To need help in picking up a pot like this would mean she had to admit to her limits that seemed to change every day. Already, Joe was helping her put her shoes on every morning and taking them off in the evening. But he volunteered each time, so Nora never actually had to admit that she needed the assistance.

She huffed, making one last grab for it. But her large stomach was in the way.

Nora groaned in frustration before Mattie scampered over to grab the pot and hand it to her. A flush spread over her cheeks, but she couldn't resist smiling at the impish look on her daughter.

While her husband was constantly worried about her and Nora was tired of being pregnant, Mattie had taken it all in stride. She had been so eager to learn that she was about to have a younger brother or sister and had been more than happy to help prepare everything from building a cradle and knitting blankets. Already, she was talking about all she wanted to do with her younger sibling, and all the things she wanted to teach them.

"Here you are," Mattie announced. "What casserole are we making?"

"Potatoes and other vegetables," Nora answered, then gestured to the back door. "Do you think you could gather some from the cellar? Carrots and anything else you like. I'll start the water boiling."

Her daughter nodded and made her way to the edge of the kitchen. But she stopped, watching Nora as she used their inside spout to fill the pot with water. It would fit several potatoes and make something they could keep for a few days. That way, Nora figured, she could put in some extra work now and less later. Already, her ankles were swelling. The thought of having a few hours where she didn't need to be on her feet sounded glorious.

"Momma? Do you need help carrying the pot?"

Nora glanced over at the girl and then back at the pot that was finally filled with enough water. She turned off the stream before shaking her head. "Nonsense. Go on, then."

Mattie hesitated, studying her for a moment, before grudgingly going away. She disappeared down the hall and out the back door. Nora listened to it open and shut before turning her attention to the pot.

It would be fine, she told herself. Joe kept telling her to be careful. Even the doctor in town had made a point to say she needed to stop bending over or lifting heavy things. Yet Nora reasoned that it had to be done once in a while. She hefted up the pot and awkwardly carried it against her large belly across the room.

She had just set the pot over the fireplace when she felt the first twinge.

Nora leaned against the wall and gasped, cradling her hand over her belly. She had felt this before. It was an uncomfortable feeling, but she knew to ride it out. She took a deep breath, closing her eyes. It would go away soon—or so she thought.

But it came back. And then another. Nora stiffened, feeling something change. And that was when it hit her.

"Mattie!" Nora cried out, wincing as another contraction came her way. "Mattie!"

****

Joe breathed in deeply as he looked around the ranch.

It was doing well. Thriving, in fact. He would be worried if he considered this competition. But Ezra Moody was successfully working his own property now, and he couldn't be happier for the man.

"This is impressive," he assured the older man. "You've brought it a long way. I can't believe it's been a year already."

The ranch house had been restructured from the mess that it had been. Joe remembered spending last winter putting the final touches on it, with Ezra and a few other men in town. Nearby was an old barn with new stables added. The fence around the property had been put in correctly and was made to keep the animals safe and not hurt others. And then, down by the stream, the water's edge had been cleaned up to allow more fresh water there.

"Thanks. I always wanted to do something more with this place," Ezra admitted. "But Kane didn't want any ideas. What a shame."

"A shame indeed," Joe echoed.

Once the trial had ended the year before, Kane and Rawls had lost everything they owned. This included the ranch that Kane had built and that Ezra had once worked on. It had been up to the town to put it up for sale, though no one had the money for it. Not even Ezra, at first.

The ranch was a large spread with a few hundred head of cattle. All the ranch hands were left to find new jobs.

After talking about it one night, Joe had learned that his foreman had always wanted his own land. And he was over halfway to the total requested. So, Joe was willing to put up the rest of the money. They made a plan for it to be paid back over the next couple of years. He didn't even ask for interest. He just wanted the man to succeed.

Taggert was the foreman for Joe's ranch now, and he was growing well into the role.

"Come on over here," Ezra invited him. "I've taken a few acres west of here to start preparing land for farming. Ronnie, my foreman, grew up in Montana and knows a good deal about planting. We've ordered the seed and it should be ready for us to start in early spring, once the ground is soft again."

Impressed, Joe led his horse after the man as they started down the path.

Ezra had made a good home for himself. He couldn't help but be amazed at how much it had improved and how much his friend still had in mind for his land. This made him wonder if he should be doing more to grow his ranch.

Right now, he felt fairly comfortable with all that he had. The ranch was flourishing and the cattle were healthy. He paid his men well and so everyone worked hard. The work went a lot more smoothly now that he knew what was going on and there was no one trying to mess around with his property.

Joe looked around to see the beautiful landscape before them. It was a snowy white world with clear skies and a warm sun. *A lovely day for a ride*, he thought. Though he knew he couldn't stay much longer, he followed after Ezra as they talked about the future.

"We'll have squash in this row," the man was explaining, "and corn over here. Ronnie has a few ideas of trying new vegetables out here that we could sell, so we'll have a small plot over there to figure out how to grow them in our soil. And… who is that?"

They squinted in the sunlight to see a horse galloping past the ranch house, headed in their direction. Shading his eyes, Joe frowned as he realized it was one of his men.

"Pedro?"

The young man had only been in his employ since the summer. He was hardly fifteen years old and, having come up north with his family, was eager to learn. His favorite thing to do was to ride fast. Joe was always telling him to be careful so he didn't stir up any cattle.

"Boss!" Pedro hollered once he was within hearing range. "Boss!"

Joe glanced at Ezra before steering his horse toward the young ranch hand. "Pedro! What's going on?"

"Your wife!" he panted as he grew closer. "Sir, the baby. It's coming!"

He was thunderstruck. "What?"

Behind him, Ezra started laughing. "Go, then. Ride, Joe! Nora needs you. Let's go!" He let out a sharp whistle and started moving.

Joe automatically followed as the shock faded. Once it did, he leaned into his saddle to push his horse faster. Pedro whooped loudly and Ezra let out another whistle, chuckling as the three of them started racing toward the road.

The baby. His baby was going to be born. Joe could hardly believe it. He scolded himself for having left the house at all. The child was due any day now. Yet Nora had insisted he keep his appointments. He went to see Ezra every other week to catch up and explore the ranch. It was nice seeing his old friend, but he didn't want to miss the birth of his child.

He quickly sent up a prayer to God so that Nora and their little girl or boy would be all right. His wife had been close to bursting for a while now and he knew how it weighed on her. She just wanted to hold her baby in her arms. Joe didn't blame her.

His heart skipped a beat as he realized that it would be today that they finally held their baby. Inhaling sharply, Joe felt an overwhelming sensation of gratitude soar through him.

They rode quickly around the outskirts of town before finally making it over to his ranch. Joe slowed his horse just enough outside the house so that he could jump down. Another horse was parked near the porch. That had to mean the midwife was there, he hoped. He left Pedro and Ezra with the horses as he took the porch steps two at a time and then burst in.

"Nora?" he called.

A loud cry that broke down into a groan sounded from down the hall. He ran over to find Mattie standing outside his bedroom door with extra towels in her arms.

The young girl brightened when she saw him. "They said they can see the head!"

His mouth turned dry. His child. He kissed Mattie's head and ruffled her hair before turning to the door. The birthing process was never a place for men, he knew, and Nora had been adamant about not having him there. But now that it was happening, he wanted nothing more than to be by her side.

"Nora?" Joe knocked on the door. "Can I come in?"

"No!" she shouted at him. "Don't you dare!"

Mattie giggled as he made a face. She elbowed him lightly before shifting her grasp on the towels. "I have the towels," she offered loudly.

Joe couldn't help but feel impatient. He wanted to be there to help his wife. There was nothing he could do while standing there.

"Too late," the midwife hollered to them. "It's coming!"

When Nora cried out again, Joe put his hands on the door. It took all his strength not to barge in to be there for her. If they had any more children, he told himself, then he would try to talk her into letting him be there at her side. He didn't care about the blood or the screaming. He just wanted to be with her.

Then, Joe noticed there was no more screaming. Frowning, he jerked his head up and pressed his ear to the door.

And then he heard it: a strong wailing coming from a new voice he had never heard before. But it was not a sound he would ever forget. His heart sang as he looked down to share a grin with Mattie. The newest member of their family was born.

Just a moment later, the door opened. The midwife nodded to each of them before grabbing the towels. She hesitated and then yanked the door open further to admit both of them.

He ran to his wife's side immediately.

Nora gave him a tired smile. Her face was streaked with sweat that made her curls stick to her cheeks. She was wearing only her shift while sitting up in bed with all the blankets and pillows around her. Though she appeared tired, Joe wasn't certain that she had ever looked more beautiful.

He sat on the edge of the bed and brushed his hand against her cheek as she sighed.

"Is it a boy or girl?" They turned to see Mattie on the other side of the bed.

Cradled against Nora's other arm was the tiniest living human Joe had ever seen. It was swaddled so tightly only a face was revealed. Joe inhaled, staring in disbelief.

"It's a boy," Nora announced. "Meet your little brother, Billy."

A tear made its way down Joe's cheek. He hurriedly wiped it away as Nora gently lifted the newborn and handed it over to him. The baby, his son, weighed nothing in his arms. He stared down in amazement.

"He's here," he murmured in disbelief. "Billy."

****

Nora woke up early a few weeks later to a quiet room.

That didn't happen too often anymore. Frowning slightly, she shifted herself up and looked around to see if something was wrong. But her fears faded as she found Joe on the edge of the bed, carefully rocking little Billy in his cradle.

She climbed onto her hands and knees to join the two men in her life. Putting a hand on her husband's shoulder, she gave him a sleepy smile before looking down at their baby.

Never before had she believed she could have more love in her life. But she had been proven wrong and couldn't be more grateful for it. Little Billy had his father's eyes on the cutest little squished face that she had ever seen. His button nose was perfect. So were his ten toes and ten fingers, and every other part of him. Nora couldn't get enough of him and, clearly, neither could Joe.

"Couldn't sleep?" she whispered.

He shrugged. "Didn't want to. Not anymore. Just look at him, Nora. He's perfect."

Resting her chin on his shoulder, she smiled. It was impossible not to. Though she was still exhausted and her body still ached, all of that was worth it just for a moment like this one. A warm sensation of peace spread through her body to wipe away the sleep lingering in her eyes.

Billy was perfect. As her stomach had begun to swell over the summer, the two of them had playfully argued about the gender and name for their child.

She vaguely recalled liking one boy's name in particular. But one morning, she had been woken up by Joe's arm on her shoulder. He was gently shaking her awake. Nora remembered feeling a chill and wrapping the blanket around herself.

"Joe?" Nora had asked. "What is it?"

"I had a dream. A dream about Billy. He was talking to me, Nora." Then, he had paused. "I should let you sleep. I shouldn't have tried to wake you."

A sleepy smile had crept up on her face. "It's all right, Joe. I'm awake now. You said something about Billy?"

He nodded as he laid back down beside her. They faced one another, laying close enough so that their noses were nearly touching. With the room still dark, she felt cozy and warm. Nora reached out a hand to her husband under the blankets and placed it on her stomach. The baby kicked and he smiled.

"He was here," Joe had whispered to her quietly. "He came and wanted to talk to me. He asked me how you were and how Mattie was doing. We talked about how smart our little girl is. It felt like an entire day that I had my brother back to talk. I apologized to him, too. He said he never blamed me for a thing."

She nodded. "I told you he loved you."

He grudgingly nodded. "I know. It just felt so real. I felt like I had my brother back, Nora. It's been so long..." Joe trailed off, falling quiet for several minutes. Nora was nearly falling back asleep by the time he spoke up again. "Nora? I was thinking. If our child is a boy... what if we name him after my brother?"

It had felt perfect in that moment, and it felt perfect now as she sat beside her husband and watched their little boy sleep. Billy pouted and had one of his tiny hands curled up under his chin.

"All right," Joe said before glancing over at her. "It's time to get up. For me, at least. I have to get ready."

She relaxed on the bed as she watched him pull his shirt on. "Get ready for what?"

Her husband just gave her a grin. "It's a surprise."

Immediately, she was intrigued. But no matter what she tried to say, no matter how she teased or prodded Joe to tell her what he was up to, he said nothing. Nora was forced to carry on with her day without a clue what her husband was doing. It was light-hearted fun, but she couldn't help but be annoyed.

It was midday, as she was putting Billy down for a nap after his feeding time, when there was a knock at the door.

"I'll get it!" Mattie sang, watching her baby brother carefully. If she was awake, the only place she wanted to be was at his side. Her excitement since the announcement of his impending birth had yet to dampen. Nora chuckled as she watched Mattie run off, wondering why she hadn't chosen to stay beside the baby.

She fixed the baby blanket on her shoulder before turning to the front door.

Nora stopped in the hallway, wondering if she was imagining the view before her. Stunned, she stood there, unable to speak.

Lauren was standing in her doorway. Lauren and her husband Daniel, and their one-year-old girl, Daphne. Her dear old friend beamed at her before hurrying inside to hug Nora as tightly as she could.

"What is this?" Nora cried out in surprise when her friend stepped back.

Everyone laughed as Joe came over to wrap his arms around her. "I wanted to give you an early Christmas present," he murmured. "You deserved something special."

****

Joe waved to the little family as they boarded the train. It only took a few steps before they disappeared.

He dropped his hand and sighed. Time seemed to be moving too fast lately, hardly giving him a chance to do everything that he wanted to do in his life. He had to remind himself every morning to embrace every moment that came his way.

Soon, Nora's dearest friends were back on the tracks, headed back to New York City. The last two months had been thrilling. They'd had the holidays, a baby in the house, and Nora had Lauren with her husband and baby. It had been a lot for Joe, who had come up with the idea in the first place. But he was grateful for the time. Nora appeared rejuvenated every day, and Mattie had loved having more people in the house.

After fixing the scarf wrapped around his neck, Joe turned his horse back for home.

Though Nora had wanted to come, little Billy had come down with a cold the day before, and she had been too worried to leave him behind. So, he hurried toward home, eager to be back with his family.

Joe arrived home and swung by the cabin for his ranch hands to see how everyone was faring. He promised to purchase them more coffee and rope soon before leaving them to do their work. Once the horse was brushed down and fed, he hastened up to the house. He opened the door and closed it to immediately feel the warmth coming from the large fireplace.

"I'm home!" he called out softly. "Everybody here?"

"In here," Nora responded from the kitchen.

He took off his jacket, hat, and scarf before making his way over to his wife.

Billy was in his small cradle on wheels as Mattie played with him quietly while Nora worked at the counter slicing carrots. She looked up and gave him a broad smile. Joe stopped to look at his family, wondering if life could get any better than this. Warmth flooded his chest as he studied the scene in amazement. Two years ago, he would have never imagined this could have happened. There was so much love in his life now that he felt as though he were living in a joyful dream.

"Did they get onboard the train safely?" Nora asked him hopefully.

Nodding, he stepped forward to pop a carrot slice in his mouth. "Yes, they did. I watched them leave the station. They'll be home in a few days and I'm sure you'll be getting a letter from Lauren telling you all about her journey back home."

Nora giggled. "She always has a good story, doesn't she?"

"She really does," he agreed as he leaned forward to give her a kiss. She tasted salty, making his lips tingle. He gave her a second kiss for good measure.

"Will I ever go on a train?"

They pulled apart as Mattie asked her question. Joe glanced at Nora, who looked back at him with an amused expression.

He supposed that meant it was his turn to give her an answer. "If you would like to, then yes," he said simply. "Someday. You can go wherever you want. How does that sound?"

Mattie bit her lip and nodded slowly. She turned down to look at Billy thoughtfully. The baby had a tight grip on one of her fingers. The young girl adored her brother and Joe knew that Billy would love her, as well. The siblings would be the best of friends as they grew up.

"Okay," she replied. "Yes, I want to."

"Where would you want to go, Mattie?" Nora prompted.

Their daughter thought about this seriously for another minute with a furrowed brow. It was hard not to smile when Joe saw it; she looked so much like her father right then. But while the pain of losing Billy would never completely fade, he knew, he could be grateful for the life that he had been given that now included her. Joe owed everything to his brother, and he tried every day to keep that in mind.

"I want to see my parents. Where they were buried," Mattie added. She smiled tentatively up at them, as though not entirely sure how they might react.

Nora reached out and touched his arm.

A lump formed in Joe's throat as he considered the growing child before him. He supposed she had been to the cemetery right after her father's passing. Dan had told him there had been a respectable and short service. Joe had visited the moment he'd arrived in town before ever stepping foot on the ranch. He had also been there to see Sophia.

Though they had talked about Sophia and Billy before, whenever Mattie wanted to, the conversation had rarely brought up their passing in any form. Joe had tried to ask her last Christmas, their first one together, if she wanted to go to the cemetery. But the little girl had seemed anxious and refused to answer the question. He didn't want to press it, so they had never gone there together.

He blinked, trying to think.

Of course, they could go see her parents. Two wonderful people had brought her into this world and deserved to be remembered kindly. Joe would never forget that. His heart ached for the loss that he and Mattie shared so deeply in their souls.

"Of course." He swallowed hard, trying to keep his voice from breaking. "I would really like that, Mattie. We don't need a train to go there, and we can go whenever you like."

His daughter met his gaze shyly and then glanced at Nora. "Can we go tomorrow? And can we bring Billy?"

Beside him, Nora sniffled and then turned to Mattie, leaning forward to wrap the girl in her arms. Mattie returned the hug as tightly as she could. "Of course, Mattie. I think that would be perfect."

It took them a few minutes to pull themselves back together.

Joe helped the girls prepare supper as they slowly turned to discuss lighter topics, ones that made them smile. They ate as a family and cleaned up together before sitting down to read. It was a quiet evening as they retired.

"Do you think Mattie is happy?" Joe asked quietly in the dark once he had laid down beside his wife.

She shifted to look at him. "Of course, Joe. You know she is. If this is about her parents, well, I think it's natural. She needs closure. She needs us and our love and our support."

He kissed her nose; Nora always seemed to know what to say. The two of them talked for a few more minutes before he could tell she was terribly tired; her words were beginning to slur. Nora went to sleep as he considered their afternoon conversation until he dozed off, as well.

In the morning, Joe rose early to work with his men. He talked with Nora beforehand to make sure he could get in some tasks before they went to town for the cemetery. After hitching up the wagon, he went inside and retrieved his family.

Their ride was quiet.

"You brought a basket?" Joe noted when Nora clambered down carefully onto the ground with Billy in her arms. "What for?"

She tutted before telling him, "Just bring it, won't you?"

He obeyed. Picking up the basket, Joe took Mattie's hand and led the way to where his brother and sister-in-law were buried. Their graves were covered in snow. He leaned forward and brushed it away until he could see their names.

It felt like a punch to the gut. No matter how many times he told himself this, there were still moments where he was surprised that his brother was not around.

Joe struggled to rein in his emotions as Mattie crept forward to slip something out of the basket he held. There were flowers, he realized. Just a few of them that Nora had rescued from the frost over and over again. He watched the tender sight of the young girl placing the flowers down for her parents.

"Hello, Papa," Mattie said in a whisper just loud enough to be heard. "Hello, Mama. I brought my new Papa and Mama here. And Billy. He's my brother and I love him. Thank you for bringing him to me. I miss you."

Nora leaned into Joe's chest and he wrapped an arm around her. Their baby was asleep in her loving grasp. Snow began to fall silently and peacefully around them.

As Mattie crouched down and talked to Billy and Sophia, Joe marveled once more on his life. There was so much good to be experienced. He prayed this joyful dream of his never faded away. Everything was perfect right then, and he wouldn't give up anything.

"I love you," Nora whispered to him. "We're so lucky, aren't we?"

His lips curved up to find she had been thinking the same as he was. "We really are. I thank God every day for this." Then, he looked at her and kissed her delicately. "For you. I love you, Nora."

THE END

Also by Ava Winters

Thank you for reading "**An Unexpected Bride for his Scarred Heart** "!

I hope you enjoyed it! If you did, here are some of my other books!

Some of my Best-Selling Books

#1 Brave Western Brides [Boxset]

#2 The Courageous Bride's Unexpected Family

#3 Healing the Rancher's Cold Heart

#4 A Redeeming Love in the West

#5 The Rancher's Unexpected Love

#6 A Bounty on Their Scarred Hearts

Also, if you liked this book, you can also check out **my full Amazon Book Catalogue at:**
https://go.avawinters.com/bc-authorpage

Thank you for allowing me to keep doing what I love! ❤

CPSIA information can be obtained
at www.ICGtesting.com
Printed in the USA
LVHW032333040423
743524LV00021B/381